ONE LAST GAME

DAVID ARCHER

ONE LAST GAME

This is a work of fiction. Names, characters, places, brands, media, and incidents are either the product of the author's imagination or are used fictitiously. Any resemblance to actual events, locales, or persons, living or dead, is coincidental.

Published by: David Archer

ONE

SOMETHING SOFT WAS touching the right side of my face, and I smiled. Dex was kissing me good morning, the way he sometimes did, and I loved it. I opened my eye and turned my face to kiss him properly, and Critter's paw smacked me in the mouth.

"Critter! What are you doing?" I spit a couple of times, just in case cat fur had gotten into my mouth.

"She's trying to tell you to get up," Dex said from behind me on the bed. "She's not used to us sleeping in this late, her bowl is probably empty."

I picked up my phone from the nightstand and glanced at it. Holy cow, it was almost noon! I didn't panic because it was Saturday and I was off, but I still couldn't believe it was that far into the day. "How on Earth did we manage to sleep so late?" I asked. "It's eleven forty-nine."

"Probably has something to do with how late we got in," Dex replied. "As I recall, it was around four o'clock this morning."

"Yeah, but I never sleep this late. Even when I'm up most of the night, I still wake up when the sun shines through the windows. I always do."

Dex rolled over toward me and wrapped an arm around me, pulling me back to him. "Then maybe it has something to do with after we got here," he said, nuzzling the back of my neck. I tried to pull away, because he knows what that does to me, but there was no hope. The tickle and the tingle began at the same time, and I told Critter she was gonna have to wait.

Luckily, neither of us was up to any long-term gymnastics. It was only about twenty minutes later when I made it to the kitchen in my bathrobe. Critter was waiting, sitting patiently beside her bowl. I reached into the cabinet and pulled out a can of cat food and showed it to her, then watched her face as the can opener made the music she loves to hear.

I don't care what anybody says, a cat can smile. Critter does it all the time.

"I agree with Critter," Dex said as he made it into the kitchen. "It's lunchtime." He opened the freezer and looked inside, then closed it again. "What have we got that's quick and easy?"

"I can make chili-mac," I said. "Or you could put some clothes on and run down to McDonald's. I think they still have the rib sandwiches."

"Or we could both put clothes on and go out to lunch. I like that idea better." He smacked me on the butt as he turned and went back toward the bedroom.

I turned and looked at him as he walked, a mock look of annoyance on my face just in case he cast a glance over his shoulder. When he didn't, I started after him. I caught up with him in our bedroom and stood with my hands on my hips, just staring at him.

"In what universe did I ever give you permission to slap my bottom?" I asked.

That got him to look my direction. "And in what universe did I ever ask? You know how it works when two people get together. What's mine is yours and what yours is mine. Why would I ask permission to slap my own bottom?"

I couldn't help it, I burst out laughing. Dex has that effect on me, and pretty damned often. My boss at the counseling center where I work, Marsha, says he is the best possible therapy for someone who's been through the things I've been through.

Just in case you don't know, my name is Cassie McGraw. A few years earlier, while I was in college, I was engaged to what I thought was a wonderful man. To give you the short version of a very long story, it wasn't very long before I discovered that he was actually a monster. Mike, despite being a decorated police detective, was the type of man who thoroughly enjoyed abusing women, to the point that he and four other cops had raped and murdered several prostitutes. That was before I met him, of course, but when he began to abuse me, I stumbled across evidence of his crimes. I took the evidence and fled, then reached out to a close friend to help me decide what to do.

The two of us got together and decided to contact his superiors in law enforcement, but Mike found us. He and one of his buddies took us to a cabin in the middle of nowhere, intending to kill us. At some point, though, Mike had a change of heart and didn't want me to die. His buddy killed him, and then poured gasoline on me and Abby, my friend, and set us on fire.

Abby died from her burns. I survived, but the flames somehow took hold of the left side of my body. From the right, I look perfectly normal, and a little girl once told me that was my "pretty side." On the left, however, all of the skin on my leg, my left arm, my side, and the left side of my neck and face was burned away. I lost my left ear and my left eye, and the two outer fingers of my left hand are fused together. Doctors said it was the only way to avoid amputating them.

After I recovered, I returned to college to get a bachelor's degree in psychology. After what had happened to me, I decided to devote myself to helping other women escape abusive situations. My degree allows me to work as an abuse counselor.

To finish out this short version, the city of St. Louis, where Mike had been a detective, ended up giving me a massive settlement, based on the fact that other cops had actually suppressed evidence that would have gotten Mike arrested and convicted long before I ever met him. As a result, I don't need money, so I work as a volunteer.

And then, in a weird twist of fate, I ended up rescuing a young girl who had been kidnapped and was being abused by her stepfather. I was forced to kill him in the process, but somehow that turned me into some kind of hero. More than one person suggested that I consider becoming a private eye, but I basically just laughed it off.

After that, Dex, a man I had met while working on that case, asked me to try to locate a missing friend of his, which ended up solving another mystery and allowed a young woman to regain a life she thought she lost. It was another feather in my cap, as far as local law enforcement was concerned, and I started to actually think about getting my PI license.

And then, someone started abducting the women I was counseling. The police couldn't come up with any valid leads, but I'm the sort who can't sit back and wait. I talked to my friend Dex and another friend at the police department, and another private investigator Dex knew helped me to get a provisional PI license, which allowed me to investigate without breaking any laws. I've already told that story before, so I won't go through it all again, but I caught the men who were doing it and saved several women in the process.

Of course, those men sort of died. In my defense, I only killed one of them. The other one died as I was being rescued, but I can't say I lost any sleep over it.

It was after that when Dex and I, who had somehow sort of become friends-with-benefits, decided that we liked being together enough to share a place. Since I had bought my house and he was only renting, he moved in with me. That was about three months ago, and I have to say that I think it was a good decision.

Besides, Dex is the only guy I know who can stand to look at me. Men don't get misty for a girl who's gone crispy. Dex says my scars don't scare him a bit, and he's proven that to me over and over. He was also burned, years ago when he was a kid, and even though his burn scars are covered by his clothing, he has some sense of how I feel. I'm not really self-conscious about the scars on my face and arm, the ones that show, but some of the ones that don't show are kind of disturbing. Dex is the only person I can stand seeing them.

Besides that, he just happens to be a fantastic lover.

It took me a couple of minutes to get my laughing under control, and then I just started getting dressed. I probably needed a shower, but I didn't feel like taking the time at that moment. As Dex had said, we had come dragging in not long before dawn. We had been out celebrating our three-month anniversary of moving in together, and even though the club had to stop selling drinks at two a.m., the dance floor stayed open until three thirty and the band kept playing, so we kept dancing.

"You ready?" Dex asked. "I was thinking about going to the Cracker Barrel."

I finished brushing my hair, or what was left of it, and dropped the brush on the bathroom counter. "Cracker Barrel sounds good to me," I said. He took my hand—my burned left hand—and we walked out the front door together.

The day was nice and warm, with the sun shining beautifully. Even though it was late March, the last few days had been warmer than usual for this time of year, and I was enjoying it. Dex opened the passenger door of his gorgeous '65 Mustang for me, and I just about bounced inside. He shut the door while I buckled my seatbelt, and then came around and got behind the wheel.

I always like riding in the Mustang because the people we pass can't see Freda. Freda, in case you don't know, is what I call my burned side. I tell everybody she's Freddy Krueger's twin sister, hence the name: Freda Krueger.

I've been living in Tulsa for about a year, now, and most of the places Dex and I go have gotten accustomed to seeing me. Sometimes the waitresses still tend to look away when they're taking my order, but I don't hold that against anyone. I have a mirror, and I know what I look like. The little sparkly things I put on my eye patches don't really do much to detract from just how ugly that side of my face really is.

Cracker Barrel, however, is one of the places where the staff is always gracious and welcoming. We probably eat there at least once a week, and we've gotten to know just about everybody who works there. As it turned out, one of the women I saved in the recent adventure I mentioned was the sister of the manager of the restaurant, and he recognized me from the photo they published in the newspaper. I guess he told all the rest of the employees that I was the private investigator who rescued his sister and several other women, and Dex and I have been treated like royalty there ever since.

This day was no exception. Clarice, the hostess on that shift, looked up and saw us and broke into a huge smile.

"Cassie, Dex," she said. "It's good to see you. Is it just the two of you today?"

"Yep," Dex said, "just the two of us."

"We're kind of busy today," she said, "but I got a table for two that's open. I'm afraid it's right in the middle of the dining room, is that okay?"

I shrugged. "It's fine with me," I said. "Just don't hold me responsible if other customers get up and run out the door."

She stuck her tongue out at me. "If they do," she said, "we don't want their business anyway."

She led us to the table she had in mind, and it definitely was right smack in the middle of the dining room. The conversations around us suddenly got quieter, as some of the customers saw my scars. I confess to feeling a moment of self-consciousness, but then Clarice looked a couple of people in the eye and they all seemed to go back to discussing whatever it was they were talking about before.

Dex and I picked up the menus as Clarice went to get the iced tea we ordered.

"Hey," I said, "they've got the campfire chicken on the menu today. That's what I want."

"Oh, yeah," Dex said. "I'm having the same thing."

"Good, you can have my carrots. I love the chicken and the potatoes, but I've just never been a big fan of roasted carrots."

"I'll take 'em," he said. He started to say something more, but Clarice came back with the tea at that moment and took our orders.

Dex, who was sitting across from me, suddenly flicked his eyes to my left and frowned. He turned back to me almost instantly, then reached across and took my hand. I didn't need him to tell me that someone was staring at me, because I could feel it.

"Don't look," he said softly. "It's a couple of kids, but apparently their parents haven't taught them any better manners."

"Don't worry about it," I whispered back. "You think it's the first time kids have stared at me? I look like a monster to them, it's natural."

I turned my head and looked their direction, and two kids, a boy and a girl who might have been ten years old, met my gaze steadily. That was unusual, so I smiled.

"Are you Kathy McGraw?" the boy asked.

I chuckled. "My name is *Cassie* McGraw," I said. "You guys must be from around here, right?"

Both of them nodded, and their parents turned to look at me. Their father smiled and leaned slightly toward me.

"It is you, isn't it?" he said. "Please forgive my kids, but you're something of a hero to them."

My eye shot open. "I am?"

"Yeah, I'm afraid so. We lived next door to Kendra McCoy and her daughter Melanie. I'm afraid the kids heard all about how you rescued Melanie from her stepdad. To hear Melanie tell it, you're tougher than Batgirl. All three of them clipped your picture out of the newspaper and have it on their walls."

"Oh, great," I said with a grin. "I'm surprised it doesn't terrorize them in the night."

"Not at all," his wife said. "Forgive me if this comes out the wrong way, but we actually used your picture, and their fascination with it, to point out that being scarred or injured or different in any way shouldn't matter. What matters is who a person is, and you're the kind of person we would prefer them to have for a hero. Especially compared to pop stars and other celebrities, and especially with the way some of them act nowadays."

My smile grew wider. "There's nothing to forgive," I said. "In fact, thank you. That's something that a lot of us with scars would like people to know. It's nice to hear that children are being taught something like that."

"Can we get your autograph?" the boy asked. He held out a napkin and a crayon toward me, and I smiled as I reached for it.

"What are your names?" I asked, and then I wrote, "To Bobby and Lisa, All the Best, Cassie McGraw!" When I handed it over, both kids beamed from ear to ear as they showed it to their parents.

We chatted with the family a bit until their food arrived, and ours showed up just a few minutes later. We lingered over our lunch and an extra cup of coffee afterward, and were surprised when we asked for a check to find out that it had already been paid.

"The couple with the kids?" I asked Clarice.

"Actually, they tried, but somebody beat them to it. It was the older couple that was sitting behind them. As they were getting up to leave, they pointed you out to me and asked for your check, too."

Dex pulled a twenty dollar bill out of his pocket and pressed it into her hand. "Well, I can at least leave the tip," he said.

She pushed it back at him. "Believe me, you don't need to. The old gentleman was quite generous." She smiled and insisted he take the money back.

We left the restaurant feeling grand, delighted to have run into a couple examples of the good parts of human nature. Too many times in my line of work, I see the other side.

We sat in the car for a moment and talked about what else we might do for the afternoon, but both of us were still pretty tired after our late night. We stopped at a Red Box and got a couple of DVDs, then headed for home.

The rest of the day went pretty nice, as well. We actually went back to bed for a while and took a nap, then got up around five and made popcorn to munch while we watched our movies. We sat on the couch, with me leaning comfortably against Dex, and Critter curled up in the spot where our laps met. It was a wonderful Saturday, and I remember telling myself to hold onto the memory of it.

Maybe there was a part of me that knew it was going to be the last good Saturday I would have for a while.

TWO

SUNDAY WAS OUR LOAFING day, so Dex and I stayed around the house all day on Sunday. He went out and mowed the yard, first time in the year, and I fiddled around the house. I did a little cleaning, washed a couple loads of clothes and folded them, but mostly I sat on the back deck and watched Dex pushing the mower. He had his shirt off because he was sweating, and I could see his own burn scars that came up to the middle of his chest.

When I was a kid, Sunday was the day my parents took me to church. As that thought drifted through my mind, I looked up at the sky and whispered a little prayer of thanks to God for letting me have Dex in my life. I wasn't sure how long it would last, but I wanted to be grateful for him while I had him.

Weekends pass, and I woke up again to a Monday morning. Dex had to leave for work before I did; he's a mechanic at the Ford dealership, and they get backlogged if he isn't there. From what his coworkers have told me, it seems he has to solve a lot of the problems the other mechanics run into.

I kissed him goodbye and he left, and then I went back to the bathroom to get my shower and make myself as presentable as possible before heading to the counseling center. I volunteer my time at St. Mary's Outreach for Battered Women and Children, and sometimes it's hearing the story of what happened to me and gave me the scars that gives these women the strength to encourage them to get themselves and their children out of abusive situations.

When that happens, I do two things. First, I thank God that my story might help save a life. Second, I tell Abby that we managed to save another one.

That's because they can tell you know what you're talking about, Abby replies, or something like that. Yes, you're not mistaken and you don't need to look back at the first chapter. Yes, I did say Abby died the night we were burned, and I'm fully aware that the voice I hear in my head is nothing but my own subconscious trying to reassure me that she doesn't blame me for her death. I do have a degree in psychology, remember? Now, let it go.

I decided to dress as if it were already spring. I put on a bright yellow skirt and added a light pink top. A yellow sweater and a pair of pink boat shoes seemed to go just right with it all, and I finished it off with a pink leather eyepatch I had made. I grinned at myself in the mirror, then walked out and got into my little Kia Sportage and headed off to the Outreach.

There was an awful lot of traffic that morning, and I was running a little late. This was compounded by the fact that I seemed to hit every red light between my house and the Outreach, and I was really starting to get frustrated by the time I got to the corner where I would turn so I could reach the alley behind it. I always parked in the back, because the one time I had parked my car on the street, the driver side mirror got broken off by a kid on a skateboard.

Don't laugh, it cost me almost 200 dollars to get it fixed.

Of course, the light at that intersection was red, so I had to stop before turning, and then I had to wait a moment as a van with a cloud on the side cruised past me. The Outreach was actually half a block ahead of me, and I was just about to turn when the most horrendous noise made me slam on the brakes.

At first, I thought someone had hit my car, because it felt like the whole world was shaking for a moment. I looked around, but there was nobody even terribly close, so I shrugged and was going to go ahead and turn.

That's when I saw the billowing smoke up ahead of me, and my gut twisted into knots as I realized it was coming from the Outreach.

The light turned green, and I floored the car and shot straight ahead, cutting off the car in the lane beside me. I pulled up in front of what was left of the building and threw the car into park, turned on my emergency flashers and jumped out.

The building was a shambles. Half the front wall was gone, and there were flames everywhere. I stood there in shock, just wondering what in the world could've happened, and suddenly there were dozens of people around me. Some were asking what happened, others were trying to get the rest of us to move away, but I pushed aside one man who dared to try to move me.

Sirens rent the air, and two police cars slid to a stop around my Kia. One of the cops recognized me and asked if I knew what happened, but I only shook my head. I was in shock, I just couldn't believe what I was seeing.

The cop was talking to me, but I couldn't make out what he was saying. I turned and looked at him and forced myself to focus.

"What? What did you say?"

"I asked you if anyone was in there," he said. "Do you know if..."

I whipped my face back toward the ruined building, and then I screamed.

"My God, yes," I said. "I was running late, that's the only reason I wasn't in there when it happened. Marsha, Angie, Nicole, Brenda... Oh my God, you have to get them out!"

Fire engines had arrived without me even noticing them, and firemen were hooking up hoses and water began spraying into the building. Two of them put on oxygen masks and special clothing and actually went into the building, and I dropped to my knees where I stood and began praying.

There was a fireman standing close to me, holding a radio. It suddenly crackled to life, and a voice came out of it.

"Found a body," the voice said. "looks like the receptionist, maybe."

The receptionist? I thought. *A body? But that means Angie—Angie is dead?*

Everything went black.

When I woke up, I was in the back of an ambulance. The paramedic was holding an oxygen mask over my face, but I pushed it away.

"Cassie, take it easy," I heard, and looked up to see Dex. He was standing just outside the ambulance and looking in at me.

"What are you doing here?" I asked.

"It came over the radio in the shop," he said. "A special news bulletin. They said a bomb went off at St. Mary's Outreach, and I just dropped my tools and ran for the car. I got here a few minutes ago and one of the cops told me you passed out and they put you in an ambulance, and that's how I found you."

I was staring at him. "A bomb? They said it was a bomb?"

He nodded. "That's what it looks like at the moment," he said. "They found Nicole, she's alive but hurt. From what they tell me, they think she's going to be okay, but a big section of the ceiling fell in on her. Some of the others weren't so lucky."

I looked at him, my one good eye boring into both of his. "Marsha?"

He grimaced, and I knew. Marsha was the director of the Outreach, my boss. She was the driving force that kept it going when even the bishop wanted to shut it down. The place would be finished without her, even if the diocese would provide the money to rebuild it.

I started to cry, then, and I didn't even bother to try to hold it back. Marsha was more than my boss, she was also my friend in many ways. Angie Milligan, the receptionist, had taken a while to become accustomed to Freda, but she and I had also become friends. There were other counselors who would have been there, as well.

"Oh, Dex," I cried. I pushed myself up off the stretcher and climbed out of the ambulance, and he wrapped his arms around me and held me as I bawled myself dry of tears.

I felt a tap on my shoulder, and looked around. Alicia Perkins, the police detective who handled domestic abuse cases, was standing there.

"Cassie? Are you okay?"

"Hell, no," I said. "Marsha is dead, and so is Angie. I don't know about anybody else yet, except Dex said Nicole is still alive."

"I know," Alicia said. "I'm not really on this case, but when I heard what happened I came anyway. I—I was afraid you were inside when it happened."

"I should have been," I said. "I was running late because I wanted to get dressed up nice, and then I hit all the red lights. If not for that, I would've been inside the building at my desk when this happened." I let go of Dex and forced myself to stand. "Dex says they're saying it's a bomb?"

"It looks like it," she said. "The firemen say the damage seems to have started a few feet behind the reception desk, probably right about where your office was. Jim Pennington is taking lead on the investigation, and I might as well tell you now, he's asked me if I think someone might have been trying to target you."

I stared at her. "Me? He thinks someone was trying to kill me with a bomb?"

"I told him I doubt it," she said quickly. "He's just looking at all possible motives, Cassie. That's his job, don't get upset."

"I'm not getting upset, I'm wondering if he could be right. Geez, do you think he could be? I mean, let's face it, there are a lot of men out there who hate my guts. Every time I get a woman to leave her abusive husband, I'm the one he blames. Do you honestly think one of them might have tried to get back at me this way?"

"I told you, I don't think that," Alicia said. "Jim just has to consider all the possibilities. Cassie, don't get yourself all torn up over this. We're going to need your help just to figure out what happened."

A thousand thoughts raced through my mind in a matter of seconds, but the one that stood out from all of them was this: if someone planted a bomb to try to kill me, then all of the others who died would have been nothing but collateral damage to him. It would mean they didn't matter, and the more that thought bounced around the inside of my skull, the angrier I became.

"Where's Pennington?" I asked. "I'm going to help, all right. I'm going to find the son of a bitch who did this."

Alicia started to say something, but I guess she thought better of it. She closed her mouth and motioned for me to follow her. I didn't need to look to know that Dex fell in right behind me.

Pennington was a big man, probably six foot six and a good two hundred and eighty pounds. He wasn't fat, not by any stretch of the imagination. Everything about him was solid, and I guessed he probably spent hours each week at a gymnasium.

"Jim?" Alicia said. "This is Cassie McGraw."

Pennington looked me up and down, but I didn't see the disgust I normally spotted in someone's eyes the first time they got a good look at me. Instead, I saw that he was measuring me up, trying to decide whether I was going to be worth putting any effort into.

I guess he liked something about what he saw, because he held out a hand. "Detective Jim Pennington," he said. "I understand you worked in there. First, let me say I'm sorry for your losses. I didn't know any of these women personally, but I respect the work they were doing here. That you all were doing here."

"Thank you," I said. "They were my friends, not just my coworkers." I looked him in the eye. "You probably already know, but I'm a licensed private investigator. I want to know how I can help."

"Yes, I know," he said. "It's probably going to be a little while before I get time, but I'm going to need to sit down and talk with you. From what I've been told, the bomb was apparently planted somewhere around your office, possibly even inside it. That makes me wonder if someone was trying to get you. Can you think of anyone who might want to blow you to hell?"

"Our records are all backed up in the cloud," I said. "When I get to a computer, I can print you out a list, but it may be pretty long. Every husband whose wife left him over abuse after she talked to me would probably love to see me blasted this way. Unfortunately, I can't point to any particular one who might actually try it, but it's definitely a possibility."

Pennington nodded. "That's pretty much what I thought," he said. "I've already got our IT department trying to track down your records, but if you can get into them, that will help."

I nodded my head. "I can," I said. "If you get them on the phone, I'll give them my login and password."

He took out a phone and dialed the number, then handed it to me. I spoke with a girl named Melissa and told her how to get into the cloud server we had used. A moment later she told me she was in, and would begin printing everything out for the detectives to look over.

I gave the phone back to Pennington and looked at him. "Now, how else can I help? And don't tell me to go home and stay out of it, because that's not going to happen. I want this bastard caught."

"Cassie, I understand that," he said. "At the same time, you need to let us do our job. However, it's pretty obvious to me that you have no intention of doing that, so I'll make you a deal. You promise to share anything you find out with me, and I'll do the same with you. Shake on it?" He stuck out his hand again.

I grabbed it and shook it firmly. "You got a deal. When do you want to sit down and talk?"

He looked around at the scene for a moment, then looked back at me. "There's not really anything for me to do here," he said. "How about now? You got time to come to my office?"

"You bet," I said. I turned around and found Dex standing right behind me, and I threw my arms around him. "Thank you for coming," I said. "It means a lot to me."

"Yeah? Well, thank you for not being inside that damn building when it blew up. Cassie, I don't know what I would do if anything happened to you. I know you're not ready to hear it, but..."

I put a finger to his lips to stop him. "Dex," I said, "I know. I know, but right now I have to concentrate on this.

You go back to work, and I'll call you when I get done with the detective."

He pushed my finger away gently, then kissed me and turned to walk away. I started toward my car as I heard the Mustang fire up and drive away.

It took a few minutes to get to the police department, and it still seemed like I was hitting every red light. Pennington had made it back before I did and was waiting for me in his office when I arrived. He had a print out of all of the clients of the outreach on his desk, and was concentrating on my cases.

"You have been a busy lady," he said. "If I'm reading all this correctly, you've actually gotten more than a hundred women to leave their husbands and boyfriends and go into shelters. Does that sound about right?"

"A hundred and seven," I said. "I don't know if you're aware of my history, but the way I look is connected to my own abusive relationship years ago. I'm very proud that I had something to do with the fact that a hundred and seven women, and an awful lot of their kids, are no longer suffering from abuse."

"You should be," Pennington said. "I've worked abuse cases, and they suck. Half the time, you can't get the victims to show up and testify."

"That's because they're terrified of what the abuser will do if he gets out," I said. "Unfortunately, the vast majority of them do get out. Sometimes it's on bail, but all too often it's just because the jail is overcrowded and the courts don't consider domestic abuse to be that serious a crime."

"Well, I damn well do. That's why it pisses me off when the victims fail to even show up at court. I can't keep them locked up if nobody will testify against them."

"Next time you run into a case like that," I said, "you call me. Let me talk to the victim, and I just about guarantee I can get her to show up. They seem to look at me and start to think about just how bad it really can get. That's why I have such a high success rate."

"Yeah, I know. Alicia told me I should Google you, so I did. By the time I got done reading, it was a good thing your ex was already dead. I wanted to shoot the bastard myself."

I couldn't help it, I chuckled. "And you didn't even get to read the whole story," I said. "I Google myself every now and then, so I know what's out there. There's a lot more that isn't public knowledge, but we don't need to go into that. Now, how can I help?"

THREE

WE SPENT THE NEXT TWO and half hours going through all of my cases, all the way back to when I started working with the Outreach almost a year earlier. Some of the men I had dealt with were what I call "opportunity abusers," which means they were actually cowards who can only be abusive to someone they consider much weaker than themselves. Unfortunately, most men feel that way about their own wives and girlfriends. Those men, I told Pennington, were highly unlikely to ever have the nerve it would take to try to build and plant a bomb. We made a list of them, anyway, but then we moved on to the ones I considered genuinely dangerous.

That list was smaller. Of the two hundred or so women I had counseled, only about thirty-five of them had abusers that I believed were capable of extreme violence. These men were often psychopaths, with no natural moral compass to guide them. Their actions and decisions were based only on their own desires, and it would never occur to them that beating a woman into submission was wrong.

Don't misunderstand me, they knew it was against the law. They just didn't feel that the law should apply to them. After all, such a man would reason, it's his own wife he's beating. To him, being "his wife" meant that she was a possession, that he had all rights where she was concerned.

We talked about those men at length, and Pennington asked me to rate just how dangerous I thought each one was on a scale of 1 to 5. When we were finished, he turned the sheet of paper around to me so I could look at it. Of the thirty-five men on the list, I had pegged all but one as being extremely dangerous—number five.

"My question is," I said at that point, "do you honestly think it was one of these men who planted the bomb? I mean, there were five other counselors in the Outreach. I don't know about their cases, how dangerous the men might be, but it could have been one of those."

"Or it could be somebody completely unconnected to any of you," he said. "It's quite possible that whoever did this simply doesn't like the kind of work that you all do. That would be no different than the people who bomb abortion clinics. I can't say for sure that one of the men on your list is our bomber, but I have to start with those who can be identified as having at least a motive. If it turns out one of these men bought the things necessary to build a bomb, then we look at him a lot more closely."

"And what kind of things would that be?" I asked.

"Lots of things," he replied. "One of the most common homemade bombs uses diesel fuel and liquid fertilizer. Others use things like pool cleaners, which contain nitric acid or sulfuric acid. Model airplanes run on a fuel called nitromethane, which is pretty highly explosive itself, but when you mix it with ammonium nitrate, the fertilizer, it can be several times more powerful than TNT. You'd be quite surprised at how easy it is to make an explosive right in your own kitchen. Mothballs, drain cleaner, some aerosol sprays—it's not that hard to come up with stuff that goes boom if you really want to, especially when you can look up the recipe on the Internet."

"So, you're going to look and see if any of these men bought some of those things?"

Pennington nodded. "That's where we start. If we find that anyone on our suspect list purchased the necessary supplies, that gives us a reason to pull them in for questioning. We dig deeper, and we keep digging until we find evidence of guilt, or of innocence."

I shook my head. "Well, I'm going to be talking to some of these men myself. I've come face-to-face with most of them at one time or another, and they already know they don't scare me. Some of them even have a hard time looking at me, one of the few advantages you get when you look like Frankenstein."

"Yeah, Alicia said you'd want to sink your teeth into this. Just do me a favor, and be careful. If you start to get a bad feeling about any of these men, call me in. There's nothing wrong with asking for backup, you understand me?"

"I understand," I said. "Don't worry, I don't have a death wish. And, I have a secret weapon. My boyfriend, Dexter Tate? I don't know if you know him, but he has an incredible knack for knowing when somebody is lying. When he was in the Army, his commanding officer used call him the human lie detector. I'll set up my meetings for after work when I can, so he can go with me."

"I don't know if I believe in human lie detectors," Pennington said, "but if you do, and he indicates somebody is being untruthful about anything connected to this, I want to know it. Okay?"

"Absolutely," I said. "If I come up with a suspect, you'll know it as quickly as I can get hold of you."

He reached into his shirt pocket and pulled out a business card that he passed it to me. "My cell number is on the back," he said. "I don't care what time it is, if you think you've got something, you call me."

I smiled as I slipped it into my own pocket. "Thank you, Detective," I said.

"Hey, none of that," he said. "You might be a private eye, but I've heard enough about you to be able to say that we're both cops. It's just Jim, all right?"

"Thanks, Jim," I said. I gave him another smile and got up to leave his office, but then I stopped. "Hey, Jim? Can I have a copy of that list of names?"

When I got out to the car, I took out my phone and called Dex. He answered on the first ring. "Cassie? Anything new?"

"I sat down with Pennington and went over all my cases," I said. "We got about thirty-five men who I think could possibly be violent enough to do something like this. The trouble is, we don't have any way to judge how dangerous the men from the other counselors' cases might be. Pennington says they're going to go through all of their credit card transactions, see if any of them bought the kind of stuff it takes to make a bomb."

"I guess that's a good start," he said. "Can I make a suggestion?"

"Of course," I said. "Go ahead."

"Why don't you call Alfie and give him those names, let him run the same kind of search? I will guarantee you he can do it a lot faster, and a lot more thoroughly, than the police can."

"Do you think so? I guess it's worth a try. I'll give him a call and see if he's got time today."

"He'll do it for you," Dex said. "In fact, why don't you pick up some pizza and just head over there? I can take off for lunch in about fifteen minutes, I'll meet you there."

That got me to smile. "Okay, great," I said. "Alfie likes pepperoni, right?"

"Alfie likes any kind of pizza."

Twenty-five minutes later, I pulled up at Alfie's apartment building and made my way inside, carrying two large supreme pizzas. I knocked shave-and-a-haircut, and Alfie answered the door a moment later. He grabbed the pizzas out of my hand and carried them inside, then turned and looked at me.

"I heard what happened," he said. "I called Dex as soon as I heard, but he said you were running late and didn't make it into the office. Do you ever feel like the world's luckiest bitch?"

"All the time, lately," I said. "Dex is on the way, he's going to join us for lunch. You got time to do some computer work for me today?"

"Soon as I heard what happened, I said to myself that you were going to ask that question today. Yeah, come on. Give me what you got."

I told him about my conversation with Pennington, then showed him the list of the top thirty-five names. It was actually a list of more than two hundred names, but the ones I had identified as potentially dangerous were highlighted in red. The nice thing about that was that it included the name, the address, and even the phone number in most cases.

"Hey, you actually brought me something I can work with this time. Here, read them off to me." He bounced up onto his stool—Alfie is a dwarf, only three and a half feet tall—and opened the program on one of the many monitors that surrounded him. "Okay, go ahead. Give me the first one. Name and address, both."

"Okay," I said. "The first one is Gary Cohen, two fifty-nine Gordon Street, apartment 6 G."

"Got it," Alfie said. "Next one."

"George Davis, fifteen forty-nine Broken Arrow Boulevard."

"Next."

I read off all of the names to him, finishing the last one just as Dex knocked on the door. Alfie pointed at the door without moving from his stool. "That's Dex, let him in."

I went and opened the door, and Dex grabbed me and pulled me into a hug.

"Mmm, I could do this all day," he said.

"Not here, you can't," Alfie said. "Get a room."

"You're just jealous," Dex said, chuckling. He kissed me quickly, then came in and shut the door behind himself. I handed him the open box of pizza and he grabbed two slices. I took a couple more and sat down on the couch beside him.

"Alfie," I said, "the pizza will get cold."

"That's okay, I like cold pizza," he said, his eyes intent on the monitor in front of him. "I've got my Spybot set to pull down all the Social Security numbers for these guys," he said. "Soon as I get those, I can find all of their financials and start searching for purchases that could be suspicious."

He spun the stool around and hopped off, grabbed a slice of pizza, and flopped onto a beanbag. He shoved the pizza into his mouth and took a humongous bite, then struggled to chew it up.

Besides being a dwarf, Alfie is sort of my other boss. In order to get my provisional PI license, I had to be employed as an investigator, and Alfie already had his full private investigator license. He had even set up his own investigation company, Centronic Investigations, Inc. He hired me as an unpaid intern, signed a letter confirming this fact, and sent me off to Oklahoma City. I got my provisional license that day, and I'd been studying for the test for my unlimited license ever since.

Alfie is a professional computer hacker. He got his PI license because he is often hired by attorneys and even government agencies at times to find things that people want to keep hidden. Sometimes, that's finding the people themselves. Other times, it means finding any assets they may have hidden, or evidence that can be used to prosecute them. In return for my occasional assistance doing legwork, Alfie only charges me half his normal rate for computer work. It's a symbiotic relationship, Dex says, because we're each dependent on the other at times.

Personally, I think Alfie is getting the better end of the deal. Even at half rate, it costs me a lot of money when I need him to dig out some information for me.

Usually, it's just when I need to find out something about my clients or their abusers. Alfie has been instrumental more than once in helping me get orders of protection for my clients, by finding hateful things their abusers had posted online. A couple of times, he even found things that put the men in jail; one of them was doing thirty-five years after Alfie discovered he was running a meth distribution ring.

His computer made a noise, and he bounced up off the beanbag and hopped onto the stool again. "Okay, got their socials. I'm feeding them into the search database now, and we should have their credit cards and bank accounts in a few minutes." He hopped back down and grabbed another slice of pizza.

Thirty minutes later, he was shaking his head. "None of these guys has purchased anything online that would be even slightly suspicious," he said, "except for Rodney Kirkman. Rodney has been buying a lot of female type underclothing, but I don't think it was for his wife. From the sizes, I'd say he's probably wearing the stuff himself, and he just started buying it after his old lady moved out."

"Yuck," I said. "I'm pretty sure I really didn't need to know that, Alfie."

"Hey, I'm just giving you my report. That's the only unusual purchase any of these guys made in the last month or so." He spun the stool around and looked at me. "Of course, I can only check on what they buy using credit or debit cards. If they pay cash at the local grocery store, there's not much I can do about that."

"Well, thanks for trying, anyway," I said. "It was worth a shot. Unfortunately, it leaves me back at square one. Somebody planted a bomb, and I have no way to figure out who it was."

"Don't be so hasty," Alfie said. "For one thing, we don't even know what kind of bomb it was, yet. Any idea when the police will get a report back on that?"

I just looked at him. "I'm afraid it didn't occur to me to ask," I said. "Why? Does it take a while?"

"It can," Alfie said. "Depends on how busy the crime lab is. The fire department would have gathered up some of the materials from around where the blast happened, and they might've even found pieces of the explosive device. The crime lab can figure out from that kind of junk just what type of bomb it was. If we knew that, it might suggest other searches I can run on these guys. I don't think you should rule any of them out, but I can't hand you information right now that definitely proves any of them guilty."

"I'll check with Pennington the next time I talk to him," I said. "Any other suggestions on how I should approach this?"

"Yeah," Alfie said. "Approach it gun first. I'll be honest, when I heard about the explosion at St. Mary's, I thought you were a goner. I called Dex because I figured he'd be falling apart, he said he had already found you okay, so I relaxed a bit."

"Don't listen to him," Dex said. "When he called me, he was crying like a baby."

"I was not!" Alfie shouted. "I was having sinus problems, that's all. My allergies were flaring up."

"Allergies to what?" Dex asked. "Maybe you haven't noticed, but nothing is actually growing outside just yet."

"It's a cat, dammit. The lady in the apartment next door has a freaking cat, one of those long-haired things that everybody is allergic to."

"Oh, shut up and admit it, you big baby," Dex said. "Cassie, I swear to you, he was crying and couldn't even talk. He kept saying your name over and over, and I finally had to yell to make him listen when I told him you were okay."

Alfie glared at him, but then he turned and looked at me. "Okay, okay, so maybe I was a little upset. I don't have a lot of friends, you know, I really don't want to lose any."

"Well, I don't want you to lose me, either," I said. "I'm okay, though, and I plan on staying that way."

FOUR

"I GOTTA GET BACK TO work," Dex said. "What are you going to do for the rest of the day?"

"I think," I said, "I'm going to go home and get on my computer, and call all of my current clients. I need to let them know that I'm still around if they need me." I shook my head. "I don't think the diocese is going to bother trying to reopen the Outreach, but I don't want to quit working with these women. Would I have to have any kind of special license to set up my own counseling center?"

"Nope," Alfie said. "I anticipated this question, so I looked it up. You can do it one of two ways. You can go into private practice as a counselor and specialize in abuse cases, or you can set it up as a charity organization, a 501(c)3. In private practice, you can charge a fee for your services if you want to."

"I don't need to charge anything," I said. "Is there any advantage to being a charity?"

"Only if you want to take donations to help offset the costs. Otherwise, the paperwork you have to file with the government periodically can be a royal pain in the ass. If you don't want to take donations, then you can do it as personal pro bono work, and still get a decent tax write off."

"See?" Dex said. "I told you, Alfie is the man with all the answers."

I looked at both of them, bouncing my eye from one to the other. "I don't need anybody else's money," I said. "I think what I need is an office. I can combine them, right? Use one office for counseling and for my PI license?"

"Sure you can," Alfie said. "As soon as you pass that test. Until then, you're mine, baby, all mine. That temporary license you've got can't be moved from this office."

I stuck my tongue out at him.

Dex left, and I followed a moment later. I went home and let Critter try to trip me at the doorway—that's her way of saying, "welcome home"—then went into the kitchen and microwaved a cup of the leftover coffee. I carried that back into the living room and sat down on the couch, opening my laptop on the coffee table.

That was when my phone rang, and I picked it up to see that it was my mother calling. It suddenly hit me that she follows all the news from Tulsa, especially since I became a private eye. She probably got a notice about the Outreach being bombed and was on the verge of panic.

I answered quickly, keeping my voice upbeat. "Hey, Mom," I said. "How's your day going?"

"Never you mind about my day," she said. "Oh, God, Cassie! I just needed to hear your voice! I got on the computer a little while ago and the first thing I saw was a notice that the place where you work got bombed this morning. Cassie, are you okay?"

"I'm fine, Mom," I said. I spent the next twenty minutes telling her what had happened, and slowly listening to her get a grip on herself. I should have thought about the fact that she would be notified, because she has a newsfeed set to look for anything with my name in it. The radio and TV station websites would already have the story up, and they were bound to mention me in one way or another.

It turned out that they only mentioned that the Outreach was the place where I did volunteer work. They didn't bother to say that I was alive and well, the bastards.

After Mom calmed down, I went back to what I was doing with my computer. It only took me a couple of minutes to get logged in to the cloud server, and then I was looking at all of my client records. I downloaded them so that I'd have them on my computer, then took out my phone and began calling each one.

Most of the women had heard the news, and thought I was dead. I got every reaction from screams of joy to tears to one lady who kept asking if I was a ghost. I assured her that I was not, but I'm not a hundred percent certain she believed me.

I explained to each of them what had happened, and that the Outreach was probably no more. However, then I explained that I would be opening my own office and would be happy to continue working with them, and that got some pretty big thank yous. I promised to let them know as soon as I found a location, and then called the next woman on the list.

It took me almost two hours to get through all of them, but it was worth it. Some of them were actually terrified, afraid they'd never be able to escape the abuse they were living in without me. It dawned on me that all of the other counselors had clients, as well, but I just didn't have the energy to sit down and call them all at that time.

Instead, I ran a Google search for offices that might be for rent in Tulsa, and found a gazillion of them.

There were offices in fancy high-rise buildings, but that didn't appeal to me. Most of the women who would be coming to me lived near or below the poverty level, so I didn't want them to feel intimidated by the surroundings. I saw a few that looked interesting, basically just storefronts, and called a couple of the real estate agents who were handling them.

That got me three separate appointments that afternoon, so I gave Critter a quick belly rub to calm her down, then grabbed my purse and hurried out to the Kia again.

I went to the first appointment on Admiral Boulevard, and then called to cancel the other two. The building I found was perfect. It was only a thousand square feet, but it had a nice little reception area out front, a beautifully decorated office behind that, and a big conference room that actually had a small kitchen in it. There were also bathrooms, two of them. That was important, since a lot of these women had little boys.

The place was available for only six hundred a month, so I signed the lease and paid a year in advance. The previous tenants had actually left some furniture behind, including a decent reception desk and chair and their conference table, so all I really needed was my own desk and chair, plus chairs for the clients, and a few decorative accents.

I sat down at the reception desk and made the calls to get power, water, phones, and Internet turned on in my name, and then I drove off to a big office supply store on Harvard Avenue and picked out a desk, a luxurious chair for myself, and four comfortable wingback chairs for clients, several smaller chairs for the reception area, file cabinets and lots of office supplies, a big commercial copier and printer, a computer system with two terminals, and a lot of decorations. The salesman was extremely happy, so I guess he must work on commission; he promised to have it all delivered to my new office by nine o'clock the following morning, and even assured me that his delivery guys would set everything up for me.

After I left, it dawned on me that he might have been so helpful and friendly because he wanted me to leave. Oh well, that's life.

I checked the time and it was just short of four thirty. I had just enough time, so I hurried down to the Ford dealership and was waiting when Dex got off work.

"Hey, good looking," I said. "Care to take a ride?"

Dex looked at me, and he grinned. "You already got an office, didn't you?"

That man can be so infuriating at times. He can read me—correction, he can read just about anybody like a book.

"Oh, shut up and get in," I said. "Yes, I got an office, and I want to show it to you."

We drove back to the office and I gave him the grand tour. He looked around carefully, then nodded.

"For six hundred a month," he said, "you got yourself a pretty good deal, here. It's a decent neighborhood, but not too upscale. Not a lot of crime in this area, so that's a plus. I wonder why it was so cheap?"

"I asked the agent that question," I said. "She told me that the previous tenants were running some kind of a scam out of here, so the cops had it boarded up for a few months. They just got all the legal tangles untangled, and the owner is desperate to get rent coming in from it. They only put it back on the market for rent this morning, so I was just at the right place at the right time."

"Well, it's a great place to get started. You're gonna need some office furniture..."

I held out the receipt from the office store. "It'll all be delivered tomorrow morning," I said. "I can't wait for you to see it once I get everything set up."

He stood there and looked at me for a moment, then reached out and put his arms around me.

"Cassie, have I ever told you that I'm proud of you?"

He was looking into my eye, the way he does when he's feeling romantic. I've asked him not to do that, because he knows that it turns me on, but he does it anyway.

I stood there, looking back at him and breathing heavily, so he finally quit waiting for an answer and kissed me. It was a long, drawn-out kiss, and when it was finished I dragged him out the door, locked it behind me, and pushed him toward the car. We got in and I drove straight home, telling him to shut up, we could go pick his car up later.

We did, about three hours later. We stopped at one of the Mexican fast food places for dinner while we were out, then went back home to eat it.

We found a movie on Netflix that sounded interesting, then kicked back to watch it. We sat on the couch the way we usually do when watching TV, with Dex on one end and me leaning against him. It was a really nice way to watch TV, I thought.

Six months earlier, if anybody had told me I would enjoy cuddling with a man again while I watched television, I would've said they were crazy. Back then, the closest I got to intimacy was the assortment of toys I kept in my nightstand drawer. The thought of even letting a man touch me, after the things I had been through with my former fiancé, would send me into spasms of pure revulsion.

Sometimes, though, changes creep up on you when you least expect them. Dex had started out as a mildly annoying acquaintance, but then it turned out that the reason he was so persistent was because he hoped I could help him locate a missing friend. A former girlfriend of his had gone missing after dealing with a stalker, and the stalker had also disappeared. The police had concluded that the two of them simply ran off together, but Dex wouldn't buy it.

After I rescued the first little girl from her stepfather, Dex had talked me into looking for his missing friend. The deeper I dug into it, the more convinced I was that the girl was dead, but then I stumbled across an even more surprising and chilling revelation. I found the answers he was looking for, and a friendship began. I finally gave in to his persistence and agreed to a night out on the town, and it slowly dawned on me that my scars didn't put him off a bit.

We went to a bar and he managed to drag me onto the dance floor, and between that and the liquor, his gentle seduction got through the barriers I had erected around myself. Without even really thinking about what I was doing, I went home with him for the night and suddenly felt alive again.

At that point, since neither of us really had time or inclination for the pursuit of romance, we calmly and bluntly agreed that being friends-with-benefits was exactly what we needed. We started hanging out together on weekends, which often resulted in one of us staying overnight with the other. It was just a way to deal with our need for human contact, and nothing more.

Or so I thought. Over a few short months, I found myself thinking about Dex a lot during the week, and finding excuses to call him. He is a pretty smart guy, and could often help me figure out ways to help my clients, things like that.

At the same time, though I didn't know it then, Dex had begun to realize that he was more attracted to me than he had expected to be. He hinted a few times that he wanted to take our relationship to another level, but I wouldn't even hear of it.

Then, a few months back, I decided to go undercover in my search for the people who were abducting abused women. I have a prosthetic mask that actually makes me look perfectly normal from the neck up, and I put that on, put in my glass eye (ugh) and got Dex to pretend to be my abusive husband. I rented an apartment under a phony name and we put on an act so that all the neighbors could hear me being "abused." Alfie was able to rig it so that when I called a certain abuse hotline, it went directly to the perpetrators, and I became their next target.

I got the bad guys, but then Dex and I had to deal with the fact that we had enjoyed the short time we were living together. We talked it over, and that's how we ended up living together at my place and cuddling on the couch.

"This is nice," I said softly.

"Yeah," Dex said, "it is. I wasn't sure you were going to be able to relax tonight."

I shivered as I remembered the friends who had died that morning. "Life goes on," I said. "Whether we like it or not, life still goes on."

"It does, indeed." His arm, which was wrapped around me, pulled me a little bit closer. "So, are you excited about your new office?"

I broke into a smile, then. "Yes! I really am. I think I can really do some good, you know?"

"Have you thought about what the other abuse clinics are going to think?"

I turned and looked at him. "Why would I? I mean, this isn't a business, I'm not going into competition with them. Am I?"

"Remember what Alfie said once? People set these places up as charities so they can get grants and such, and have tax write-offs. They're making money in some ways, so any clients they lose to you are likely to be money they're not going to get. They might not care at all, but I'm just suggesting you might want to give it a little thought."

I frowned. "It's not supposed to be about making money," I said. "It's supposed to be about helping these women and children get out of bad situations. I can't say I'm going to lose any sleep worrying about whether New Beginnings or the Freedom Center can't give themselves a bonus at Christmas."

I settled back to watch the movie, but suddenly my mind wasn't really into it. I was thinking about what Dex had said, about the possibility that some of the other centers might resent what I was about to do.

On the other hand, St. Mary's Outreach had employed five paid counselors, and had a couple of other part-time volunteers. I was the only full-time volunteer they had, but I was also the only one that didn't need the income. Between all eight of us, we handled a total of around five hundred clients a month. There was no way I could handle them all, so the other programs would probably see an upswing in their clientele, rather than seeing fewer of them. I put the question out of my mind and finally managed to get back into the movie just in time to see Will Smith save the day once again.

FIVE

I WOKE THE NEXT MORNING to a cloudy, overcast day, but I was too busy thinking about my new office and the things I would need to do to let it bother me. Dex was already up and showered by the time I rolled out of bed, so I got my own shower and then went to the kitchen in my bathrobe.

"Sit," he commanded. I raised my eyebrow and thought about a snappy comment, but then he turned around and set a plate of waffles on the table. For waffles, he can get away with talking to me like that.

Holy cow, he'd even melted the butter! I couldn't help wondering how many women were as blessed as I was, but I quashed the thought quickly. I knew that road, and I didn't want to go down it. It's the one that leads to thoughts of chapels and vows, and I certainly wasn't ready for either.

With butter and syrup, waffles are one of the greatest things God ever gave to man. I've often wondered who invented the first waffle iron, and what could have led to the idea, but not knowing the answer hasn't hindered my enjoyment. I cut into the stack and shoved a big forkful into my mouth, and that caused me to moan in sheer delight.

"Oh," I said, "oh, these are so good. Did you do something different this morning?"

"Secret ingredient," he said mysteriously. "I used an old family recipe that I learned from my grandmother."

"Then call your grandmother and tell her I love her. These are incredible. What's the secret ingredient?"

"If I tell you that," said, "it won't be a secret anymore. You can't ask the guy to give up all his culinary secrets, now can you?"

My eyebrow came down, giving me the stare of a one-eyed psycho. "Tell me," I said. "Tell me, now."

He grinned. "Mayonnaise," he said. "Instead of using two eggs, like it calls for, I used two heaping tablespoons of mayonnaise. Makes the batter come out a lot smoother, and for some reason it really brings out the natural flavor of the waffles."

"Whatever it is, it works." I shoved another forkful into my mouth and tried to grin at him at the same time, but it didn't quite work. I don't think he noticed, he was too busy slathering butter and syrup onto his own.

Having breakfast together was one of the benefits of sharing the house. Sometimes, our easy banter actually reminded me of my parents. They had always gotten along well when I was a kid, and I could look back now and see that Mike and I had never achieved that kind of comfort level with each other. Even before he started being abusive, even when I thought he was my knight in shining armor, we just never quite reached the point of being able to joke and tease the way Dex and I could do.

Shake that off, Abby said in my head. *Last thing you need to do is start comparing Dex to Mike! In fact, you shouldn't be thinking about Mike at all. Put that behind you, and everything that went along with it.*

I'm not comparing, I said back. *I was just thinking that it should have been a warning sign, but I didn't recognize it.*

"Abby again?" Dex asked. He had once asked me why my face would occasionally go blank, and I had finally confessed about hearing Abby's voice in my head.

"Yeah," I replied. "Don't worry, she was just telling me what a great guy you are. She never had a boyfriend who would make her waffles."

That got me the look, the one that says he's not quite sure if I'm joking or not. As I said before, I'm fully aware that it isn't really Abby talking to me, and I've explained that to Dex, too. It's just that now and then, I wonder if he believes me, or if he thinks I'm just crazy enough to believe she's living inside my brain.

"Relax, Dex," I said. "It's all good."

We finished off our breakfast, and then he had to rush a bit to make it to work on time. I stood in the bathroom and talked to him while he shaved and sat on the bed while he got dressed, and he kissed me quickly as he hurried out. It was only seven thirty, so I had a little extra time.

I decided that day was going to be about getting the office all set up, so I climbed into a pair of blue jeans and a T-shirt. I slipped my feet into my sneakers and went back to the kitchen to feed Critter, then grabbed my purse and my jacket and headed out the door.

I got to the office well before nine, and went inside to get all the lights on and make sure nothing was in the way for the delivery guys. I found a broom and dust pan, so I swept the place and carried the sweepings out to the dumpster in the back alley. It was one that was provided by the city, and all the businesses on my block paid a fee for it on our water bills.

It was a big dumpster, and had a door in it that had to be opened by hand to throw anything in. The handle was stiff but I got it after a moment, then reached in to empty the dustpan. I was just about to close it again when I heard a sound, and I had to stretch a bit to look inside.

A woman was laying among the trashbags in the bottom of the dumpster, and she had obviously been severely beaten. I dropped the dustpan and grabbed my phone to call 911.

"Nine one one, what is your emergency?"

"This is Cassie McGraw, I'm in the alley behind 1525 Admiral Boulevard," I said. "I just found a badly beaten woman in the trash dumpster."

"I'm sending police and an ambulance immediately," the dispatcher said. "Does she appear to be breathing?"

"Yes, she's breathing, but she seems to be in a lot of pain." I leaned my head into the opening. "I got help coming," I said. "Can you tell me your name?"

She tried to say something, but nothing came out except a grunt.

"She doesn't seem able to speak," I said to the dispatcher. "She's breathing and moving around, but I don't think she's in very good shape."

"Police officers will be there within two minutes," the dispatcher said, "and there's an ambulance on the way now, probably five minutes out. Can you remain there until the police arrive?"

"Yes, I'll stay right here," I said. I could hear sirens off in the distance.

"Do you know the victim?"

I was still looking inside the dumpster, just trying to be sure the woman kept breathing and didn't die on me. I took a good look at her face, then, and got the eerie feeling that she did look familiar. I leaned in a bit further, and then I gasped.

"Yes! Yes, I know her! Her name is Marsha Wyatt, she was the director of St. Mary's Outreach, the place that got bombed yesterday."

"What? Give me that name again, please."

I gave her Marsha's name again, and then the police arrived. I got off the phone with the dispatcher and immediately called Detective Pennington.

"Pennington," he said as he answered.

"Jim, it's Cassie McGraw," I said. "I just found Marsha Wyatt, the St. Mary's Director, alive." I quickly explained to him about finding her in the dumpster, and he told me to stay where I was.

One of the police officers had climbed into the dumpster, and was squatting down beside Marsha. The other one was standing just outside and looking in, but he turned to me as I got off the phone.

"You're the one who found her?"

I nodded. "Yes, sir," I said. I pointed to my dustpan. "I came out to dump that, and I heard her groans."

"Good job on calling for help," he said. "Any idea who she is?"

I told him, and pointed out that Detective Pennington was on the way. The ambulance arrived at that time, and the officers got out of the way to let the paramedics do their job.

It took them several minutes to get her onto a stretcher, and then it took all four of them to lift her out. The opening in the dumpster was too small, so they had to take her up and over the top, about eight feet off the ground. It was actually quite an operation, and if she hadn't been strapped onto the stretcher, I'm pretty sure she would have fallen off. They had just gotten her into the ambulance when Pennington arrived, and he went right past me to try to talk to her.

"Ms. Wyatt," he said, "can you tell me what happened to you?"

"She's not gonna be able to talk," one of the paramedics said. "Her jaw is broken in a couple of places, and I think she has a pretty bad concussion. She's in shock, right now. Let us get her to the hospital and stabilized, and you can try to talk to her later this afternoon."

Pennington scowled, but nodded. He turned around to me and motioned for me to follow him to the side of the alley.

"Is it just me, or does it seem a little odd that you were the one to find her?"

"It's not just you," I said. "That was the first thought that went through my mind." I pointed at the back door of my office. "I just rented this place yesterday afternoon, because I'm going to open my own office to work with the women I was helping at the Outreach. Seems like a pretty big coincidence that she would turn up in the dumpster right behind my new office."

"It does seem that way, don't it? I spoke with Alicia a bit more yesterday afternoon, and she told me some of the details about your last big adventure. Do you make a habit of being targeted by crazy people?"

I rolled my eye. "Not on purpose, I assure you," I said. "I can't really argue with you, though. First you tell me the bomb was in my office, and now I find Marsha all beat up in the dumpster behind my new place? There's obviously some kind of connection, and it has to be me."

He made a face. "I'm waiting for a report back on any purchase history from the possible suspects you and I identified yesterday," he said. "I..."

"You won't find anything," I said. "I got my boss at Centronic to run the same searches, but he can do it a lot faster and better. Unless they paid cash somewhere, none of them bought anything that could be used to make explosives."

That got me a frown. "I'll take a look at the report when it comes in, anyway. I was gonna be calling you before too long, because I just got the report back from the fire department. They only found two bodies inside the building, other than the lady who survived. She still hasn't woke up yet, so we can't get any answers out of her. From what you told us, though, there should have been at least four people inside there. Right?"

My eye was wide. "Yeah," I said. "Of course, one of those was Marsha, but there should have been Angie, Nicole, and Brenda, as well. They said they found Angie's body..."

"Actually," Pennington said, "that body was identified as Brenda Birch. The receptionist might be the other body, but it was so badly burned that they haven't made a positive identification, yet."

I shook my head. "Poor Brenda," I said. "She was another one of the counselors. If I remember the schedule correctly, only she, Marsha, and I were on duty as counselors. Nicole is actually a child psychologist, a volunteer. She comes in two days a week to work with the children the women often bring with them."

Pennington nodded, then turned and looked toward the ambulance. They were closing the doors, and then it drove away a moment later with siren blaring.

"I'm wondering," he said, "if you opening an office is really a good idea. I hate to say this, Cassie, but it's really starting to look like you were the target. Whoever did this must have taken Ms. Wyatt yesterday morning, for some reason we don't know yet. The question is how he found out about your new office so quickly. Looks to me like he planned on somebody finding her dead, in your dumpster."

"Oh, God," I said. "I guess it does look that way. The shape she was in, she probably wouldn't have lasted a lot longer. You think he left her for dead, figured the garbage men would find her or something?"

"No, from the look of her, I suspect he thought she was already dead. It's probably nothing short of a miracle that she was alive enough to make a noise for you to hear." He looked away for a moment, then turned back to me and looked me in the eye. "I need you to understand something," he said. "I have to consider the possibility that her injuries are your work. I'm not saying I believe that, but I'm going to need to know everything you've done for the last few days."

I let Freda give him her icy stare. "Jim, you need to think. If I beat her up like that and put her in a dumpster to be found after she died, do you really think I would've called 911? She's alive, and there's at least a decent chance she's going to stay that way. If I did it, I sure as hell wouldn't want her able to talk, now would I?"

He had the grace to look sheepish. "Like I said, it's not that I believe it. It's just due diligence, all right? I admit you make sense, but I still have to look into it."

I shrugged. "It's okay, I really do understand. I'm more worried about what you said a minute ago. How on Earth did this guy find out about the office so quickly?"

"Did you tell anyone?"

"Well, I told my boyfriend. Other than that, I haven't told anybody about it yet. Wait, I take that back. I did call all of my current clients yesterday and tell them that I was planning to open an office, but I hadn't even looked at one yet. I didn't have an address or anything to give anyone."

"Let's take a look at the place," he said. We walked in through the back door, and I locked it behind us. I led him through the back utility room and into the office area, and we both jumped when somebody yelled out, "Hello?"

It was the delivery guys, of course. I had lost track of time after finding Marsha and waiting for the police and everything, and they had been there for about ten minutes.

"I'm sorry about that," I said. "We had, well, something of an emergency out back." I didn't feel like going into detail with these perfect strangers, so Pennington simply waited while they carried everything inside. Once they were in my office setting up the desk, he and I sat down in the reception area.

"I'm going to need the list of people you called," he said. "It's possible one of their husbands could be our perpetrator. If he overheard you talking to her, or she mentioned that you were getting an office, he might have followed you or something." He pointed at the sign on the window. "The real estate agent plastered 'No Longer Available' over the for rent sign. That would have been enough to tell him this is probably the one you got."

I frowned. "You know what? I've gotten pretty sensitive to people following me, and I really don't think there was anybody on my tail yesterday. I could be wrong, but I don't think so."

"And I could be wrong. I'm just trying to think of how he might have known that this was going to be your place. It's just too much of a coincidence to believe he put her in the dumpster behind your office just by chance."

"Oh, I agree. There's no doubt in my mind that you're right, he was planning on her being found dead right behind my new place of business. Nothing else makes any sense, but none of this really makes any sense, anyway. I mean, if he's after me, why did he bother taking her? If he was planning on her ending up dead, why not leave her in the building when he blew it up?"

"Those are all good questions," Pennington said. "I'll be sure to ask them, when we catch the bastard."

I turned Freda loose again. "If you get to him before I do," I said. "It was bad enough when I thought he might have blown us up at random, and then you said the bomb was probably in my own office, so that made it kind of personal. Now, he dumps my friend in the trash behind my new office? That's not just personal, that's war."

SIX

PENNINGTON LEFT A FEW minutes later, going out the back to speak to the crime scene technicians that were digging through the dumpster. I stepped out with him for a moment, just long enough to hear them explain that they weren't finding much of anything that was of value. I closed the door and locked it again, then went back toward the front.

I looked into my office and saw that the desk was fully assembled. They were in the process of setting up the credenza that came with it, and I stood in the doorway and just admired it all for a moment. One of the guys turned around and looked at me, but then he looked quickly away.

I was used to that, so I went back up front to the reception area and sat down in one of the chairs they had brought in. I took out my phone and checked the time, saw that it was almost 10:30, and called Dex.

"Hey, sexy," he said. "How's it going?"

"I'm half surprised you haven't heard on the radio," I said. "I swept up some dirt and carried it out to the dumpster behind my office, and found Marsha Wyatt laying inside it. She looks like somebody beat her with a ball bat, and the police think whoever did it probably thought she was dead when they put her in there."

Dex is one of the fastest thinkers I have ever known. "Somebody is sending you a message," he said. "There's no way it's a coincidence, but who could have known that was your office?"

"That's what the cops and I are trying to figure out," I said. "Whoever did this must have had some kind of reason for taking Marsha out of the Outreach before the bomb went off, but it obviously wasn't to keep her safe. She's in pretty bad shape. They took her to the hospital, but the paramedics said her jaw is broken and she has a concussion. Might be a while before she's able to talk."

"Yeah. Anything new about Nicole? Jimmy left yesterday while I was out with you, and he's been at the hospital ever since."

Jimmy Hanks was a friend of Dex's, a coworker there at the Ford garage. We had introduced him and Nicole sometime back, and they were still dating several times a week. Nicole had actually told me a few days earlier that she was falling in love with Jimmy, but swore me to secrecy. Naturally, I went home and told Dex exactly what she had said, and he laughed because Jimmy had said the same thing to him that very day.

"Detective Pennington said she hasn't woke up yet," I said. "Must be hard on Jimmy. I hope she's okay."

"Yeah, me too. What are you going to do the rest of the day? Are you going to stay there, all by yourself?"

"Of course not," I said. "I'll be staying here with Mr. Smith and Mr. Wesson. Don't worry, Dex, I can take care of myself."

"I know that," he said. "Can't help being cautious, though. I'm a guy, remember? It comes with having a girlfriend."

"Well, yeah, but most guys don't have a girlfriend with a PI license and a concealed carry permit."

"And I'd be a lot happier if she added a black belt that list. Listen, it's not that long until lunchtime. I'll grab us something to eat and come down there on my break."

"Okay," I said. "See you then."

I cut off the call and leaned back, thinking about Marsha and wondering just what she had gone through. From the look of her, it must've been horrible. I remembered the paramedic saying it look like the work of a ball bat, and I shivered.

The delivery guys finished up a few minutes later and left. One of them seemed to have no problem with me at all, even shook my hand. The other just wanted to get out of the building as quickly as he could. He hurried out the door as I was signing the ticket that said they had done a good job.

"Sorry about my partner, there," the guy said. "He's a little..."

"He's perfectly normal," I said. "Most people react that way the first time they see me, I've gotten used to it."

He gave me a halfhearted grin and shrugged. "Listen, would it be rude if I ask..."

I smiled. "It was my former fiancé. I found out about something horrible he had done, something that would have sent him to prison for the rest of his life. He decided he didn't want me to talk, so he called a friend of his who poured gasoline on me and set me on fire. Somehow, I lived through it."

His eyes were wide and he shook his head. "That's horrible," he said. "What are you going to be doing here? I mean, is this for a business?"

"Actually, I'm a counselor for women in abusive relationships. Having been there, I can understand what it is they're going through."

His eyes somehow got a little wider. "Really? Do you have a business card or something? I got a sister who needs to talk to you. Her old man, he's nuts."

I still had some of my Outreach business cards, so I scribbled my cell number onto one of them and gave it to him. "Tell her to call me on that number," I said. "Unfortunately, the Outreach was the one that got blown up yesterday."

He nodded his head. "Will do," he said. "By the way, my name is Jason, and my sister is Tammy. I hope I can get her to call you, she really needs to talk to somebody who can get through to her."

"I'll do my best if she calls."

Jason hurried out the door and got into his truck, and he and his partner drove away. I looked around my new office for a couple of minutes, then locked the front door and started putting out the decorations I purchased.

There was a knock on the door a few minutes later, and I looked out to see a man standing there. He was from the telephone company, and he barely even got up the nerve to come inside after getting a look at my face. He installed my phone system, with a phone on the reception desk, one on my desk, and one in the conference room. He managed to give me a quick instruction in how to use the three lines and the hold button, and then he was gone.

I went back to hanging paintings on the wall and putting out fake plants, but then there was another knock. This time, it was Dex standing there with a bag in his hand. I hurried over and unlocked the door to let him in.

"I felt like fish," Dex said. He handed me a basket of fish planks, six of them with hush puppies and fries.

"Where's the sauce?" I asked. He reached into the bag and came out with a small bottle of malt vinegar sauce, and I rewarded him with a smile. I twisted off the cap and dumped a generous amount onto my fish, then handed it back to him so he could do the same.

We sat at the reception desk and ate, and I filled him in on more of the details surrounding finding Marsha. He shook his head at the appropriate spots, then asked if I was going to try to see her that afternoon.

"Yeah, I think I will," I said. "A part of me is just relieved that she didn't die in the blast, but another part wonders if what she went through might not be even worse than that. My God, getting beaten like that would be torture."

"Yeah," Dex said. "Have you called Alfie yet?"

I guess I looked confused, because he chuckled. "Why should I call Alfie?"

"Somebody has managed to find out you got this place before any record of it could exist. You ask me, that sounds a lot like something a computer hacker could do. You ought to check with Alfie and see what he can find out."

I narrowed my eye. "You're thinking maybe somebody got into the realtor's computer?"

"No," he said. "I'm thinking somebody has gotten into your cell phone. You said you called several real estate agents and made appointments, but then you canceled the other ones after you saw this place. If somebody was listening in to your calls, it wouldn't have been hard to know which place you took."

I stared at him for three more seconds, then yanked out my phone and called Alfie. I told him the entire situation, and he agreed with Dex.

"Somebody is listening in on your calls," he said. "They might even be tracking your GPS signal, checking where you've been. Let me do a little digging and I'll see what I can find out."

"He's going to check it out," I said. "Can he really do that? Find out if somebody hacked into my phone?"

"If anybody can, he can. Alfie knows more about computers than anyone else I've ever known. I don't know how many times I've heard him going off on somebody who thought they were some kind of computer expert, explaining to them just how stupid they really are. It never fails, but he's right and they end up apologizing."

We talked for a few more minutes, and then he had to get back to work. I gave him a kiss as he was leaving, then followed him out the door and locked the office behind me. I had decided to go to the hospital and see if Marsha was able to have visitors yet.

I should've called first. Because she was obviously the victim of violence, and possibly connected to the bombing case, there were two police officers stationed outside her hospital room. The front desk refused to tell me anything about her, so I took out my phone and called Pennington.

"Hey, it's Cassie," I said. "I came to the hospital to see if Marsha might be awake and coherent, but they said you got her under police guard. Any way you could let me in to see her?"

He let out a sigh. "I probably shouldn't," he said, "but I will. Give it a minute, and then they should tell you to go on up to her room."

"Okay, thanks."

The phone on the desk rang, and the lady picked it up. She was speaking softly, but I saw her look up at me and nod to herself. She put the phone down, then turned to me.

"That was the detective in charge of this lady's case," she said. "He said to put you on the list that can go see her. She's in room four twenty-seven, fourth floor. If the officers up there haven't been told yet, just tell them to call the detective."

I thanked her and went to the elevator, rode it up to the fourth floor, and got out. It was easy to spot which room must be Marsha's, because the two cops were in plain sight. As I walked toward them, one of them noticed me and nudged the other.

"Hi," I said. "I'm Cassie McGraw, and..."

"Yes, ma'am," one of them said, staring at my face. "We were told. You can go on in, but I don't think she's awake."

I smiled and thanked him, then stepped inside the room. The lights were dim and the machines were beeping as I walked up and stood beside the hospital bed.

Poor Marsha! Most of her head was wrapped in bandages, and there was literally some sort of bracing around her jaw. There was a tube going into her nose, and she was black and blue all over. I noticed that her right arm was strapped to a board, and there were two different IVs run into it.

"Marsha?" I asked quietly. At first, I didn't think she was awake at all, but then her eyes fluttered open and she looked up at me. She grunted something, but her jaw wouldn't move. "No, don't talk," I said. "You've been hurt pretty badly. Your jaw is broken, and it looks like they've got it braced so it can heal."

She blinked a couple of times, and I saw tears starting to run from her eyes.

"Marsha, do you know what happened?"

Slowly, carefully, she shook her head from side to side.

"Did you see whoever did this to you?"

This time, she nodded. I gave her a smile, and I saw her lips twitch as she tried to return it.

"Did anyone tell you about anything that happened yesterday?"

Her eyes squeezed shut, and her tears flowed steadily. I took that to mean that she'd been told about the bomb.

"Marsha, we're going to find whoever did this. The police are working on it, and so am I. Did you know the man who did this to you?"

She shook her head again, in the negative.

"Okay, I just wondered. Detective Pennington is in charge of the case, I'm sure he'll be down here to see you soon. You just need to rest, and he'll tell you more about what's going on. I just wanted to come by and see how you were doing."

Her left hand reached across and grabbed hold of my right hand, which was laying on the rail of the bed. She gripped it tightly, and pulled me toward her. I leaned closer and looked into her eyes.

"What? Is there something you're trying to say?"

She nodded.

"Okay," I said. "Do you think you could write something down?"

She nodded, quicker this time. I looked around and found a piece of paper, something that had apparently been left by one of the hospital staff. I flipped it over and found a pen in my purse, then grabbed a magazine that was laying on a side table. I put the pen in her hand, and held the magazine to support the paper.

Marsha is right-handed, but she did a fair job of printing with her left. She wrote slowly, and I was following the letters, reading upside down as she wrote.

N... O... T... K... N... O... W... She finished writing those letters, then pointed at them with the pen and looked up at me.

"You are saying you didn't know the man that did this?" I asked. "It was a man, right?"

She nodded her head slowly, deliberately. She looked back at the paper and began writing again.

A... N... G... I... E... She pointed at the paper again.

I stared at her, my single eye big and round. "Angie did this to you?"

She shook her head.

"Then what are you trying to say about Angie? They think they found her body in the wreckage, but they're not sure yet."

She shook her head again, then went back to the paper.

A… L… I… V… E…

I stared at the word she had written. "Angie is alive?"

Marsha nodded.

My eye still wide, I stared at her for a couple of seconds, letting the implications sink in.

"Marsha, are you saying the guy who did this has her?"

She nodded again.

SEVEN

I GRABBED MY PHONE and called Pennington, and he answered on the second ring.

"Jim, it's Cassie," I said. "I've been talking to Marsha, and she says the guy who took her took Angie, too, at the same time. Marsha thinks Angie is still alive."

"Stay put," he said. "I'm actually on my way there, now. Can she talk?"

"No, but she can write. Printing, with her left hand, but she can answer you. Hurry up and get here." I cut off the call and took hold of Marsha's hand again. "He's on the way. Marsha, do you know where he has her? Where he took you?"

She shook her head, and then pulled her hand away and picked up the pen. She seemed to be gaining some confidence with her left hand, because she wrote more quickly this time.

Somewhere close

"Close to where the office was?"

She nodded. Her hand started writing again.

Short ride

"Okay, that's good. Can you describe him?"

Tall young 25-26 brown hair brown eyes

She closed her eyes for a second, as if concentrating, then started writing again.

Green pants green shirt

"Okay. We're getting somewhere. What about the vehicle, what kind of car was it?"

Old car blue big

"An old car? Any idea what kind it was? Ford, Chevy?"

She shook her head.

I picked up the paper she'd been writing on and looked it over. She said the guy was tall, mid twenties with brown hair and brown eyes, wearing green pants and a green shirt.

Green pants and shirt. "Was he wearing some kind of uniform?"

She nodded.

"Okay, think," I said. "Was there any kind of company name on it? Maybe a logo or something, or did it have his name on it?"

She closed her eyes tight and kept them that way for moment. When she opened them, she snatched the paper back, but this time she didn't write. She drew a cloud, with what looked like a lightning bolt slashing down from it.

It was a logo, and I suspected it had something to do with electricity, but it wasn't anything I'd ever seen before. I took out my phone and snapped a picture of it, and emailed it to Alfie.

See if you can find out what company uses this logo, I said.

Pennington came in a few minutes later and came to stand right beside me. He looked down at Marsha and smiled.

"Good to see you're awake," he said. "Bet you hurt like hell, right?"

The grunt that came from her that time was probably her body's attempt to laugh at the absurdity of his comment. She winced, then nodded slowly.

"Well, I've always heard that hurting means you lived through whatever happened," he said. "And you did, and a lot of that is thanks to this gal." He indicated me with a flick of his head. "You were lucky she needed to take out the trash at that moment. Couple more hours without medical attention, and you probably wouldn't have made it."

"Geez, Jim," I said, "a little tact, maybe?"

"Ignore her," he said to Marsha. "You were lucky, and that's the truth. I was really hoping you'd be able to talk a bit, but I can see that's not going to happen soon." He looked at the paper she was holding. "I brought you a notepad. Think you can write out answers to my questions?"

Marsha nodded. Pennington took the paper and pulled a notepad out of the pocket inside his jacket and handed it to her. She laid it on the magazine.

"Okay, I see Cassie has already been asking some of the right questions. This is a description of the guy who did this?"

Marsha nodded.

"The drawing is a logo," I said. "The green pants and shirt were part of a company uniform, and it had that logo on it. Any idea what company that could be?"

"Not at the moment, but we got people who can find stuff like that." He turned back to Marsha. "You know that your office was bombed, right? Did you see this guy plant the bomb?"

Marsha looked at the paper and started writing.

Had a bag. Put it in hall.

"Okay, that fits with what we know. It would have been in the hall, real close to where Cassie's office was?"

Marsha nodded her head.

"Did he say anything to you before he took you out of there?"

Where is Cassie? Asked about Leanne.

Pennington glanced at me. "Leanne?"

My eye had gone wide. "Oh, Lord," I said. "Leanne Downey. She was a client, one of Marsha's clients. Marsha, was Leanne there?"

She nodded, and tears began to flow again. She picked up the pen and started writing once more.

He had gun. Shot Leanne and Brenda. Made me and Angie go with.

Pennington's face was grim. "She's right," he said to me. "We hadn't released that information, yet, but both of the victims we found inside the building had been shot." He looked at the paper she had originally been writing on. "You're saying that wherever he took you was not far from your office? Can you guess how long it took to get there?"

2-3 minutes

Pennington nodded. "Well, that gives us a radius. Excuse me, I've got to go make a phone call."

He stepped just outside the room and took out his phone, but I couldn't make out exactly what he was saying. At one point I heard him mention Leanne Downey, so I figured he was telling someone to try to confirm her identity. He was on the phone for about ninety seconds, then came back into the room.

"Ms. Wyatt," he said, "the other woman, Angie. Was she injured when you saw her last?"

Marsha shook her head, and started writing.

He said I was message. Said he was sorry before he hit me.

"What did he hit you with?" Pennington asked.

Metal bar

"You said he told you you were a message. To Cassie?"

Marsha nodded.

"Did he tell you why he was so interested in her?"

This time, she shook her head in the negative. She looked at me, and started crying again.

"Marsha," I said, "oh, my God, I'm so sorry."

She wrote again.

Not your fault

I couldn't think of anything to say. I looked at her for a few seconds, but then my cell phone chimed to tell me I had gotten an email. I yanked it out and looked, and sure enough, it was from Alfie.

That is the old logo from Lightning Electric Supply. Company went out of business three years ago. No joy on your phone. Whoever hacked it didn't leave fingerprints.

I handed the phone to Pennington and let him read it. He grunted, then handed it back.

"That mean anything to you?"

I shook my head. "No, nothing. They would've been out of business before I ever came here."

"It's just kind of odd that a guy doing something like this would wear the uniform from a defunct company. If he's connected to that company, that's like giving us a free clue."

"Might be something he picked up at a thrift shop," I said. "My boyfriend buys old work uniforms, because they can stand up to the grease and stuff."

He nodded. "Maybe." He turned back to Marsha. "Ms. Wyatt, can you think of anything else that might help us catch this guy?"

Marsha closed her eyes tight again, but she opened them a moment later and shook her head.

"Well, I'll let you rest. I'll probably be back with more questions..."

I interrupted him. "I got a question. Marsha, when did he beat you? Was it this morning?"

She nodded.

"How did he treat you before that? Was he hurting you at all?"

She shook her head, then started writing.

Put us in room and locked it. Brought sandwiches at lunch and chicken last night. Gave us water.

"What about going to the bathroom? Did he let you?"

Bathroom in room. Like in motel.

I looked at Pennington. "What kind of buildings that close to downtown would have bathrooms in the rooms?"

He shrugged. "Could be a lot of them. You know how many offices are empty downtown? There are probably a dozen small office buildings that are completely vacant in that area, but you can bet I'm going to get someone checking them, now. Good job, Cassie."

A nurse came in. "Hey," she said. "Doctor said she needs to be resting. We understand you have to talk to her, but you need to make it just a little at a time, okay?"

Pennington looked at the nurse and nodded. "We were just about to leave," he said. He turned to Marsha and told her he'd be back, then motioned for me to follow him out of the room.

When we got out into the hallway, he stopped and looked at me.

"Alicia was right," he said. "She told me you're a natural investigator. I missed a good point there, and you picked it up."

"I did?"

"Yeah," he said. "The part about when he beat her. That tells us that he made the decision to try to send you that message sometime this morning, rather than last night. If he'd thought of it last night, she would have been dead by the time you found her."

"What gets me," I said, "is that he was treating them decent up until that point. And she said he told her he was sorry. Sorry that he had to do it? Sorry that he was going to kill her?"

"I don't know," he said. "About the only thing we do know for sure, now, is that this son of a bitch is out to get you."

I looked at him for a moment, and then I shook my head. "No," I said, "he's not. I'm not sure what it is he's doing, but he would have known I was going to be at my office, alone, this morning. If he wanted me, that was his chance. Why didn't he take it?"

"He asked where you were before he left the bomb in the building," Pennington said, musing. "I took that to mean he was upset that you weren't there, but maybe I got it wrong. Maybe he was making sure you hadn't arrived, yet."

"But that doesn't make any sense either," I said. "Any other day, I would have been there. If it hadn't been for all the red lights, I would've made it, I would've been inside the building before that bomb went off."

He looked at me and chewed on the inside of his cheek. "This is one of the most confusing cases I've ever seen. Maybe he was planning to grab you with them? That might be why he'd ask where you were."

"But then I have to go back to the fact that he could have grabbed me this morning. Well, he could've tried."

More cheek chewing. "No, I'm going to stick with my gut on this. I think he was making sure you weren't there."

I looked at him. "Wait here a minute," I said, and I turned around and walked right back into Marsha's room. The nurse looked up at me, but the look on my face told her not to say a word and she didn't. I went straight to Marsha's bedside.

"Marsha," I began, "when did he ask you where I was? Was he already starting trouble?"

She shook her head and started writing.

No. Asked if you were there, then asked where you were. Angie said late and he took bag into hall. Angie yelled for him to stop and I came out. Leanne and Brenda came out. He looked scared and pulled out gun. Shot them and made me and Angie go with him.

Something wasn't adding up, but it took me a second to realize what it was.

"Marsha, they found Nicole inside the building. She was alive, but she's in a coma. Why didn't she come out?"

No idea. Didn't see her.

"Okay," I said. "You get some rest. I'll try to come back and see you tomorrow, okay?"

She nodded, and I left the room, letting Freda glare at the nurse one more time on my way out.

"Okay, here's what I found out," I said to Pennington. "The guy came in and asked if I was there, and Angie said no. He asked where I was and she told him I was running late. That's when he went through the door to set the bomb down, and Angie yelled at him to stop. Marsha and Brenda came out to see what was going on, and I guess Leanne followed Marsha. She said he looked scared, and that's when he pulled out the gun and shot Leanne and Brenda. The thing that's getting me is that Nicole didn't come out of her office. Marsha said she never saw her yesterday morning, but they found her inside the building."

"I might be able to explain that part," he said. "You're talking about the woman who was still alive, right? CSI thinks she had just come in the back door when the blast went off. A lot of the building caved in on her, but she didn't actually get caught in the blast itself. That's probably why she's alive."

Suddenly, I felt kind of stupid. It hadn't occurred to me to ask where Nicole had been inside the building, I had assumed she was in her office.

"Okay, that makes sense, then."

"And what you just told me," he went on, "backs up my theory that he wanted to be sure you were not there. I don't know why, but he didn't want you to be caught in the blast. Apparently, he didn't want to abduct you, either. All that leaves us with is knowing that you are somehow connected to all this, but with no information on how or why."

I shook my head. "That's what I want to find out," I said. "Just what is it that makes him ask about me?"

He stood there and looked at me for another moment, then shrugged. "I don't know," he said. "If you come up with any theories, I want to hear them." He turned and walked away, and I stood there, trying to think of what to do next.

I rode the elevator down to the first floor, walked back to the front desk, and looked at the woman sitting there again.

"There's another patient here," I said. "Nicole Rayburn. What room is she in?"

"She's also under police guard," the lady said. "But I guess, if you can see one of them, you can see the other one. She's in 509."

Back in the elevator, and up to the fifth floor. The officers standing in front of Nicole's room looked at me for a moment, then one of them smiled. I recognized him from my big undercover case; he was one of the responding officers who came to help with the women I had rescued.

"Ms. McGraw," he said. "Good to see you again. I heard you might be coming up here."

"Hi, there," I said, frantically looking for his name tag. "Officer Landers, right?"

"Yes, ma'am," he said. I think I detected a hint of pride that I remembered his name, so I hope he never figures out that I had to read it off his chest. "The doctors ran in here a few minutes ago, I guess the lady finally woke up."

I broke into a bigger smile. "Really? Can I go in?"

He held the door open for me and I stepped inside. Jimmy was sitting on the edge of the bed, holding Nicole's hand, and she was looking up at him. She heard the door and glanced my way, and suddenly started to cry.

"Cassie," she said. "Oh, God, I'm so glad you're okay. Jimmy said there was a bomb..."

I walked around instead of the other side of the pack. "Yes, there was. Brenda was killed, and one of Marsha's clients, Leanne Downey. The guy who did it kidnapped Marsha and Angie, but Marsha has been found. She was in pretty bad shape, she's here in the hospital, too. How are you doing?"

"The doctors say I've got a concussion, and had some swelling on the brain. I guess it's going down, now, but they say I have to stay a day or two."

"Nicole, what do you remember about what happened?" I asked.

"I can't say I really remember anything," she said. "I remember walking in the door, and then I woke up here just a little bit ago."

"Okay," I said. "I was just told a little bit ago that the crime scene technicians thought that's what had happened. They said it looked like you had just come in the back door when the bomb went off."

"I guess so. God, I wish I could remember. How bad is Marsha hurt? You said she was in bad shape?"

I didn't think I should go into too much detail, so I just told her that the guy who did this had beaten Marsha pretty badly and left her to be found. I also told her that Detective

Pennington would probably be coming to see her, and I explained about the police guards on her door.

"It's always possible that the perpetrator might think you know something," I said. "Probably not, but just in case he might try to get to you, they decided to give you police protection."

Jimmy looked at me. "He'd have to get past me," he said. The look in his eyes told me he meant business.

"See?" I asked. "Between Jimmy and a couple of cops, you couldn't be safer."

I stayed and chatted for about twenty minutes, mostly just to reassure her that she was going to be okay. When I told her I needed to go, she pulled me down and gave me a hug.

Jimmy walked out to the hall with me and followed me to the elevator.

"Cassie," he said. "I want to hire you to find out who did this."

"You don't need to, Jimmy," I said. "I'm already on this case, and so are the police. Trust me, we're going to get this guy."

He looked down at the floor, then raised his eyes back up to meet mine. "Look, I don't know for sure how Nicole feels, but I'm just crazy about her. It makes me nuts to think somebody would have killed her so callously. If you need anything, and I mean anything at all, don't you hesitate to call me. I don't care what it costs, I'll sell everything I've got if that's what it takes."

I reached out and patted his shoulder. "It's already covered, Jimmy," I said. "Go back in there and take care of her. That's what she needs right now."

He looked like he was going to say something, but then he turned and walked away. I pushed the button for the elevator and waited for it to come up to me.

I walked out the front door and across the street to the parking garage, then took that elevator up to deck three. I stepped out and looked around, because I couldn't quite remember where I had parked the Kia.

There was a horrendous explosion, and the shockwave knocked me on my ass.

EIGHT

I SAT THERE, STUNNED, wondering just what had happened, and then it dawned on me that the blast had come from the other side of the deck. That was where I had parked the Kia, I remembered suddenly, and the blast came just after I stepped out of the elevator.

Alarms were going off on half the cars on the deck, and the noise was deafening. Well, it would have been, had the blast not already set my ear to ringing. I was trying to get to my feet when several people came running, some of them from further down the deck and some out of the stairwell beside the elevator.

Hands were grabbing me and trying to lift me up, and I saw people trying to talk to me, but I couldn't hear a word they were saying. The ringing was so loud that I could barely even detect the noise of the alarms, so I just kept shaking my head. I remember thinking how strange it was as a blue van passed us, driving calmly and slowly down and toward the exit. The driver, a man with a hat on, seemed to be looking straight at me, but it didn't really register at that moment.

There was a bench beside the elevator, and a couple of men walked me over and made me sit down. A lady produced a bottle of water out of her purse and handed it to me, and when I saw that it had never been opened, I gratefully twisted off the top and took a drink.

I'm not sure how long I sat there, but police and firemen arrived pretty quickly. Sure enough, it was my Kia that had exploded, and while my ear wasn't ringing quite as badly as at first, my anger was suddenly through the roof! That was my Kia, I had that car since high school. Well, longer, in a way. It had been my mother's car, and I sort of inherited it when Mom got a new one from Dad for their twentieth anniversary. I'd kept it for sentimental reasons, even after the settlement with the city of St. Louis made me relatively wealthy.

One of the police officers figured out quickly who I was, and it wasn't long before Jim Pennington showed up. He hurried over and asked me if I was all right, and I assured him that I was.

"Well, this just gets weirder and weirder," he said. "We'll check the security camera footage, maybe we can get a picture of the guy. He must've planted the bomb while you were in the hospital."

"You think? I'd say he's definitely trying to finish the job he started yesterday. Dammit, he blew up my car."

"Finish the job? You think he was trying to kill you?"

I looked at him as if he had purple hair. "He blew up my car," I said. "I don't think he was trying to tell me he has a crush on me."

"But it blew up while you weren't in it," Pennington said. "If he wanted to kill you, he would've waited until you got in."

I stopped and thought about what he had said. "You could be right," I conceded. "I had just stepped out of the elevator when it blew up."

His eyes registered comprehension. "He had to have been watching for you, then," he said. "I'd say that kind of confirms that he isn't trying to kill you, but maybe we should put protection on you for a while, anyway, just in case."

"Oh, the hell you will," I said. "I want the little bastard to keep coming after me." Suddenly, I got a grip on the raging anger driving my thoughts. "Wait a minute, was anybody hurt when it blew up?"

"Doesn't look like it," Pennington said. "We were lucky on that, I guess. There wasn't anybody else close to it when it went up, but several other cars were damaged. The two right beside it were totaled, but there's probably eight or ten cars with broken windows and other damage. Your insurance company can expect to get sued."

I leaned against the back of the bench, relieved. "Thank God nobody was killed," I said. "I meant what I said, though. If he's after me, then hiding me away isn't going to do any good. We need to do whatever we can to catch him while he's trying to get to me."

Pennington sat down on the bench beside me and looked at me for a moment. "You might be right," he said. "But let me know if you change your mind. I could put a surveillance detail on you. Four different people, four different cars. Nobody would notice them, but they'd be watching you and keeping an eye on your car when you're out of it. I mean, assuming you have another car?"

I sighed. "Not yet, I don't," I said. "Can you give me a lift to the Ford dealership?"

"Sure," he said. "But are you sure you want to involve your boyfriend in this?"

"Trust me, you won't keep him out of it. The reason I need a ride, though, is because I need to buy a car. I'll deal with the insurance company on the Kia later."

"Okay. Just let me know if you want police protection, so I can start the surveillance."

The crime scene technicians had arrived and were going over what was left of my little Sportage, so he led me to his car and even held the door open for me. It was the first time I had actually been in a police car—well, in the front seat, anyway—and I was surprised at how crowded it was. There was a shotgun standing straight up from the floor, right beside my left knee.

I had him drop me off at the service entrance, and I walked up to the cashier's window. The girl who works there looked up at me and grinned.

"Hi, Cassie," she said. "You need to talk to Dex?"

I grimaced. "Yeah, kinda," I said. "Is he real busy?"

"Always, but I'll get him for you." She picked up the telephone and pushed the button, and I heard her calling for Dex over the intercom. I felt a sense of déjà vu, because I'd gone through the same exact thing the first time I ever met him.

Dex came out front a moment later and broke into a smile when he saw me. The smile vanished a split second later, when he saw the thin line that my lips were set in.

"What happened?"

I didn't want everyone in the place to know, so I motioned for him to step outside with me for a moment. When we were out in the parking lot, I told him about the Kia getting blown to smithereens.

He shook his head. "How are we going to stop this guy?" he asked me.

I sighed. "I don't know, Dex," I said. "At least, this time, all he did was blow up my car. Nobody was hurt, thank God."

"It could've been a lot worse," he admitted. "He probably did it with a remote, just waited until he saw you coming out and pushed a button." He shook his head. "You ever think it might be a miracle that he didn't decide to wait till you were in it?"

"Trust me, I know what a miracle it was, okay? I've already said my little prayer of thanks, but now I need to buy a car. What's the best one?"

He grinned. "That depends on what you want," he said. "You want another SUV? Or would you rather have a sports car?"

I looked at him for a moment. "Maybe something sporty," I said.

"Well, they don't let me out on the sales floor. Go up front and talk to Jake Hogan. I'll buzz him and let him know that you get my price."

He grabbed my shoulders and pulled me in for a quick kiss, then turned around and was gone. I walked around to the front of the building and stepped inside, and four salesman tried to descend upon me at once.

"I'm looking for Jake," I said.

"I'm Jake," said an older man. "Relax, guys, this is Dex's girlfriend. He told me to take care of her."

The other three grumbled as they walked away, and Jake stuck out his hand without a moment's hesitation. I shook hands with him.

"Cassie McGraw," I said. "I'm here to buy a car."

"Well, then, you came to the right place, because that's what we do. We sell cars. Any idea what you're looking for?"

"I was talking to Dex, and I think maybe something like a Mustang. Something sporty, you know?"

"We've got quite a selection of them. Have you got a particular budget in mind?"

"No, not really," I said. "Why? Are Mustangs expensive?"

Jake laughed. "They can get that way," he said. "What we can do is start you out looking at the less expensive ones, and then see what kind of options you might want to add in."

I looked at him for a moment, and thought about all the stories I'd heard about the car salesman trying to take advantage of women.

"I got a better idea," I said. "Let's start with the absolute best Mustang you've got on the lot. Which one would that be?"

His face took on a sly look. "Well, most people would say that's the new Mustang GT fastback. I got to warn you, though, that is an extremely powerful car."

"That's okay," I said. "I'm not scared."

Jake grinned, grabbed a couple of things, and we walked out onto the lot. He led me right up to an absolutely beautiful new Mustang, used the smart key to unlock it, and then held the driver's door open for me. I got behind the wheel and adjusted the seat as he got in the passenger side, put on my seatbelt, and pushed the button to start the car.

The engine roared, and I felt a thrill go through me. Dex's Mustang was one of the original ones, a 1965 model that he built from one he pulled out of a junkyard. This machine was brand spanking new, showing only six miles on its digital odometer. The whole car vibrated with the engine, and I felt myself starting to fall in love.

"We can take it for a drive," Jake said, but I was already putting it in gear. I pressed gently on the gas pedal and it pulled out smoothly, and I drove it cautiously to the exit onto the street. I turned onto Sheridan, then gave the pedal a much firmer push.

The car leaped forward, and Jake and I were both thrown back into our seats. I let out a laugh, curved onto the ramp for the Broken Arrow Expressway, and then floored it.

The car took off as if it had been standing still. A quick glance at Jake showed me that his eyes were wide and he was staring through the windshield, but I had been a farm girl. If there was one thing we learned how to do, it was drive like a bat out of hell.

This car was built for it, there was no doubt in my mind. I was weaving in and out of traffic like a professional race driver, and I was shocked when I glanced at the speedometer and saw that I was doing over a hundred miles an hour. I swear it didn't feel like we were going a bit over eighty, so I eased down on the brakes and brought it down to the speed limit.

Jake seemed to be catching his breath about then, so I peeled off the next exit and turned around to go back. As we pulled into the dealership lot again, I looked over at him and said, "I'll take it."

He gave me a funny-looking smile, and acted like he couldn't wait to get out of the car. I parked it right up near the showroom and we walked inside. Forty-five minutes and a lot of money later, I was the proud owner of a new, shiny black Mustang GT.

And then Jake told me I could pick it up the following day.

"I beg your pardon," I said. "I need it today."

"Well, there are some things we have to do to it before you take it," he said. "It's normal procedure, like making sure it's clean and..."

"Then do it now," I said. "I have to take the car with me when I leave today."

He looked at me again, then let out a sigh and picked up the phone on his desk. I'm not sure who he talked to, but the next thing I knew, they were rushing my car into the service center, and Jake told me it would be ready in about an hour.

"Okay, thank you," I said as sweetly as possible. I got up from his desk and found my way back toward the service department, and the girl in the window showed me where I could sit and watch as the prep guys got my new car ready for me.

I took out my phone and called Pennington. "It's Cassie," I said. "I just bought a new Mustang GT. They're getting it ready for me right now."

"Wow," he said. "Alicia said you weren't hurting for money. I've looked at those but I can't afford them. Which one did you buy?"

"A shiny black one. It's really beautiful, and absolutely awesome."

"All right, then," he said. "Incidentally, we checked the security video in the parking garage, but there is no sign of anyone getting close to your car. If he knew where the cameras were, though, it wouldn't be hard to avoid them. And I've got your surveillance detail all set up. They'll be on you by the time you get home, and they'll stay on you twenty-four hours a day until this guy is caught."

"If you really think it's necessary," I said. He insisted it was, and we said goodbye.

Dex came walking up to me a couple minutes later. "You bought the GT?" he asked.

"Yep," I said. "Have you ever driven one of those? Oh, my gosh, it is awesome! I took it for a test drive and decided I wanted it before I even got out of the parking lot."

He stood there grinning at me. "Okay," he said. "It is a good one, I'll say that. And it's one of the most powerful cars we've got."

By the time the prep guys were finished, it was Dex's quitting time. We drove home together, his classic Mustang right behind my own new one, and we ended up parking side-by-side in my driveway.

Normally, my car goes in the garage, but my garage remote had been in the Kia. The new Mustang had buttons that could be programmed to work with my garage door opener, but I didn't know how to do it and didn't feel like taking the time to read the book and learn.

Dex, on the other hand, had apparently been busy. While I was buying a car, he was talking to Alfie and running down the street to some electronics shop. He spent ten minutes crawling all over my car, hiding little sticky-backed things up underneath it, inside it, and under the hood.

"Mind telling me what you're doing?" I asked.

"I'm going to show you in a minute," he said. "I called Alfie and told him about your car getting blown up, and after I got him down off the ceiling, I asked him how to prevent it happening again. He told me about these little gizmos. They're a combination of motion sensors and micro cameras. If something moves the car or gets in front of one of these things, it'll record video and send it to your phone." He placed the last one, and then took my phone from me. He fiddled around with it for a minute, downloading some special app, and then handed it back. "Now, watch."

He got down on his knees and stuck his arm up underneath the car, and my phone made a funny noise. I looked down at it and saw a video of his arm and hand moving around.

"Hey, that's cool," I said. "So, if somebody tries to put a bomb on my new car..."

"The app will tell you something is up, and you'll get a video of whoever is messing with it. The app records the video so you can look at it again later, or show it to the police. They cost a pretty penny, but a whole lot less than a funeral. Yours, or some innocent bystander's."

I looked at Dex, and suddenly got this overwhelming feeling. I wasn't about to put a label on it, but it meant I wanted to hold him close and kiss him, right then and there.

So I did.

NINE

SINCE I WANTED TO CELEBRATE buying my new car, I convinced Dex to let me take us out for dinner. It was interesting, watching him sit in the passenger seat of my new Mustang. He was trying to see everything going on in the car at once, and he finally shook his head.

"Way too much technology in here for me," he said. "I have to deal with all that at work. Give me my old school hot rod."

"Yeah?" I asked. "Tell you what, I'll let you drive home. We'll see how you feel, then."

After dinner, I honored my promise and let Dex drive the GT back home. He showed me some things I hadn't already discovered, like how to use the paddle shifters and the built-in apps that keep track of just about everything the car does. If my new car ever got stolen and recovered, its onboard computer would be able to tell me exactly where it was taken, how long it stayed there, and how much fuel it used. It actually recorded a lot more information than that, but I was quite impressed.

Dex figured out how to set the garage door opener when we got back home, and pulled the car inside for me. It was a little bigger than the Kia, so I was going to have to move some things around to make it fit better. We managed to get out of the car and into the house, though, and finished our celebration in a more private way.

With all the excitement over finding Marsha in the dumpster, I had completely forgotten about getting the utilities taken care of in my office, so that was going to be my mission for the following day. Luckily, it turned out that only the telephone guy had needed to get inside, to hook up the phones and internet router. By the time I arrived at eight, I had already received emails telling me that the electricity and water had been transferred to my name, and I was all set.

Now, I needed to think about getting the word out. I set up the computer on my desk and googled for sign companies, then, not sure about trusting my cell phone, I used my new office phone to call one and arranged to have a sign done on the big glass window at the front of the building. "Cassie McGraw—Abuse Counselor." I would add "and Private Investigator" once I got my own license.

A call to a local print shop took care of ordering business cards, letterhead stationery, and such, and then I called the cloud company that had provided services for St. Mary's and asked to speak to a sales representative.

"Hamilton Pro-Cloud," said a voice. "This is Maggie, how can I help you today?"

"Maggie, my name is Cassie McGraw," I said. "I need to set up an account for client files and business records."

"Hi, Cassie," Maggie said. "That's great, I'll be glad to help. First, can you tell me how you heard about us?"

"Yeah, that's easy. I worked for St. Mary's Outreach, and I know that they use your services. I decided to call you because I'm familiar with them, and how to use them."

"Okay, great. Now, I should tell you that the company was recently purchased by a new owner, but it shouldn't affect the way we operate, or how the software works or anything. It's all still the same, but we've just been a local service company for the last several years, and Mr. Hamilton decided it was time to sell it and retire. It's all still going through the legal stuff, but we'll probably be changing our name pretty soon. We'll still offer the same great service, though."

"That's good enough for me," I said. "I just didn't want to have to start all over and learn a new system."

"Well, okay then, let's get started."

I arranged the same kind of backup St. Mary's had used, then used the computer to log into their old account and download all of my client files. A moment later, they were backed up in my own new account, and I started calling each client to let them know that I was open and available.

That led me into a whole new world of problems. Telling these women that I had set up my own private practice made them think I was going to charge them for my services, so I learned quickly to make sure I explained that there was no fee involved before I even mentioned setting up my own office. All but two of them thanked me for letting them know, and I had three appointments set for that afternoon by the time I got done.

The door had one of those electronic chimes on it, and I heard it go off as someone came in. My first thought, naturally, was that the bomber had realized I was there alone and decided to make his play. I got quietly out of my chair and reached behind my back to get my hand on the grip of my pistol, then quickly opened my office door and stepped out into the hall.

Detective Pennington stood there, and Alicia Perkins was with him.

I let go of the gun and smiled. "Hey, guys," I said. "Welcome to my new office."

Alicia gave me a half smile, but Pennington didn't bother. I invited them to sit down, and they took the reception chairs.

"There's been a development in this case," Pennington said, and I felt a sudden chill go down my spine. "Based on the information you got from Ms. Wyatt yesterday, we had officers do a sweep of vacant offices and office buildings within a five minute drive time from where the bomb went off. In one of those buildings, officers found a body."

I gasped, and my knees buckled. I had to sit down in the chair at the reception desk. "Oh, God," I said. "Angie?"

"No, it wasn't Angie," Alicia said.

"The body they found," Pennington went on, "was of a young man who fit the description Ms. Wyatt gave of her assailant, right down to the green Lightning Electric uniform. He'd been bludgeoned to death, to the point that his face is completely unrecognizable. There was a metal bar found near the body, and it was covered in blood and other tissues."

I looked from Pennington to Alicia and back. "Are you thinking Angie beat him to death?"

"We're not sure," Pennington said. "The only thing we know at the moment is that there was no sign of Angie Milligan where the body was found. CSI is checking the area for any indication that she or Ms. Wyatt had been there, but it may take a while to get any definitive results."

I sat there, a dozen thoughts trying to run through my mind at once. "Is it just me," I asked, "or does this just seem a little too pat? You've got a body that seems to fit the description of the bomber but his face has been obliterated, so you can't get a positive identification out of Marsha. If it really is the same guy, Angie should either be there, or would have escaped and been screaming for help. Did anybody check Angie's place, to see if maybe she got away and went home?"

"First thing we did," Pennington said. "She lives alone in an apartment, and there is no sign of her."

"And no ID on the body?"

"Nothing. We got fingerprints and will be running those through AFIS, but it'll take a couple of days minimum to get results back."

I grinned. "You mean it's not like they show on TV, where they get a positive identification in fifteen seconds? How much would you bet that when you identify this guy, he'll turn out to be some local druggie with no connection to St. Mary's or me?"

"That's what we're thinking," Pennington said. "This looks like a set up, a ringer. Our perp probably paid this guy to put on his clothes, then hit him in the back of the head when he wasn't looking."

"He's trying to make us think he's dead," I said. "I just can't see the sense in it. Do you think he honestly believes you'd just close the case?"

"Yeah, probably," Alicia said. "By giving us a body that seems to be our suspect, he probably thinks we'll just be glad he's gone and give it up."

"I don't think so," I said, shaking my head. "This guy is smart enough to build a bomb, he managed to kidnap two women in broad daylight, then he planted another bomb on my car without being seen. He's no slouch in the brains department, I'm telling you. Doing this, he's trying to make you think he's stupid, but he's not."

"You could be right," Pennington said. "And like you said, it still leaves the question of what happened to Angie Milligan. If she had managed to catch him off guard and beat him down, she should have turned up."

I shook my head. "All this does is make more questions. If we could just figure out what he wants with me, we probably could get a handle on who he is. This is going to drive me crazy."

Alicia chuckled. "Welcome to our world," she said.

A thought struck me. "Not that I wasn't glad to see you guys," I said, "but why did you come all the way over here to tell me this? A phone call would have been just as effective."

Pennington looked uncomfortable. "Cassie, to be perfectly honest," he said, "we needed to see your reaction when we told you. It's not outside the realm of possibility that you might have identified the suspect and decided to take matters into your own hands."

I nodded, letting Freda give him her own version of the evil eye. "So you consider me a suspect? I suppose I blew up my own car, too, right?"

"Again, that's not outside the realm of possibility. If you were the perpetrator, something like that could be a forensic countermeasure designed to throw us off. Even you admit that it was a miracle that you weren't in the car when he blew it up."

I looked at Alicia. "*Et tu, Brute?*" I asked.

Alicia shook her head. "Hey, don't look at me," she said. "I told him he was full of crap, but that's why he wanted me to come along. If he got the feeling that you already knew the guy was dead, he wanted me here to offer a second opinion."

I looked back at Pennington. "And?"

He grimaced and rolled his eyes. "I don't really believe you're involved in this thing," he said, "at least, not voluntarily. You're obviously involved, because the perpetrator is deliberately targeting you. He's got some kind of grudge against you, and I'm not sure it's related to your work at St. Mary's at all."

If he had slapped me in the face with a wet rag, he couldn't have shocked me more. It hadn't occurred to me that there could be any other connection; after all, what I did was guaranteed to piss off men, and a lot of them. Every abuse counselor has heard horror stories of vengeful abusers coming after the person they blame for helping their victims get away.

But who else might have a grudge against me? To be honest, I couldn't think of a single soul.

"Cassie?" Alicia asked. "You okay?"

I shook it off and looked at her. "Yeah," I said. "I guess it just hadn't occurred to me that somebody might be after me for any other reason. I mean, there are a lot of men out there that probably hate my guts for helping their wives stand up and leave them, you know? If Jim hadn't said that just now, I wouldn't even have considered the possibility that this might be about anything else."

"Have you got some idea what else it could be about?" Pennington asked. "Is there somebody from your past, maybe, that would have a grudge against you?"

I rolled my eye. "The Dalai Lama might never have pissed anyone off, but I'm sure the rest of us have. I think everybody has people who hold grudges against them for one thing or another. I'm trying to think of who it might be in my case, though."

When I'm really thinking hard, I have a tendency to twirl my hair with my fingers. It's just a nervous habit, one of those things you do without even thinking about it, but I suddenly caught myself twisting a strand around my index finger. I yanked it out of my hair and looked at Pennington.

"Well, the first things that come to mind are the two cases I solved. The first one was about six months ago, Roger McCoy. He was the man who tried to run off with his stepdaughter into the woods, and when I caught up to him he had killed a deputy sheriff. I ended up using the deputy's gun to shoot him. The other case was about three months ago, just before Christmas. That was about the two men who were abducting women who had left their abusers. They had caught me, and I killed one of them by dumping a few tons of wooden pallets on him. My boyfriend actually hit the other one with a car, just before he was going to kill me. I suppose either one of those cases might be connected. If Roger or those other guys had family or friends who got angry about them being killed, I guess they might come after me."

"I had already looked up those cases," Pennington said. "McCoy has a brother, but he's at home in Florida. We're looking up any friends he might've had, but most people described him as a loner. Frank and Michael Rawlings, the two kidnappers, don't seem to have any remaining relatives, and we don't know about friends just yet. Can you think of anything else that might be connected, any other situation that might make somebody hate you this badly?"

A thought went through my mind, but I shut it down. There was no way I could believe the thing I was thinking.

Speak up, girl, Abby said. *You can't afford to hold anything back, not now. This guy has already killed two people because of you for sure, and you don't know if Angie is alive or not. You can't hold anything back.*

She was right, even though I hated her for it. "There's one other possibility that I can think of," I said. "It goes back to when I..." I waved a hand at my left side. "To when I got burned. My ex-fiancé was a cop, a detective like you. He and three of his buddies were involved in raping and murdering prostitutes, but I have to wonder if there might have been more than just the four of them. If there is another one out there who wasn't caught, it's possible he might still be worried that I know something. That would be the biggest motive I could think of for somebody coming after me, but I would think they'd want to shut me up permanently."

Pennington and Alicia looked at each other, and then looked back at me.

"Cassie," Pennington said, "did you have any reason to believe there were others involved?"

"No, not directly," I said. "On the other hand, the reason the city of St. Louis gave me such a big settlement was because they said other police officers had actively worked to conceal evidence that should have gotten those guys caught long before. There were almost a dozen cops who were indicted over that, but I remember my lawyer saying that a few of them were only going to get reprimands."

"That would definitely be sufficient motive," Alicia said. She turned to Pennington. "We need to get all over this. We ought to look at the officers who were charged with concealing, as well. Some of them might have gotten light sentences, or probation. Even if they weren't involved in the murders directly, being convicted of covering it up would've ended their careers. That could also be a motive."

Pennington got to his feet, and Alicia followed. "Cassie," Pennington said, "you need to be as careful as possible. I'm like you, I think finding that body was just too easy. No matter what reason he had for leaving it for us, our guy is probably still out there, and still seems to be aiming his violence toward you."

"I know," I said. "As you can see, though, I'm not that easy to kill."

Alicia reached out and put a hand on my shoulder. "And I want to keep it that way."

TEN

THE NEWS ABOUT THE body hit the radio around ten thirty, and Dex called me at a quarter to eleven.

"Radio says they found a body that fits the description of the bomber," he said. "You know about that already?"

"Yeah. Detective Pennington came by, with Alicia Perkins. They told me."

"You honestly think the dead guy is the one who was behind it?"

See what I mean? Dex sees through things.

"No, and neither do they. It was just too obvious, you know? Alicia thinks the bomber is hoping they'll think he's dead and give it up, but I don't buy it. This guy is too smart for that, so I think he's just trying to make himself look dumb."

"That's pretty much what my gut says. Baby, I don't like this. I'm thinking about taking some time off, so I can stay beside you."

"Oh, come on, Dex," I said. "You said it yourself, I'm tough. On top of that, I'm a survivor; this guy comes near me, I'm either going to arrest him or put a bullet through him, one of the two."

"Yeah, you're tough," he said. "But that only works when you see it coming. I hate to be this blunt, but you've only got one eye. That means you got three times as many blind spots as most people."

"And you want to watch one of them for me? Dex, you took time off to help me with the abduction case. You don't have any vacation days left, you told me that yourself. You take time off, you might not have a job."

"So what? I was looking for a job when I found this one. There's other jobs out there, and I've got a damn good reputation as a mechanic."

"Dex, I..." I stopped. It suddenly occurred to me that Dex was only working so he wouldn't be dependent on me to support us. He knew how much money I had in the bank, and one of the things I really liked about him was that he didn't seem intimidated by it. Most men get this macho, alpha-thing going on when their woman makes more money or has more money than they do, but not Dex. He would even let me pay for dinner, sometimes, a clear sign that my money wasn't freaking him out.

"Dex, if you could do any kind of work you wanted, what would it be?"

"Me? I'd probably have my own shop, and do nothing but build classic cars. Build them right, and you can make a fortune doing that."

"Then why aren't you doing it?"

He chuckled. "I think I know where you're going, and I think you know what I'll say. The reason I'm not doing it now is because it would cost a hell of a lot of money to get started. If you're thinking of offering to bankroll me..."

"I am, but not just for the reason you think. If you had your own business, then you could be available if I needed you, right?"

He was quiet for a moment, and I started to worry that I had insulted him.

"That's true," he said. "To get set up right would probably cost a hundred grand, maybe more, and that isn't even counting what it would take to buy a car to start with."

"I could write the check today," I said. "Interested?"

"I'd have to think about it," he said. "My problem would be that it might be quite some time before I make any money doing that, so I wouldn't exactly be able to make payments back to you, like on a loan."

"You wouldn't have to pay me back," I said, but he cut me off before I could say any more.

"Cassie, I couldn't handle taking your money that way."

"Would you let me finish a sentence? What I was going to say was that you wouldn't have to pay me back, because we could be partners. You can run it however you want to, and someday when it makes money I get my share." I thought for a moment about just how stubborn and independent he could be. "You take sixty percent, give me forty. Would that work?"

There was silence on the phone for ten whole seconds. "Give me an hour," he said. "I'll come to your office for lunch again, okay?"

I smiled. He was hooked, and we both knew it. "Okay, honey," I said sweetly. "See you then."

I sat back in my chair and put my feet up on the desk. I was suddenly feeling a lot less stressed, and I needed only a moment to figure out why. See, as independent as I am, I'm not stupid.

Dex was in the Army, and he's a pretty tough guy. I had asked Alicia to check him out when I first met him, which is how I found out that he had earned two medals for bravery, and once kicked the snot out of six gang bangers in a bar because they were threatening a couple of women with unnecessary roughness. If there was anybody in the world I would trust to watch my back, it was him, so my sudden lightness of heart probably had to do with the fact that his presence would help me stay alive and healthy.

He showed up right on time, and brought pizza with him. We took it into my office and ate at my desk, and I didn't even bring up the idea. I waited until we were done eating, then just looked at him.

"So," he said, "I really thought long and hard about what you suggested."

"Okay. And what did you decide?"

"I have to go back this evening and pick up my tools. It means I'll have to go rent a truck after you close down for the day, and I'm afraid they're going to take up a lot of your garage until I find a shop building. Cassie, are you sure about this? It's not too late for me to go back and tell the boss I changed my mind and want to stay."

I smiled, then leaned forward and kissed him. "I'm sure," I said. "Dex, having you to watch my back for me is going to mean a lot to me. There's nobody else I would trust that far, do you know that?"

"Good," he said. "There's nobody else I would trust that far, either. If anyone is going to watch your back, it's going to be me."

"I'm just surprised you got away with quitting already. Didn't they demand a two week notice?"

He grinned. "Jerry tried," he said. "I explained to him that somebody was apparently trying to kill you, and that I needed to be with you, and he understood."

The look in his eyes told me that he probably said more than that, but I suspected it was things I wasn't ready to hear. One of the agreements we had made when we moved in together was that we wouldn't talk about any long-term future plans until we were both ready to do so. I just wasn't ready, yet, and Dex knew that.

Dex did not have a concealed carry permit. It's not that he couldn't get one, it's just that he never wanted one. He told me once that he didn't trust his own temper, that there had been times in his life when it had gotten the best of him. He didn't want to be armed should such a thing happen again, because he wasn't certain he would not draw a gun and use it.

Playing bodyguard to me was going to be a whole different ball game, though. I hesitated for just a moment, then looked him in the eye.

"I think it's time you started to carry a gun," I said.

He frowned. "Do you really think that's necessary?"

"I think it's like my daddy used to say," I said to him. "It's a whole lot better to have it and not need it, than to need it and not have it. I'm sure you know how to handle a gun, right?"

He snorted. "Of course," he said. "I even have a couple, but they're put away. I just don't think it's a smart idea for me to carry one all the time."

"Dex, how long has it been since you actually lost your temper on anybody?"

He shrugged. "Couple of years, I guess. That time in the bar."

"How many of them did you kill? Don't give me that look, you and I both know that the way you beat them could have been a lot worse than it was. You didn't kill any of them, and you know why? Because you're not a killer."

He looked me dead in the eye. "Frank Rawlings might disagree with that," he said.

"That was different," I said. "If you hadn't done what you did, he would've killed me. Everybody understood, remember? Nobody even threatened to charge you with anything."

"You're right, that was different," he said. "But what do I do when I get mad because some guy is flirting with you?"

I burst out laughing, and it was almost hysterical. "Oh! Oh! Oh, I needed that. Dex, you are the only man who has even attempted to flirt with me since the night Freda Krueger came into my life. Don't tell me you haven't seen it; men don't see me as a woman, they see me as a freak. The last thing in the world you ever have to worry about is some guy hitting on me, because the minute somebody does, I'm going to turn and make sure he sees both sides. Trust me, they disappear in a hurry when I do that. I can't imagine that you'd ever have a reason to get mad over somebody flirting with me."

He just sat there and stared at me for a moment, and it dawned on me that, for all his macho bravado, Dex was a bit on the insecure side. There honestly was a part of him that was afraid somebody might try to take me away, even though I couldn't imagine it at all.

"Dex," I said. "You don't have to worry. I'm not going anywhere."

He forced himself to smile. "Okay," he said. "I guess I can get a permit. You want to run to the house with me real quick, so I can grab a pistol?"

I looked at the clock I had hung on the wall. "I've got an appointment coming in about fifteen minutes," I said. "You can go get one, I should be fine until you get back."

He shook his head. "Give me yours," he said. "When your appointment gets here, I'll take it out and sit at the front desk. I'm not leaving you alone again."

I smiled as I took the gun out and passed it to him. He carried it out to the front desk and put it in the drawer, then called out to me.

"Looks like your client is early," he said. I started to get up, but I heard him unlock the front door and tell the lady that I was in the first office on the right.

Beverly Walker had been coming to see me at St. Mary's for over a month, stopping in once a week to talk about her husband, Chris. Chris would get mildly physical with her at times—never hitting, but sometimes pushing her into a chair she was trying to get out of, or refusing to let her leave the room—but most of the abuse she suffered was verbal and emotional. Beverly was short, only about four foot eleven, and just a bit on the chunky side. According to Chris, she looked like Miss Piggy.

Personally, I thought Beverly was quite pretty. She had auburn hair that she wore just down to her shoulders, and she kept it in beautiful condition and nicely curled. Her eyes were brown, and she had a pert little nose that sat over a pair of the most perfect lips I've ever seen.

"Beverly," I said as she came in. "I'm glad to see you. How are things going?"

"They actually seem to be getting a little better," Beverly said. "I tried what you suggested, just letting him rant when he starts in, and it seems like he gets tired of it pretty quickly. As long as I don't argue, he just sort of fizzles out after a couple of minutes." She suddenly smiled. "In fact, just yesterday, he got all mad about the bills because we didn't have quite enough to pay them this week, and he started yelling at me that I was lazy, didn't bother to contribute. Normally, I would always yell back that he didn't want me to go to work, but this time I just sat there and kept quiet. After a couple of minutes, he just stopped yelling and walked away, and then a few minutes later he came back and kissed me and told me he was sorry."

I nodded. "He's what we call an emotionally dominant abuser. He wants to be able to express his feelings, without having to listen to yours. When he gets what he wants, when he's satisfied, then he'll become compassionate. How has he been as far as insulting your appearance?"

"You know, it's funny," she said. "The last few days, he's actually told me that it looked like I was losing weight. He complimented my hair and said he liked the way I was dressed, yesterday."

"Beverly, how does that make you feel?"

She sat there for a moment and just looked at me, and a hint of a smile came onto her face. "You know what? Kinda makes me feel the way I did when we first got together."

I looked at her and thought carefully about what to say next. "Beverly, are you content to live like that? Keeping your own opinions to yourself?"

She cast her eyes downward for a moment, but then brought them right back up to meet mine. "I don't know if I can do it all the time," she said. "But, yes, I could live like this most of the time. I mean, maybe I was more to blame for our arguments and fights than I admitted to myself. When I just let him vent, he lets it go a lot quicker, and even acts more loving toward me." She licked her lips. "You're going to tell me that it might not last, right?"

"That depends on Chris. If he's really being satisfied by getting to vent, then you'll probably see less of his venting over time. If not, though, then he'll eventually start pushing, trying to get you to fight with him. It's what we call an escalation. If he escalates, then there's a strong likelihood that the escalation will continue over time, and the abuse will eventually return and may become worse."

"But you don't know that for sure, right?"

"Of course I don't," I said. "I'm not a fortune teller, I'm a counselor. My job is to help you understand the situation you're in, and to help you get out of it if that's what you choose. Unless I honestly believe that you're in danger, I'm ethically bound to leave it entirely up to you. Frankly, I don't think Chris is dangerous, not at this point. He may never be dangerous to you, but I want you to be aware that it's a possibility. If you can handle letting him vent, and it seems to be making things better between you, then I think you might have a chance to work things out. If he starts pushing you into fights, though, it might be time to insist on marriage counseling."

Beverly smiled. "The thing is, I really do love him, and I believe that he loves me. I just can't really handle the fighting and yelling and everything, but so far this seems to be working." She leaned forward, as if to get closer to me. "Cassie, I don't know how to thank you. It's talking to you that gave me the strength to try doing things your way, and just seeing him apologize—that was such a change, such a difference from the way things have been lately."

I winked at her. "Has it made any difference as far as intimacy goes?"

She giggled, and she blushed. That was pretty much all the answer I needed.

Every once in a while, one of the women that comes to me is willing to listen to some advice and try some things to see if the situation will improve. It's extremely gratifying to me when I see even the slightest sign that a marriage might turn around. Chris and Beverly had a chance, now, and I truly hoped they could find happiness together again.

But I still scheduled her for another appointment the following week.

I followed her out front and waved goodbye as she left, then sat down in one of the extra chairs and looked at Dex.

"So, how do you like your new position as receptionist?" I asked.

"The job is easy," he said. "Of course, the pay sucks, but I have a great boss."

I giggled at him. Sometimes, this man knew exactly how to make my day.

ELEVEN

DEX WAS LOOKING AT something on the computer, so I moved my chair to let me look over his shoulder. "What're you doing?" I asked.

"Taking you at your word," he said. "I'm looking for shop buildings that might be available at reasonable rent. Look at this one."

He turned the monitor slightly so I could see it better, and showed me an old gas station.

"It's got three full mechanical bays, with a lift in each of them. It sits on a corner lot that's a full acre, and it's already fenced in. It's just about ideal for what I've got in mind, but would you like to hear the best part?"

"Sure," I said. "What's the best part?"

"If you go out your front door here and turn right," he said, "then go to the corner and turn right again, you will walk right into it. It's on the other side of this block."

My eyebrow went up. "Really? You'd actually be that close?"

He nodded. "Yep. I could install a panic button in your office and out here in the reception area, so if something was going wrong, you could push the button and it would sound a buzzer or something. If I came to the back door, I could be here in less than thirty seconds."

I smiled. "Call them," I said. "Let's get it."

"Not so fast, Ms. Moneybags," he said. "The rent is pretty high for this area. They want fifteen hundred a month, but I think that's because they're trying to sell it."

"But it's a whole acre? How much are they asking for it, to buy it, I mean?"

"A hundred and fifty thousand," he said. "That's why I think the rent is too high. At that price, it should go for less than a thousand a month."

I smiled at him and took out my phone, then dialed a number from my contacts.

"Hey, who are you calling?" Dex asked, but I held up a finger to tell him to wait.

"Tulsa Maxwell," a receptionist answered. "How may I direct your call?"

"I like to speak to David LaBarre, please. Tell him it's Cassie McGraw calling."

She put me on hold for a moment, and then David came on the phone. "Cassie? Hey, how are you?"

David LaBarre was my personal banker. When I moved to Tulsa, I brought my money along, and put it into investment accounts at Tulsa Maxwell, an investment bank with an outstanding reputation. The principal in my accounts earned me eleven percent interest, giving me close to three hundred and twenty-five thousand a year to live on, after taxes and everything.

In reality, more than half of that went back into the principal each year, so it was actually growing. David was the guy who monitored the investments my money was tied up in, to make sure that it continued to grow for me. He also handled all of my other banking business.

"I'm pretty good, David," I said. "How are you?"

"I'm great," he said. "My wife and I just had our third baby, a girl."

I gave him my congratulations and we chatted for a couple of minutes, then I got down to business. "David, the reason I'm calling is because I want to make a direct investment into something. There's a piece of property I'm interested in buying, and I'd like to set the financing up through you."

"Sure, Cassie," he said. "Give me the particulars."

I gave him the address of the property, and the MLS number from the webpage. As my investment banker, David had my power of attorney for investment purposes, so he could actually handle the whole thing on my behalf. He told me to hold on for a moment while he looked it up on the Internet.

"Oh, the old Amoco station. Back when I was a kid, my parents used to buy gas there all the time. It's been a towing service the last few years, but I guess they went out of business."

"I guess so. I have a tenant all ready to rent it, so I'd like to get this locked down pretty quickly."

"Okay, not a problem. Do you have an idea what you want to offer on it?"

"Now, David, you know I'm no good with money. I'll let you handle that, all right?"

He chuckled. "I was kinda hoping you'd say that," he said. "To be honest, I think I can get it for about a hundred, maybe a hundred and five. Let me get started, and I'll call you back."

I thanked him and ended the call, then looked at Dex. He was staring at me.

"What?" I asked.

"I didn't expect you to just up and buy it," he said. "Isn't that going to take a bite out of your principal?"

"Oh, not at all," I said. "David will negotiate the best price he can get for the place, then he'll set up financing for it. Because I have so much money in his bank, I'll get an extremely low interest rate, so the payments won't be very high at all. Since we're partners, I just figured this was the best way to handle it. We don't have to worry about the owner deciding to sell the place out from under us sometime down the road."

He gave me a lopsided grin. "And I just heard you say you were no good with money."

My next appointment showed up about then, so I took her back to my office. This was a more serious case than Beverly's, because this woman was often covered in bruises. Her makeup that day was so thick that it looked like she put it on with a spatula.

"Regina," I said as we got into my office, "Bob's been hitting you again. What happened this time?"

She let out a sigh, then reached up to adjust her sunglasses. "Kenny, my oldest boy? He came home Saturday from hanging out with his friends, and Bob spotted a pack of cigarettes in his back pocket. He went ballistic, of course, and so did I, but Kenny kept insisting they weren't his. He said they belonged to another boy, and that he was just holding them for him, but Bob didn't believe it. He yelled at Kenny to tell him the truth and Kenny argued, so Bob slapped and knocked him down. I got in the middle of it, trying to get Bob to chill out, but it just made him even angrier."

I looked at her. "Did you call the police?"

She hesitated for a second, then shook her head. "Cassie, I'm afraid to. He gets so damned angry, and I just can't afford to move away. If I tried to break it off with him now, I'm literally afraid of what he might do."

I leaned forward. "I know," I said. "I remember what that feels like. I hardly even admitted to myself at the time that I wanted out, I kept telling myself that I loved Mike and that everything was going to be perfect once we were married, but I was already wearing as much makeup as you and keeping long sleeves on even in the summer. I thought about leaving a few times, but it scared me so badly that I convinced myself I was just imagining that there was a problem."

"Oh, I know there's a problem," she said. "I don't lie to myself about it, if that's what you're thinking. I just know that Bob can be—he can get a lot worse than this. This is nothing, compared to some things I've been through. If I try to leave, I'm not just afraid of what he'll do to me, but what he might do to the boys. All three of them hate him, and I'm pretty sure he knows it. He just wants the whole world to believe that he's got the perfect little family, and I don't want to think about what would happen if he had to face the truth."

"Regina, we can go to the courts and get an order of protection. The court would tell him to stay away from you, and if he violates that order..."

"What good is it going to do me for him to go to jail if I'm dead, or one of the boys is in the hospital? Cassie, I know you mean well, but there have been three stories in the news in the last six months about women being killed by their ex-husbands in spite of restraining orders."

"Then let me put you in a shelter," I said. "There's a family shelter in Sand Springs where they help you get back on your feet. They'll help you find a job, help you move into a new place of your own, get the kids in school, everything."

"And what happens when Bob finds us? And he would find us, too many people know us around here. It probably wouldn't take him a week, and then he'd be in a real rage. What happens then?"

"What happens then is the shelter security will have him arrested. He'd go to jail, and you'll get your chance to testify about the abuse you've been suffering. The courts are getting very serious about domestic abuse nowadays, so he wouldn't get just a little slap on the wrist. He'd be looking at doing some time."

Regina smiled sadly. "Bob is a hunter," she said. "I don't know how many of his buddies have told me how he can drop a deer from five hundred yards away. He wouldn't even have to come near the shelter, all he'd have to do is wait until I stepped outside, or one of the boys."

I sighed. "Then we can move you away from here," I said. "There's a process that lets you change your names, get new Social Security numbers, everything. You and the boys would go to a shelter in another city, at first, and then that one will help you start over."

"I can't do that. For one thing, I can't take the boys away from their grandparents, on both sides. Bob's parents love those kids, but they're just as afraid of Bob as I am." She put a hand over her eyes. "I don't know what to do, Cassie. I'm afraid to stay, but I'm even more afraid to leave." She sat there and cried softly.

"I want to help you, Regina," I said. "But I can't, if you're not willing to involve the police. You have enough bruises on you right now to get him arrested, and an order issued. You could go to the shelter while he's waiting to go to trial, but the DA is pretty good about pushing a plea-bargain on these guys. Bob would do pretty well to get away with less than eight years. I'm certain he would do at least five years, and you could be well established by the time he got out."

The quiet crying continued for a couple of minutes, and then she opened her eyes and looked at me again. "If I did this," she asked, "how soon would he be arrested?"

"I can call Alicia Perkins right now," I said. "She's the detective with the Tulsa PD who handles domestic abuse cases. One look at you and she'd go right out to pick him up. The DA would file charges, but they've gotten good about holding them in jail for several days. It would be a week or more before he had a chance at a bail hearing, and the DA would do everything possible to make the bail so high he couldn't afford it. You could be in the shelter by tonight."

She licked her lips and thought about it for a moment, but then she shook her head. "I can't do it just yet," he said. "He's been kind of calm the last couple days, so I need to just—I need to just take some time and think. Maybe this is the best thing to do, but I need to be sure before I stick my neck and my kids' necks out there, you know what I mean?"

"Yeah," I said with a sigh. "Just do me a favor, and call me if things get bad. You got my cell number, so you can call me anytime. If it gets bad, I want to know it. Okay?"

She agreed, and then she left. I went back out front to sit down with Dex, and saw him watching her as she walked away past the window.

"She looks pretty shook up," he said.

Ethically, I'm not allowed to tell anyone what my clients and I talked about, and Dex knows that. He didn't expect a response, he was just letting me know that even he could see there was a problem.

My phone rang and I answered it quickly.

"Cassie McGraw," I said.

"Cassie, it's David. It turns out that the broker handling that listing is a close friend of the owner of the property, so I was able to get him to take an offer over the phone. The seller says he'll agree to one oh five, but he wants an answer right away."

I smiled at Dex and gave him a thumbs up. "Buy it," I said. "Do I need to do anything?"

"It's a real estate deal, so you'll have to come in and sign the paperwork. I'll have everything ready within an hour, can you come by this afternoon?"

"Yeah, but it'll probably be closer to two hours. Is that okay?"

"That'll be fine. I'll see you then."

I turned to Dex. "You have a gas station. Well, an old gas station." I told him about the deal David had made, and he shook his head in amazement.

My last appointment was set for three, but she called at five minutes till to cancel. She had been on the way to the office when her husband called, throwing a fit because she had left the house without telling him. Apparently he had gotten off work early, and she was rushing home to try to defuse the situation.

That sort of thing happened periodically, and it was always frustrating. Legally, I can't do much of anything without the client's authorization, and this was a case where I couldn't absolutely say that I thought she was in danger. Her husband had gotten physical with her a few times, but it had never been worse than a few bruises. Unfortunately, the courts don't consider that to be serious danger, so unless she ended up in the hospital, there wasn't much I could do.

Since I was free for the rest of the day, I took Dex and headed on over to David's office. I introduced the two of them and signed all the paperwork, and then David faxed it to the broker. Fifteen minutes later, we got back a signed acceptance and the real work of transferring the property over to me began.

"Listen, I got the feeling you were in kind of a rush," David said. "I snuck a clause into the contract that said you would get immediate possession. The broker has the keys, and you can go pick them up right now, if you want to."

Dex broke into a big grin, and we headed across town to Oklahoma Real Property Associates, Inc. The broker, whose name was Malachi, completely ignored me and handed the keys to Dex.

For once, I didn't mind a bit.

TWELVE

WE WENT DOWN AND TOOK a look at the inside of the building, and Dex was suddenly kicking himself. We found evidence that the roof was leaking in a couple of spots, and the pictures on the website that showed the interior of the building had obviously been taken sometime before the present. There were a couple of broken windows, and a great deal of graffiti on the inside walls.

"Don't worry about it," I said. "You were going to want to set it up your own way, anyhow. As far as the roof goes, we can get a contractor down here to look at it tomorrow. It may not be as bad as it looks."

"Yeah, maybe," he grumbled. "I can fix the roof, I just should have known that we needed to look at it before you bought it."

"Relax, it'll be fine. We'll replace the windows with those new unbreakable ones, especially if you're going to have your tools in here. The walls just need some paint, so that's no big deal. I think this is going to be great, myself."

It worked. Once I got him thinking about how to set it up this way, he was in a much better mood. We walked around inside the place for half an hour, making notes about repairs and design ideas, and then we went outside.

The lot was huge, and completely paved. The chain-link fence that surrounded it was twelve feet high and in very good condition, with barbed wire angled out over the top to keep anyone from climbing inside.

I pointed to the back of the building, which sat near the front of the property. There were two large dog houses sitting there. "Looks like you need some watchdogs," I said. "We can put in a security system, too, with video cameras and everything."

He was standing in the middle of the lot, just looking around and thinking about what he could accomplish there. I was just standing beside him, letting him establish the dream in his mind, when he suddenly spun around and grabbed me.

"I love you," he said. "Just deal with it." He crushed me against him and pushed his lips onto mine, and I didn't even get upset about what he'd said. That was a kiss, let me tell you. That was definitely a kiss!

Since the building wasn't quite secure yet, we decided to go ahead and take all his tools to my garage. We had ridden together in my car, so I drove him to a local equipment rental place to get a truck, then followed him back to the Ford dealership. I wasn't much help as he was loading up his tools, but a couple of the other guys who work there were happy to lend a hand.

Good thing they did. He had four extremely large toolboxes on wheels, and several smaller ones. I remember him telling me once that he had almost eighty thousand dollars' worth of tools, and that he was going to be paying for them for a few more years yet. Then I recalled him telling me that it would take a hundred thousand or so to set up the shop, and found myself wondering what else he could possibly need.

I asked, and he started laughing. He pointed at different machines there in the shop and told me he'd be needing one of each. I didn't have any idea what some of them were, but they certainly didn't look like they were going to be cheap.

Oh well. At least I'd be able to call him for help if I needed him, without getting him fired or in trouble.

We took the truck to the house, and found Jimmy and Nicole waiting when we got there. She had just been released from the hospital a couple of hours earlier, after they were confident that the concussion wasn't as serious as they first believed.

"The doctor says the reason I was unconscious so long was because of shock," Nicole told me. "I didn't really suffer any serious injuries, but I'm sore as hell, I can tell you that. They think it was just shock from the blast wave of the explosion that kept me out of it so long."

"Well, I'm glad you're okay," I said. "Did you happen to see Marsha? I was supposed to go back and see her today, but I didn't get the chance."

"Yes, I went down and visited with her this morning. That poor thing, she can't even talk, and I can't imagine what she must've gone through. One of the nurses told me that she had lost almost enough blood to be beyond saving by the time they got her in the ER."

"Yeah, she was a mess. She was so badly beaten and bloody that I didn't even recognize her at first."

Nicole pointed at Dex and Jimmy, who were manhandling those big toolboxes out of the truck and into my garage. "Dex says he's opening a shop to build hot rods?"

"Yep," I said. "It's what he's always wanted to do, I guess, and that means he'll be able to take time off whenever he needs to. According to him, that means he'll be available to play bodyguard for me now and then, and I'll confess that I kinda like the idea." I grinned at her.

She gave me a knowing look, with a bit of a smirk in it. "Yeah, I kinda figured you were bankrolling this thing. Did you know he was going to offer Jimmy a job?"

I chuckled. "Let's just say I'm not surprised," I said. I had figured he was going to need helpers, and Jimmy Hanks was not only his best friend, but one of the few mechanics Dex respected. I made a mental note to find an accountant to help with handling payroll and such, and that made me think of my own new office. I turned to Nicole.

"Hey, what are you going to do now, with St. Mary's gone?"

"Well, I've still got my own practice," she said. "What about you?"

"I'm opening my own office, too. I'm still going to work for free, but I just can't run out on the clients."

Her eyes went wide and she smiled at me. "Really? That's awesome. Got any room for a child psychologist to drop by now and then?"

"The place I got has a big conference room," I said, "but we could easily turn it into an office and a break room. It's got a little kitchen area in it, but it wouldn't be hard to put up a wall and a door, to give you a nice sized office."

She stuck out her hand. "Put me down for Wednesdays and Fridays," she said. "But let's start it next week, okay? I need a few days to get past the stiffness and soreness."

"You got yourself a deal," I said. I was about to say something else, but my phone rang. I pulled it out to see who was calling, and it was Pennington.

"Cassie McGraw," I said.

"I figured I'd better call you right now," he said, "before you hear it on the news."

My guts twisted up in a knot again. "Oh, God," I said. "Angie?"

"Yes," he said. "We found her. A motorist called 911 twenty minutes ago and said he saw somebody get thrown out of a car, and found a young woman who looked like she'd been beaten to death. Officers responded immediately with paramedics, and they took one look at her and figured it was too late. One of the paramedics checked for a pulse anyway, and found a faint one so they went into action. She's at the hospital, but nobody is saying whether they think she might make it."

"I'm on the way," I said. "Are you at the hospital?"

"I'll be there in about two minutes," Pennington said. "I'll see you there."

I ended the call and screamed for Dex, and he came running quickly. I told him, Nicole, and Jimmy what Pennington had said, and that I needed to get to the hospital.

"Jimmy, can you finish up for me?" Dex asked.

"Go," Jimmy said. "I got this."

Nicole gave me a hug and then Dex grabbed my hand and took me to my car. He shoved me into the passenger seat and ran around to get behind the wheel, hit the starter button and slammed it into gear. We left rubber as we pulled away from the house.

We got to the hospital and hurried into the emergency room entrance. I flashed my ID and badge at the front desk and asked where Angie Milligan was. The woman looked at me blankly for a second, so I told her bluntly that Detective Pennington had called and told me to get down there.

"Just one moment," she said. I started to say something but Dex put a hand on my shoulder.

"She's just doing her job," he said.

She spoke quietly into a phone for a moment, then hung it up and looked up at me. "Go through the double doors, then to the fourth room on the right. The detective is waiting for you there."

I barely even heard the last part. I hurried through the doors with Dex right beside me and saw Pennington standing outside the door of the fourth examination room.

"How is she?" I asked.

"Determined to live," he said. "The doctor stuck his head out a minute ago and said she's stabilizing. They've got her heart rate closer to normal and her blood pressure is up where it should be. Apparently the biggest worry is whether she's getting enough air. They said her diaphragm is ruptured and some of her abdominal organs are getting into the chest cavity, so her lungs can't expand properly. They got her on oxygen, now, but she'll be going into surgery shortly."

"That settles it, then," I said. "There is no doubt the body you found is not the killer, not if he's done this."

"We actually got an ID back on the body," Pennington said. "Guy's name was Richard Long, a local punk who's been in and out of trouble for the last few years. I don't know if he was actually involved in this or not, but we did find gunshot residue on his hand. He could be the one who took the bomb in and killed and kidnapped your friends, but I still have my doubts. I think he was a patsy, and just a ploy to throw us off."

I nodded toward the examination room. "Has she been able to say anything?"

He shook his head. "She's not conscious," he said. "Doctor says she might wake up tomorrow, if she makes it through the operation to fix her diaphragm. Then it will be a matter of waiting to see if she's suffered any brain damage."

"Head trauma?" I asked, but he shook his head.

"Lack of oxygen. With a ruptured diaphragm, I guess you can't really breathe properly. They're worried that she wasn't getting enough oxygen into her blood."

Dex had an arm around me, and I leaned into him. "Where was she found?" I asked. Something told me I wasn't going to like the answer.

Pennington frowned. "Witness said he saw a car stop in the middle of the street and the back door opened on the passenger side. She appeared to be thrown out, landed on the pavement a couple feet away from the car, and then it took off." He looked at me and sighed. "Right smack in front of your new office on Admiral Boulevard."

"Then we've got at least two people involved," I said, and Pennington nodded. "If she was pushed out the back door, that means somebody else was driving."

"Right," he said. "That's got us thinking this is related to the situation in St. Louis. There were six officers who went to prison over covering up what your ex did, and four of them are already out. Of those, there are two we haven't been able to locate, yet."

A chill went down my spine and I shivered. "Who are they?"

Pennington pulled a notebook out of his pocket and flipped it open. "They were uniform officers," he said. "William Laclede and James Linkletter. Both of them got three years and served it all out, no parole, which means they're not under supervision and aren't limited on where they can go. We got their pictures and passed them out to all of our officers. Right now, we just want to know if they're in Tulsa. If they are, they become our main suspects."

I tried to think, but I didn't recognize either name. "I don't know them," I said. "Of course, that doesn't mean they don't know me. I was all over the news for a couple of months, there. You think maybe they blame me for what happened to them?"

"That's as close as we got to a theory. If they turn up back in St. Louis, or anywhere else other than here, we're back to square one."

"I wouldn't know them if I saw them," I said. "If you can get me a copy of those pictures, I'd appreciate it."

He glanced down at his phone and poked at it a few times, and my phone chirped. I looked at it and saw that he had sent me the pictures, but I didn't recognize either of their faces.

"The funny thing is," I said, "while they were going through being arrested and charged, I was laying in a hospital bed in a coma. The closest I came to being involved in the case was a couple months later, when they sent somebody down to take a video deposition. I never even testified in court."

"That's because they all ended up taking plea bargains," Pennington said, and there was a bitterness in his voice. "That was the only way they could hope to get into minimum-security institutions. Ex-cops don't last long in the prison system unless they're in minimum."

"Lex Stuart didn't take a plea bargain," I said. "He was the one who actually did this to me. That son of a bitch went to trial and tried to claim that Mike did it, my ex, and that he was trying to save us." I snorted, a derisive laugh. "The deputy who arrested him testified that he saw Lex deliberately drop the match into the gasoline. That was all it took for the jury to convict on their first vote."

"I read about that," Pennington said. "I just..."

The exam room door opened, and we all had to get out of the way because they were bringing Angie out to take her into surgery. I got my first look at her, and Dex had to hold me up to keep me from falling to the floor.

She looked even worse than Marsha did when I found her.

THIRTEEN

THE NURSES TOLD ME that Angie was going to be in surgery for anywhere from 4 to 7 hours, and that she would be moved to intensive care after that. There was no possibility I was going to get to see her before she left ICU, so Dex convinced me that we should go back home.

The ride back was quiet. I sat in the passenger seat and leaned my head against the window, just staring out at the world going by. I wasn't actually seeing anything, though, because I was lost in my own thoughts.

It was pretty obvious that the attack on the Outreach was actually aimed at me. What was driving me crazy was the fact that this killer tried to use a bomb against me, but didn't hesitate to pull out a gun and shoot two innocent bystanders. Everything I knew about the workings of the human mind said there was something that wasn't adding up, and I was determined to figure out what was really going on.

I looked at what we knew for sure, which was that the killer had entered the Outreach and asked specifically whether I was there. When he was told that I was running late, he walked right past Angie and apparently tried to set the bomb down right beside my office door. Angie jumped up and was yelling for him to stop, which caused Marsha, Brenda, and Leanne to step out into the hall to see what was going on. The killer drew a gun and shot Brenda and Leanne, but did not shoot Marsha or Angie.

Instead, he forced Marsha and Angie to leave with him, put them into a vehicle, and drove for only two or three minutes, then took them out of the vehicle and into a building. He spent all of that day being relatively gentle with them, even somewhat compassionate.

And then he had taken Marsha, apologized to her for what he was about to do, and beat her almost to death before shoving her in the dumpster behind my new office. Now, he had also beaten Angie and left her in the street in front of my office, with the help of an accomplice who was driving the vehicle.

When I thought it through, I realized we didn't know very much, and what we did know indicated that I was the focus of whatever emotion was driving the killer.

Our speculations were that the killer or killers—we didn't know whether the accomplice was willing or forced—were after me over something out of my past. The only thing that seemed to be a credible theory was that I had exposed Mike and his friends as the monsters they truly were. If that was the case, then it was reasonable to assume that we were dealing with one or more of those who were indicted as accessories.

What I couldn't understand was why, if they were blaming me for the misfortunes that had befallen them, they hadn't come directly after me. I'm not in hiding, it would have been easier to find out where I live than it must have been to find out where my new office was only hours after I agreed to lease it. Someone fitting the description Marsha gave could have walked right up to my front door and rung the doorbell, then shot me dead as soon as I answered it.

Or, and I know this is going to sound callous, he could have simply said he needed to speak to me at the Outreach and waited for me to get there. He was obviously willing to kill anyone who got in his way, so he could have shot me down, then killed the others and walked away. Hell, he could have gone into my office with me and shut the door, bashed me over the head with something and strangled me to death quietly.

For some unknown reason, however, he decided to take out the Outreach. While that would hurt me, the fact that I wasn't present when the bomb went off meant that he wasn't accomplishing his apparent goal.

We pulled up at the house and I started to get out of the car, but Dex laid a hand on my arm.

"Give me your gun again," he said. "I just want to check out the house before we go in."

Part of me wanted to argue, but I had had so many shocks the last couple of days that I didn't have a fight in me. I handed over my pistol without a word, and he got out of the car and walked toward the front door.

I watched as he studied the door carefully for a moment before inserting his key into the lock. He turned the knob carefully, then pushed the door open very slowly. Gripping my gun with both hands, he stepped inside and started searching through the house. I saw lights come on in each room as he cleared it, and a moment later he came back to the front door and motioned for me to come on in.

"All clear?" I asked. "I don't think this guy is ever going to come here. I don't know what it is he's really doing, but this is about more than just trying to kill me."

"What do you mean?" Dex asked me.

"The police think he's out to kill me," I said, "but I'm not quite buying it anymore. He's not aiming at me directly, but he's attacking people and places that are important to me. The Outreach, Marsha and Angie, Brenda and Nicole, even Leanne. I didn't really know her all that well, but she was important to me because she was a client of the Outreach. My new office, he's attacked that twice now. Putting Marsha's body in the dumpster behind it might even have been an attempt to frame me for killing her. These aren't the actions of someone who's out to kill me; this is more like somebody trying to destroy me emotionally."

"I see what you're saying. It's like he wants you to suffer, not die."

I nodded. "Yeah. The only question is, what's he going to do next?"

I was standing in the living room. Dex set my gun down on the coffee table and put his arms around me, letting me lean against him for a moment.

"I don't know," he said. "But I know what we're going to do next. We, my dear, are going to have dinner. I don't know if you noticed, but we sort of missed it."

I chuckled. "Yeah, we did." I turned my head to look at the clock over the TV and saw that it was already after eight. "Who's cooking? You or me?"

"That depends on what you want to eat. If it's easy, it'll be me."

"Oh, so if I want something complicated, I have to cook it myself?"

"Yeah, pretty much. After today, I think I could probably manage scrambled eggs."

I pulled my head back and looked at him. "With Swiss cheese?"

"Yeah, I can handle that."

"You're cooking."

Scrambled eggs with Swiss cheese is something of an acquired taste, but mom used to make it when I was young and I had introduced Dex to it. He made a face the first time, but a week or so later he asked me to make it again, and I did. Since then, it had become a regular breakfast every couple of weeks.

Because both of us had lost body fat from our burns, we both have a tendency to eat a lot. Burning the extra calories helped to regulate core temperature, and this is something burn victims learn to live with. In fact, it's one of the reasons burn victims rarely end up getting fat, and I personally consider it some kind of compensation effect. I've always loved to eat, but I used to have to watch how much. Nowadays, I can eat what I want, and as much of it is I want. Dex and I made heaping plates of our scrambled eggs and carried them into the living room to watch some TV while we ate.

We watched a couple episodes of *Criminal Minds* on Netflix, and then decided it was time to go to bed. I was planning to go to the hospital in the morning to see Marsha and check on Angie, and Dex wanted to get started on his new shop building, so we both wanted to get some sleep.

It's one of the areas where Dex makes me jealous. That guy can lay down and close his eyes and be asleep within minutes, no matter what's been going on throughout the day. Me? I'll end up laying there for a couple of hours, letting everything roll through my mind, trying to spot something I could've done differently, wrestling with questions that don't have answers. Last time I looked at the clock, it said half past midnight.

Morning comes whether you are ready for it or not. This is probably a good thing, because it means that the world is continuing, but there are a lot of people like me who would just as soon let it stay dark until after ten. Any sunlight coming through the window is going to wake me up most of the time, and that next morning was no exception.

We decided to get an early start on the day, so we got dressed quickly and got ready to go. I played Critter's favorite song on the can opener so she'd be content until we got home, and then I followed Dex to the Dunkin' Donuts shop. We each grabbed our favorites and a big cup of coffee, and then went to the bank to set up an account for the shop.

Dex insisted on both of us being on the account, and I insisted on having it at Tulsa Maxwell. That didn't matter to Dex, and it only took a few minutes to get it established. I transferred a hundred thousand from my personal savings account into it, gave Dex a kiss, and took off for the hospital.

Nicole was visiting with Marsha when I arrived, and I was surprised to hear Marsha talking. Her jaw was still clamped in place, but she was managing to speak intelligibly, even if she did sound a little funny.

"Hi," I said excitedly. I leaned over the bed and hugged her gently, and she wrapped her left arm around me to return it. "You're talking, that's awesome."

"Yeah," she said through her clenched teeth. "It's not easy but better than writing."

"I think she's doing great," Nicole said. She looked at me. "Have you heard anything about Angie?"

"No, not yet," I said. "The doctors said she would be in ICU for a while, and probably won't even be awake until later today."

She cut her eyes toward Marsha for a moment and then back to me. "I told Marsha about it this morning. We're both pretty worried. I asked one of the nurses I know this morning, but all she would tell me is that Angie made it through the surgery. They're just waiting now to see if she is going to recover or not."

I nodded. "That's what they told me last night. I guess they're worried that she might have suffered brain damage from lack of oxygen."

Marsha made a sound, and I looked over to see that she was crying. I laid a hand on her shoulder. "Angie's tough," I said. "One of the doctors last night said she was determined to live, no matter what. I think she's going to surprise everybody and come back from this."

"But it was so senseless," Marsha managed. "Why did he do this?"

I shook my head sadly. "I don't know," I said. "Marsha—the police think that it's all about me, somehow. They think that this guy is someone who hates me over something from the past, maybe from back when I got burned. There were a bunch of cops who got in trouble back then for covering up evidence about my ex, and Detective Pennington thinks it might be some of them."

Marsha looked at me for several seconds, then closed her eyes. "Why didn't he go after you, then? Why do this to us?"

The anguish in her broke my heart. "I just don't know," I said. I rubbed her shoulder, but she suddenly pulled it away from me.

I glanced at Nicole, and she shook her head. I stared at her for a long moment, then looked back at Marsha. Her eyes were still closed, and she was still crying.

"Marsha, I'm sorry," I said. I turned, picked up my purse from where I had set it down on a chair, and walked out of the room. I made it almost to the elevator before the tears started to flow.

I pushed the button for the elevator, and the doors opened instantly. I stepped inside and pushed number one, and they closed as the elevator began to descend. I leaned against its wall and let the tears out, then quickly tried to pull myself together as it came to a stop on the ground floor.

People were running. As the elevator doors opened, I heard voices shouting and saw people running toward the emergency room doors, and as I stepped out I could hear sirens. Down the hall, where it opened into the ER itself, I saw six paramedics running out the door toward their parking area.

"Hey," I said to a nurse who was trying to push past me, "what's going on?"

She looked at me for just a second, her eyes going wide when she got a good look at my face, and then she forced herself back under control. "I'm not really sure," he said. "There's been an explosion somewhere on the edge of town. I guess it's pretty bad, they're calling every ambulance out."

My eye shot open wide. "Another bomb?"

"I don't know, they just said an explosion. Excuse me, I have to go." She ran off toward the ER.

I snatched out my phone and dialed Pennington.

"Jim, it's Cassie," I said. "What's this about another explosion?"

"Yeah, our bomber has struck again," he said. "New Beginnings Family Shelter. I'm on the scene now, and my God, this is a nightmare."

My vision blurred, and my knees felt weak. New Beginnings was exactly what it sounded like, a shelter for women with kids. "Oh, God," I said. "How bad..."

"Oh, geez, we got people hurt all over out here. Adults, kids... I've got three ambulances on site, and eight more coming, and some of them are gonna have to make double trips! Scotty? Get that boy, he's headed for the street! Sorry, Cassie, didn't mean to yell in your ear. I gotta go, there's too much to do here."

"I'm on the way," I said. "Maybe I can help."

He was already gone, so I shoved the phone into my purse and kept walking. I got to my car and climbed in just as my phone rang with an incoming call.

It was Dex. "Have you heard?" he asked.

"Yeah, I just talked to Detective Pennington," I said. "It's New Beginnings, and he says there's a lot of people hurt so I'm heading out there."

"All right," he said. "I'll meet you there." I heard his car fire up, and then he was gone.

FOURTEEN

NEW BEGINNINGS FAMILY Shelter was in a huge old house on the western edge of Tulsa. It sat on twenty-four acres of land, and could house fourteen families at a time. There were eleven counselors who worked there full time, switching up their shifts and hours so that there were always at least two of them there. It was one of the prettiest places around.

Or it used to be. What I saw when I pulled in that day looked more like movie footage of a war zone. The building was mostly standing, but a large section of the front center was gone, and I could see right into the interior of both the first and second floors. Three fire engines were there, and firemen were working furiously to put out the blazes that were burning inside. By the time I arrived, Pennington's three ambulances had multiplied to a dozen, and I had to swerve out of the way so one of them could race out of the driveway with its siren blaring.

I drove out onto the grass, so that my car would not be in the way, and jumped out. I saw people stumbling around, some of them obviously in shock, and ran toward the first one I could get to. It was a girl in her early teens, and there was a gash in her left arm. Blood was dripping from her fingers as I caught up to her.

"Hey," I said, "let me help you. Come on, you've been hurt, you need to come over here and let the paramedics look at you."

She turned her face to look at me, and suddenly started to scream. I thought that my face had frightened her, but she reached out with both hands to grab my shoulders and clutched me to her, screaming and crying. I wrapped my arms around her and started walking her toward the nearest ambulance. "Shh," I said, "come on, it's going to be okay."

The ambulance I was approaching suddenly slammed its back doors and raced away. I veered toward the next one in the line, just as a female paramedic climbed out of the passenger seat.

"Hey! Hey, over here!" I shouted at the paramedic, and she looked my way. I pointed at the girl's arm, but the paramedic shook her head and ran toward the building instead.

For a moment I was shocked, and then it dawned on me that she was running toward people who were even more seriously injured. She was doing her job, and it was up to me to do whatever I could for this poor girl. I continued to the ambulance, and another paramedic came out of the back doors.

"Hey! I know you got work to do, but give me something to help this girl!"

The guy looked at me for a moment, then jumped back inside the ambulance. He came out again seconds later and shoved a small, zippered bag in my hand. "Clean the wound, put the salve on it, and wrap it up," he said, and then he grabbed a bigger bag and took off running.

I set the girl down on the rear bumper of the ambulance, where it was big enough to use as a bench. It took a moment to untangle myself from her, and then I began looking her over. The gash in her arm wasn't her only injury, but it was the most serious.

I opened the bag he had given me and found a bottle marked "Saline Wound Cleanser," and popped open its cap. The instructions on the bottle were plain, to simply rinse the wound with it. I squeezed the bottle to squirt the solution into the gash, and some of the blood rinsed away.

I capped the bottle again and found a large roll of gauze and some scissors. I cut off a piece and wiped the gash down, then reached back in the bag for the large tube of antibiotic ointment I had seen. I squeezed some into the gash and wrapped another piece of gauze around it, then pulled out one of the half-dozen individually wrapped bandages and tore it open. A minute later, with the clips holding the bandage together, I thought that it looked pretty good.

A woman came walking toward us, and I looked up to realize that she was also bleeding. There was a gaping wound on her right cheek, and I quickly had her sit beside the girl. I looked her over, just to see if she had other injuries that might be more serious, and saw that she had blood on her right hand. It was clenched into a fist, I thought, so I turned it over to try to see where the blood was coming from and realized that she was missing three of her fingers.

I rinsed it quickly, but didn't even bother to wipe it off. I put ointment on each of the stubs that were sticking out from her knuckles, shoved gauze in between them and over them, and then started wrapping. All she had left on that hand was her thumb and her pinky, and I did the best I could for her.

With her hand wrapped up, I looked at her face again. Once more I squirted the saline and wiped away the blood, then applied the antibiotic ointment. I stood there for a moment, trying to figure out how to bandage the wound, then just started wrapping the bandage from the crown of her head to under her chin. It was just long enough to hold the gauze in place, but it was what I could do.

"Here's another one for you," said a voice, and I spun around to see Detective Pennington. He was holding a boy of about ten years old in his arms, and I saw that the boy was covered in blood from his belly up.

I jumped into the ambulance and found a blanket, then climbed out and spread it on the ground. "Here," I said, "lay him down here." He put the boy down and I saw that most of the blood was coming from a large cut on the right side of his face that extended down onto his neck. As I watched, blood squirted out in a thin stream from near his throat, and a second later it did it again.

"That's arterial," I said. I got down close and rinsed the wound off to see how bad it was, and realized that there was a small nick in what had to be his carotid artery. It squirted again, and again, and I realized that he was in danger of bleeding to death as I watched.

I looked up at Pennington to ask him to grab one of the paramedics, but he was already running back toward the house. Whatever happened with this boy had to happen quickly, and it was going to be on me. I put my hand over the cut, but the blood just squirted out around it, and if I applied enough pressure to stop it, I was pretty sure I would be choking the poor kid to death, anyway.

The cut itself looked small, but deep, and I remember learning back in high school that the carotid is actually kind of deep inside the neck. I tried pinching the hole together, but it was only a couple of seconds before I realized the blood was simply building up under the skin. There was a knot developing, and I was pretty sure that wasn't a good thing. I needed to find some way to close that hole, but I couldn't actually get to it.

Think, Cassie, think! In the few seconds I had been there with this kid, I was sure I had seen at least half a pint of blood come squirting out. If I didn't do something soon, he was a goner.

Un-freaking-acceptable! I wracked my brain, trying to think of what I could do to keep this kid from dying, and suddenly Dex was beside me. He must have gotten there a moment earlier, because he was squeezing his hands into a pair of rubber gloves that he must've grabbed from the ambulance.

"He's bleeding," I said needlessly, "his throat..."

"I see," Dex said. "This happened to a friend of mine in the Army, I'm gonna do what they did then. You've got two carotid arteries, so I'm just going to press on this one. I'll have to let up every minute or so for a couple seconds, to let blood flow, but we have to get him to a hospital fast."

Dex felt the boy's throat, and suddenly grabbed it hard and squeezed with his thumb and forefinger. I watched closely, looking for any sign that the blood was pooling up inside again, but I didn't see it. He held it tight for a minute, then let up for about three seconds, enough for two quick squirts, and then closed it off again.

It was at that moment that the paramedics came back to the ambulance, each of them holding another child. The man who had given me the bag looked down at the boy and Dex, then yelled, "Get him inside here, and don't let go!"

I started to try to pick the boy up, but Dex snatched him up with his left arm while keeping his right hand pinched on his throat. He got up and stepped toward the ambulance, then looked back at me.

"Do what you can," he said. "I'll be back as soon as possible."

The paramedic, the man, helped Dex get the boy inside and then yelled something at me. I looked up at him, and he threw me two more of the red zipper bags, like the one he had given me at first. He grabbed the teenage girl I had helped and pulled her inside, then the woman, and the doors slammed as the ambulance raced away.

I picked up the bags, including the first one, and looked around. I spotted a couple more kids standing together, both of them bloody, and went toward them.

Rinse, wipe, salve, wrap. Those were extremely simple instructions, but simple is exactly what I needed at that moment. My mind was having a hard time dealing with what I was seeing, especially when I happened to glance in the direction that showed me three immobile forms covered with blankets. One of them was pretty small.

"How many have you taken care of?"

I looked up at the voice that had spoken and saw a young man in a paramedic uniform. "I don't know," I said. "Maybe seven, eight."

"Well, you're doing a hell of a job," he said. He stood there and looked at me for a moment, and then just turned and walked away. I started to call after him, ask him what to do next, but he was obviously intent on wherever he was going.

I turned back to the man whose leg I was wrapping. He had a piece of wood stuck in it, debris from the building, but I didn't dare pull it out. For all I knew, it might be the only thing keeping him from bleeding out.

"Who was that?" I heard, and looked up at another paramedic. He was looking in the direction the other man had gone, and I turned around to see what he was staring at. The guy who had told me I was doing a good job was getting into some kind of a work van, not an ambulance, and simply turned around and drove away as I stared.

I looked back at the paramedic standing over me. "Isn't he with you guys?"

He shook his head. "Nope. Never saw him before. I noticed he was talking to you, and I thought maybe you knew him."

I got to my feet. "Take over here," I commanded, and then I jogged as quickly as I could to where Pennington was standing with a bunch of people. He saw me coming and held up a hand to tell them to wait a moment, then stepped away from them and met me partway.

"Cassie? What's the matter?"

"The son of a bitch was here," I said. "Tall guy, mid twenties, brown hair and eyes. He was wearing a paramedic uniform, but he's not one from around here. Walked right up to me and told me what a good job I was doing. Son of a bitch!"

Pennington stared at me. "You really think it was him?"

"Hell, yes," I said. "He stopped and talked to me, then walked away and got into a van, not an ambulance, and then he just drove off. He must've come in during all the confusion, and the paramedic jacket would make him just about invisible."

"Did you get a look at the van?"

I stopped and thought. "It was blue, a late-model one. Not a real big one, and I think it was a Chevy. It was some kind of work van, with this weird logo on the side. I didn't really get a good look at it."

Pennington grabbed his phone and dialed a number, telling someone to relay a message to the helicopter that was circling overhead to go look for that vehicle. I kicked myself for not realizing sooner who it must have been, for not getting a license plate number or a better look at the logo.

He got off the phone and looked at me again. "So many roads around here," he said, "the guy could go in just about any direction. If he gets into traffic, he'll be harder to spot, but the chopper has the best chance. Good job, Cassie."

I looked around for a moment, and the sheer impact of it all finally hit me. Tears started to run down my cheek. "But why! Why, Jim? This place isn't connected to me, why put a bomb here?"

He looked at me for a moment, and there was compassion in his face. "This is why," he said. "Look what it's doing to you."

I stood there, weeping and staring at him, and understood what he was saying. It didn't matter that New Beginnings wasn't part of the Outreach, or that I didn't work there.

The people it serves were the same people I serve, the abused and displaced women and children who need help to get out of a bad situation.

By striking at them, he was striking at me.

FIFTEEN

DEX CAME BACK AN HOUR later, along with the same ambulance that had taken him away. He saw me sitting on the grass with some of the women and children who hadn't been badly hurt, and came quickly toward me.

I got to my feet. "The little boy," I said. "Did he..."

"He's going to be fine," Dex said, and the relief hit me so hard that he had to catch me to keep me from falling to the ground again. "When we got to the hospital, they sprayed me down with disinfectant and told me to hold on until they got him in the OR. My hand is still cramping, but it worked."

I held onto him and tried to get myself back under control. "If you hadn't been there," I said, "I would've lost him."

"Maybe," he said. "If I know you, though, you would've thought of something. I heard five different paramedics talking about you back at the hospital, how you were doing so much all on your own. I didn't know you had medical training."

I leaned back and looked up at him. "Medical training? My medical training consisted of having a first-aid bag shoved into my hand an hour and a half ago. One of the paramedics just told me to do what I could, because they had too much for them to handle."

"And you did a helluva job."

That reminded me of my visitor. I told Dex about it, and his face took on a look of near rage. "He was that close to you? Dear God, I should have been here, I should have..."

"Stop that," I said. "You were busy saving a life, that was more important. It was just weird, the way he looked at me. I swear, when I think about it now, it was like he knew me, but I don't think I've ever seen the guy before."

Things were under control by this point. The fire department had gotten the fire out, and the most seriously wounded were in the hospital. Only three people had died, which the Fire Chief considered a miracle considering the size of the blast.

Unfortunately, one of them was a six-year-old boy. The other two were actually staff members, a cook and one of the counselors. I had actually known him; his name was Mitch, and he'd only been in the job for a few months.

Pennington found us a moment later, and I grabbed the opportunity to tell him what a hero Dex had been. The detective shook his hand, then turned back to me.

"Cassie," he said, "I'm gonna need you to come to the station. You need to work with an artist, see if we can get sketch of this guy."

"Okay," I said. "You want me to go now?"

"Yeah, the sooner the better. Dex, it was good to meet you. You got yourself a hell of a woman."

Dex grinned at him. "What? You think I don't know that?"

I poked him in the ribs, and then he walked me to my car. We were just about to it when he stopped and looked at me.

"Cassie? Where is your phone?"

I looked at him for a moment, then felt my pocket. "Oh, I put it in my purse. It's in the car." I started to take another step, but he pulled me back.

"Wait here a minute," he said.

He walked over to my car and walked around it, just looking at it from different angles for a moment. He leaned down and looked inside through the window, then got down on the ground and looked up underneath it.

He lay there for a long minute or so, and then he took out his own phone and turned on its flashlight app. I watched as he carefully reached up under the car and shined the light on something, and then he was sliding back away from it over the grass.

He got to his feet and walked over to me. "Do you have your key?"

I shook my head. "That's in my purse, too."

He let out a sigh. "Okay. Wait here." He turned around and went back over to the car, reached out carefully and took hold of the door handle and pulled. My heart was in my throat, but the door came open without incident. He reached inside and carefully picked up my purse, then carried it back over to me. I grabbed my phone and swiped it to make it come to life, and there were three alerts from the motion camera gizmos.

"There is what looks like a bomb stuck up under the floorboard by the transmission," Dex said.

I was staring at the screen on my phone. There, nice and clear, was a picture of a man's face, and I knew it was the same guy who had spoken to me. It was the opening frame of a video, and I tapped it with my thumb to make it play. It showed him sliding up under the car, first getting his hand which was holding something about the size of a loaf of bread, but then his face came just into view. He was reaching up under the car and staring at what he was doing, but as he went to slide back out, he actually turned and looked straight into the camera for a split second.

"We got him," I said, and I turned the phone around to show it to Dex. I looked around for Pennington and spotted him some distance away.

"Go show him," Dex said. "He needs to see that right now."

I nodded and started walking toward the detective. I was looking at my phone as I walked, not really paying much attention to anything else, and then I just shoved the phone in front of Pennington's face.

He looked at the screen. "What's this?"

"Dex put these little cameras all over my car," I said. "Just in case he were to try again to plant a bomb, you know? Well, he did, while the rest of us were all busy trying to deal with his last one."

Pennington looked at the screen again, then raised his eyes and looked past me. "What the hell does he think he's doing?" he asked suddenly, and I spun around to see what he was talking about.

Dex was up underneath my car, and as I watched, he slid out on his back, holding something in his hands.

Pennington and I both started running toward him at the same time, yelling for him to stop and get away from it. He sat up quickly, waving his hands and telling us to stop, and then he put his finger to his lips. Pennington grabbed my arm and jerked me to a halt, and I saw that his eyes were wide as he stared at Dex.

Dex got to his feet, then bent down and gently picked up what must have been the explosive device. He walked very slowly and very carefully to a big vacant spot a good hundred yards away from my car or anything else, then set it down and started backing away. When he had twenty feet between himself and it, he turned around and started jogging toward us.

"What the ever loving hell did you think you were doing?" I asked, smacking him on the chest when he got close enough. "You could have killed yourself!"

"That was pretty dumb," Pennington said. "I was about to call in the bomb squad when I saw what you were doing. You should have let them handle it."

Dex shook his head. "I don't think so," he said. "You know, we thought he wired it into her ignition system, and that it was starting the car that set it off, right? Well, we were half right. It doesn't have any connection to the car itself, but there's a microphone sticking out, so it's using a sound activation switch. It probably has to pick up a noise that's pretty close to it, but that's why I didn't want you yelling. If she had gotten in the car and shut the door, the sound of the door slamming would probably have set it off. If not, the sound of the engine starting certainly would."

"But you still could have blown yourself up trying to take it off," Pennington said. "Why did you do that?"

"Because somebody around here would have made a noise at some point," Dex said. "I didn't want shrapnel blowing all over the people who just survived the last bomb. Besides, when I looked at it the first time, I could tell it was wrapped up in cloth and just stuck in between the floorboard and the transmission. The cloth was probably to keep it from making any sound while he put it in place, but I figured it would work in reverse, too." He grinned. "It did."

Pennington looked at him for a moment, then shook his head. He had his phone in his hand and used it to call the bomb squad immediately. As soon as he did that, he told several of the uniformed officers who were still present to make sure nobody went near that spot.

The bomb squad got there fifteen minutes later, driving a big truck with what looked like a water tank on the back of it. Two men dressed in some kind of armor got out and walked carefully toward where Dex had put the bomb, and then they knelt down and stared at it for several minutes.

One of them got up and walked away, and the other one picked up the bomb very carefully. The first guy went to the back of the truck and opened a round door in the tank, and I saw that it was extremely thick, like a bank vault door. The second man brought the bomb up and carefully put it inside, and then they closed the door gently and quietly. They turned the locking wheel that secured the door, and then moved away and started taking off their armor.

Pennington walked up to them, so Dex and I followed. "What do you think?" Pennington asked.

One of the men looked at him and grinned. "Whoever told you it was sound-activated was right," he said. "Man, you want to feel your butt pucker up, you just walk fifty feet carrying one of those. I hadn't made it three steps before I felt like I had to sneeze."

Pennington just stared at him for a second, then shook his head. "Is it safe now?"

"Well, yes and no. Inside that blast tank, it can't do a whole lot of damage. I don't think there's any way we can disarm it, though. We're gonna have to set it off."

"How are you going to do that?" Dex asked.

The guy grinned at him and winked, then bent down and picked up a rock about the size of a golf ball. He reared back, wound up like a picture on the mound, then threw the rock as hard as he could at the tank.

There was a loud *WHOOMPH!* The truck seemed to rock on its wheels for a moment, and there was a loud series of whistling noises. The officer explained that the whistling came from narrow holes that allowed the pressure from the explosion to escape under control, rather than all at once.

"Good Lord," Pennington said. "Just how powerful do you think that was?"

The other bomb squad officer shrugged. "Not really all that big," he said. "Maybe like a stick of dynamite, maybe even a little less. Would've been enough to blow up a car, definitely would've killed anybody inside the car."

I swallowed hard and promised myself I would never leave my phone in my purse again. That baby was staying with me forever, after that.

I had sent the video from my phone directly to Pennington, and he had already sent it back to someone at the station. Every officer in the city was going to get a copy of the frame that showed the bomber's face, and they would be showing it to every snitch and informer they had, as well.

"Somebody out there knows this guy," Pennington said. "Maybe this will get someone to come forward."

I looked at him for a moment. "I think I know another way to help," I said. "Put out the word that there's a twenty-five thousand dollar reward for this guy's arrest. I'll pay the money."

Pennington looked at me, his eyebrows trying to crawl over his scalp. "Twenty-five grand? Are you serious?"

"Damn right I am," I said. "Spread the word. Hell, hold a press conference. I don't want you to use my name, but I'll be happy to pay it if we get this bastard."

There were a dozen reporters on the scene at that moment, including five different TV news crews. Pennington asked me one more time if I was serious, then started walking toward where the uniformed officers were keeping the reporters corralled.

"Hey, all of you, listen up," he yelled, and they hurried to shove their microphones in front of his face. "I just received a phone call. We're going to be giving all of you a photograph of the man we believe is behind this bombing and the one a couple days ago. We're hoping you'll publicize that photo, but also I need to announce that an anonymous donor has posted a twenty-five thousand dollar reward for information leading to the arrest of this man."

He spent the next fifteen minutes answering questions the best he could, refusing a dozen times to say who was putting up the reward. Dex stood beside me with his arm wrapped around my shoulders, and I felt like I was finally doing something right in this case.

Since we had the photo, I didn't need to go and meet with the police artist. Dex and I got into our cars—I made him crawl under his own and check, just to be safe—and we went home to get cleaned up. Both of us had blood all over us, and I even had it on my face and in my hair, from trying to get hair out of my eyes when my hands were covered in somebody else's blood.

"I'm taking a shower," I said. I stripped in the utility room and dropped my clothes right into the washer, then walked naked through the house to the bathroom. I had the water set to the temperature I like and was about to step into the shower when the door opened, and I glanced around to see Dex in the same condition.

"I think there's a water shortage going on right now," he said. "We need to conserve."

I rolled my eye, but I was giggling as I did so. "Works for me," I said. "I need somebody to wash my back, anyway."

SIXTEEN

AFTER WE GOT CLEANED up, we were both pretty hungry. Neither of us felt like cooking at that moment, so we got into my car and I drove us to Whataburger. We were sitting at a table eating when my phone rang, and I answered it to find Pennington on the line.

"What's up, Jim?" I asked.

"I just thought you'd like to know," he said, "that I just got a call from the mayor. The city is matching your twenty-five thousand, so there is now a fifty thousand dollar reward out for the bomber."

I broke into a smile. "Really? That's awesome! That ought to get some attention, don't you think?"

"It should. Around here, most people would sell out their own mother for fifty grand. Anyway, I thought it might brighten your day a little bit. God knows we could all use something to do that."

"No, what will brighten my day is seeing this piece of crap in handcuffs. Preferably mine."

"I'll tell you something," Pennington said. "I'm not sure I'd be all that surprised if you don't find a way to beat us to him. Just remember, we want to take him alive if we can. From what I've read, you have a tendency to bring them back in a vitally-challenged condition."

My mouth fell open. "Hey," I said. "For the record, I only shot Roger McCoy because he was trying to shoot his stepdaughter. And I didn't mean to kill the other guy, I just figured the pallets would slow him down so I could get away."

"Geez, can't you take a joke? You're all right, Cassie. I'll let you know if I come up with anything new."

I put the phone back into my pocket and told Dex about the mayor matching the reward. We finished eating and refilled our drinks as we left, then drove down to the shop building.

Dex had been busy. While he only had a little bit of time that morning to work, he had most of the trash cleaned up already. We walked around inside the building as he told me about various pieces of equipment he planned to get and where they would go. I listened with a smile, even though I didn't have the slightest clue what he was talking about. Okay, well, not all of it, anyway. Even I know what a tire changing machine is.

"I've been looking at some cars," he said. "On Craigslist. I've found a couple I'd like to go ahead and get, just so that I got them here to start on. Is that okay?"

"Yeah, sure," I said. "Do you need some more money to buy them?"

He laughed. "No, that's not a problem. I just didn't want to buy them without checking with you first."

"Okay, whoa, whoa, whoa. Let's get one thing straight, right now. I'm the silent partner. What that means is that you make the decisions, and I'm happy with the decisions you make. You don't have to ask me about anything, you don't have to check with me first. Dex, I trust you. I trust you completely, in fact, which almost scares me because I never thought I would ever be able to say that to anyone."

He gave me a sheepish grin. "Okay," he said. "Look, this is all new to me. I've never done anything like this before, being a partner with somebody."

I opened my eye wide. "Oh, really? I thought we were already partners of another sort. Aren't we?"

He looked at me, and it seemed like he wanted to say something but was holding back. It suddenly dawned on me that I might have accidentally said the wrong thing.

"Dex, I didn't exactly mean..."

"Yes," he said. "We definitely are partners of another sort. I'll confess that I sometimes wonder just what sort that is, but I never, ever doubt that we're in this together."

I hesitated for a couple of seconds. "In what together?"

"Whatever it is that we are in," he said. "I'm not sure you and I both see it the same way, but I'm pretty certain that neither of us is ready for it to come to an end, am I right?"

"Come to an end? What on Earth would make you bring that up?"

"I didn't bring it up," he said, "I said I don't think either of us would want that. I'm right, right?"

"Well, yeah," I said. I softened a bit. "Look, Dex, sometimes I get the feeling you want things to, I don't know, maybe move a little faster in some ways?"

"You ready for honesty?" he asked.

"I don't ever want anything but honesty from you," I said. "I couldn't handle anything else."

"Okay then, pure honesty. Sometimes I want things to move faster. Sometimes I don't. And that's the truth."

I started to tell him he was confusing, but then it hit me that I could probably say the same thing to him. There were moments when I thought about the possibility of taking things to another level. Every once in a while, I would get this incredible feeling of—this incredible feeling, and I'd entertain the thought of maybe someday making our "partnership" somewhat more official.

Fortunately, sanity would return not long thereafter. I guess there's always going to be some fear of any permanent commitment, after what happened to me, but I wasn't quite willing to rule out the possibility completely. I just wasn't ready for it yet.

"Okay. I can understand that." I turned away from him and looked around the shop again. "Now, where are you going to get all this equipment?"

"Now, see, that was a really good question. See, I could go out and spend all that money you just put into the bank account on equipment, and then I might actually have to ask for a little more now and then."

"I wouldn't mind," I said, but he held up a hand to tell me he wasn't finished.

"Have you ever heard of Snap-On? They're a tool company, and they got these trucks full of tools that come around to your shop. I can buy everything I need from them and make small payments every week, so it doesn't wipe out working capital all at once. It'll cost a little more money in the long run, but it'll make that capital last a long time. By the time the capital is gone, I should be making money here, so making the payments won't be a problem."

I nodded. "Okay, that makes sense. Have you called them already?"

He grinned again. "Yep, this morning. Just before I heard the news."

I turned and walked up to him, put my arms up and wrapped them around his neck, then pulled him down for a kiss. Somehow, I thought I was going to like Dex having his own little business, and the fact that he was just around the corner from my office made it even nicer.

The kiss lingered for a few minutes, and I'm pretty sure we both enjoyed it.

It was almost 3 in the afternoon, and neither of us actually had anything planned. I let him go and stepped back, then looked up at him with a smile.

"So," I said. "What kind of cars are you looking at buying?"

He pulled out his phone and started showing me pictures. "I've found a few that could actually be worth some money, once I get them done," he said. "Take a look at this. That's a 1959 Cadillac Series '62 convertible. Very rare car, nowadays, and they bring serious money whether they're fully restored or customized. This one," he said, swiping the screen to produce another picture, "is a 1969 Chevrolet Corvette. And then," swiping the screen again, "here's a 1957 Chevrolet Bel Air sport coupe. That car is just about an American icon. Properly done, any one of these will bring more than a hundred thousand dollars at one of the big collector car auctions."

I smiled. "So we're actually going to make some money on this deal?"

"We better," he said. "That's the whole idea."

I took his phone and was scrolling through the ads, and spotted a car that caught my own attention. "What is this one?"

He laughed. "Oho," he said, "the lady has an eye for automobiles. That, my dear, is a 1970 Plymouth Cuda. Another rare car that can bring very good money."

"I like that one," I said. "Why haven't you gone ahead and bought any of these cars yet?"

He laughed again. "Babe, you just gave me money to work with this morning," he said, "and we've been a little busy since then. I might see about getting a couple of them tomorrow, just get them here and locked up inside the fence so nobody else buys them."

I nodded. "Okay," I said. "This is all your baby, so I'll let you handle it."

He looked at me and grinned. "You are way too good to me," he said, "do you know that?"

My phone chose that moment to ring, and I pulled it out to look at the display. I didn't know the number, so I put it to my ear.

"Cassie McGraw," I said.

"Ms. McGraw," a woman's voice said, "this is Alexandra Hartwell from KTUL news. Will you comment on the rumor that whoever is setting the bombs around the city is using them to try to hurt you?"

My single eyeball just about jumped out of my skull. "I beg your pardon?" I said. "Can I ask where you heard something like that?"

"Actually, it came from a reliable source inside the Tulsa Police Department, but he's asked to remain anonymous. Ms. McGraw, if there is a mad bomber running around Tulsa because of you, don't you think the people of the city have a right to know that?"

"Ms. Hartwell, I don't think the police would want me commenting on their ongoing investigation. I suggest you speak with them, and try to find someone who would go on record. Maybe you'll get some real information for a change. Goodbye."

I cut off the call and looked at Dex, then told him what she had said.

"I think you'd better call Pennington," he said.

"Yeah, I think so." I hit Pennington's number in my recent calls list and put the phone back to my ear.

"Jim, this is Cassie. I just got a call from Alexander Hartwell from the TV news. She claims somebody at the police department told her that the bombings are all about me."

"Well, crap," Pennington said. "If I find out who did it, he's going to be out of a job. What did you say?"

"I told her she needed to try to find someone at the police department that would be honest with her," I said. "Somebody who would go on record. According to her, her source wants to remain anonymous."

"That's because they don't want me finding out who it was. The hell of it is, they'll run it as a story with or without any corroboration from you or us. That could play hell with our investigation."

"I was thinking the same thing," I said. "So I had an idea. How about if I actually go ahead and give them the statement? What if I were to hold a press conference and admit this guy is trying to tie me to his bombings, and then dare him to come face-to-face with me?"

"I don't know," he said. "First off, this guy isn't going to walk into a trap. He'd know you were trying to bait him, and I don't think he'd fall for it. On top of that, it would probably give our officers the idea that it was okay to leak information to the press. That's the last thing we need."

I frowned. "Okay, it was just a thought. I just wish I could think of some way to track this bastard down."

"We've already got his picture going out on the news," Pennington said. "All we said is that a hidden security camera managed to catch a photo of him planting a bomb, with no mention of you or any other details. I think we need to just hope that somebody out there is going to recognize him and try to claim that reward."

"Okay, then," I said. "I'll leave it alone, but if you think it might help, I'm willing."

"Cassie, to be honest, I think the only real results you would get is that the women you help would start to be afraid to come to you. From everything I've heard, this city is a lot better off with you doing what you do. I'll admit I was surprised when you decided to open your own office, but Alicia tells me that's just the kind of person you are. Don't let this guy ruin everything for you."

I thanked him for the advice and let him go, then gave Dex a quick rundown of what he had said. Dex agreed with him, especially the part about scaring off my clients. Naturally, that was the last thing I wanted to do.

"So," Dex said. "What do you want to do now?"

I had actually been standing there thinking about that very subject, and an idea had come to me.

"I want to go see Alfie," I said. "It just dawned on me that I didn't even send him the picture of our suspect. I wonder if he could figure out who the guy is?"

"Let's go find out." He led the way out of the building and locked it up, and we got into his car for the ride out to Alfie's apartment.

Alfie was actually glad to see us. When I explained about getting the video of our suspect planting another bomb on my car, he freaked out for a moment, but then he grabbed my phone and plugged it into his computer. He copied the video off of it, opened it in an editor program and took several frames that showed different angles on the suspect's face.

"I'm going to run it through facial recognition," he said, "comparing it against driver's license photographs. There are more than two and a half million licensed drivers in Oklahoma, so this is going to take a little while. My program is good, so I can filter out every female, and every male under twenty and over forty, as well as anyone who isn't as obviously Caucasian as this clown. That should cut me down to under a million, maybe as low as half a million. At sixty comparisons per second, it'll take somewhere between three and six hours just to run through them all. That'll probably give me a few hundred preliminary matches, and then we go back through those and look for more detailed comparisons."

"What do you mean," I asked, "about preliminary matches?"

"I wrote my program to be fast," he said. "The one the FBI uses works basically on taking specific identifiable points out of all the photos in their database and just looking for matches on those things. It's designed to make as exact a match as possible, which means that it's going to take more time. My system uses fewer matching points on its first run, and that's why it comes up with preliminary matches. The one you're looking for will be in there, but then I only have to run a detailed scan on a few hundred faces, rather than hundreds of thousands or millions."

"Wow," I said. "I'm impressed."

"You should be," Alfie said, "because I'm a genius."

"Oh, that always impresses me. I was referring to the fact that I think I actually understood what you just told me. That's what impressed me just now."

He flipped me a bird. "If you're going to hang around here while it runs," he said, "make yourself useful and fix dinner. I know it's a little early, but I'm hungry."

SEVENTEEN

I CHUCKLED, THEN WENT into his kitchen. Two minutes in there, where I found nothing but generic frozen pizza and ramen noodles, was enough to convince me that dinner was coming by delivery. I took out my phone and called the nearby pizza place that delivered in his neighborhood.

When I got back to the living room, Dex was excitedly telling Alfie all about his new shop and what he was planning to do with it all, the cars he was planning to buy and everything. I sat down and listened, grinning to myself at how excited they were both getting. Alfie might be a nerd, but he was apparently a nerd who knew his way around cars. He even turned the browser to Craigslist so he could look at a few of the cars for himself.

The pizza arrived in thirty minutes, as advertised, and we took a break to eat. Knowing that both Dex and I required extra calories, along with the fact that Alfie could eat more than any small person I had ever seen, I had ordered three large supreme pizzas. I ate more than half of one of them, Dex ate about the same amount, and Alfie finished everything else off. Considering the guy is only three and a half feet tall, I would love to know where he puts it.

Dex and I talked about leaving a couple of times, but a part of me wanted to be there if the computer came up with a match. I wanted to know who this guy was, and why he seemed to be holding such a grudge against me. I had gone over his face in my memory a hundred times that day, pulled out my phone and looked at his picture a hundred more, and I simply could not convince myself that I had ever met him before.

At the same time, there did seem to be something familiar about his face, but I couldn't figure out what it was. I played the video over and over, trying to see it from different angles, but that tiny little bit of familiarity just wouldn't solidify. I was almost certain that I had never met this man, and I had even gone through the articles about Mike and his buddies, and all the accessories who were charged over that mess. Absolutely none of them looked like our bomber.

Dex and Alfie were still talking about cars and other things, but I was sitting there getting sleepy. I guess it was around nine when I dozed off, sitting there on the couch beside Dex, but the two of them simply turned down the volume on their voices a bit and let me sleep. Sweet of them, if you asked me.

"Cassie? Cassie, wake up," Dex was saying. I struggled to get my eye open and looked up into his face. "The computer has done its thing, but it didn't find any serious matches."

I looked at Alfie. "Why not?" I asked.

He shrugged. "Apparently, your boy doesn't have an Oklahoma driver's license. If he did, I'm pretty sure we would have found it."

I frowned. "Well, I guess it was worth a try. Any other bright ideas?"

"I'm not giving up yet," Alfie said. "I'm going to leave the computer running tonight, and I've got it set to run the same searches on our neighboring states. That'll mean going through a lot more faces, but I should know whether or not it finds anything by tomorrow afternoon, sometime."

I let Dex help me up off the couch, and we stumbled out to his car. He insisted on checking it over, since we had not put security cameras on it yet, but he didn't find any signs that it had been tampered with. We got in and buckled up, and headed for home.

Critter was delighted to see us, of course, though she was cussing me out in kitty talk. Mama had been gone too long, and the food and water dishes were shamefully empty. I rectified both horrible situations for her, and she forgave me.

Dex and I went to bed, and I actually beat him to sleep.

I woke to the ringing of my phone on my nightstand, and slapped the top of it a couple of times before I found the damn thing. I looked at it, but didn't recognize the number.

"Cassie McGraw," I said. My voice was a little raspy, because my throat was dry.

"That was pretty good," said a voice, and I recognized it instantly. It was the same voice that had spoken to me the day before, the one that I didn't realize in time was the bomber. "Getting my picture, I mean. I never would have expected you to put cameras on your car, so kudos to you."

"Who are you?" I asked. "Why the hell are you doing this?"

"Well, now, that's for me to know, and you to find out if you can. I mean, you're supposed to be some hotshot private investigator, now, right? Yeah, I follow the news about you. I know all about you, Cassie, and all about what you do. Matter of fact, I wouldn't be surprised if I know more about you than you do."

The arrogance in his voice was pissing me off. "Oh, yeah? Well, in that case, you know I'm going to put you away for the rest of your life, right?"

"No, that's not how this is going to play out. Like I said, Cassie, I know all about you. Your enemies don't go to jail, they end up dead. You want to stop me, bitch? Then you're going to have to kill me."

"Oooh, is that a challenge? I love a good challenge. How about this? You and me, all alone, you name the time and place."

Dex was up on his elbow, staring at me. I held up a finger to tell him to be quiet.

"Now, that's more like what I have in mind. The trouble is, if I tell you when and where, I'm not sure I believe you'll show up alone."

"I will," I said. "You know, it looks like everything you're doing is aimed at me, anyway. Even if things go bad when we meet, at least you'll be able to stop hurting innocent people once you got me, right?"

"See, there you go again. That's not how this works. You want me to stop? Then you have to stop me. Cassie, I'm way too smart for the cops, I know way too much about how they work. You, on the other hand, you don't think like they do. You do things your own way, and that's why you might actually manage to stop me."

"Wait, you want me to stop you?" I asked. "Is that what this is really all about? You're some kind of serial killer, right, addicted to it?"

He laughed. "That would be pretty convenient for you, wouldn't it? I guess there might even be a little truth to it, because there is something pretty exciting about knowing you have power over life and death. Isn't there?"

It's not all that often than I'm left completely speechless, but he managed it for a moment there. "You son of a bitch," I said. "Don't you even imply that I'm anything like you. I've never killed anyone for fun, for a thrill."

"Nobody ever does, the first time," he said. "The trouble is, that's when you realize that there is a thrill, that it makes you feel alive and powerful. I'll bet you just about wore your boyfriend out after you shot that guy. Am I right?"

He did it again. Left me speechless. As much as I hated to admit it even to myself, that was the night I had actually let my guard down and allowed Dex to take me home with him. I hadn't been with a man since Mike, I even told everybody I hated men, but that night...

Nobody likes to admit it, but it's true. Violent death, especially when you are the one who caused it, makes you horny as hell. I always blame the fact that Dex and I had been drinking, but the truth was that I needed that sex that night. I needed it bad.

All of that went through my mind in a split second. "God, you're disgusting," I said. "Like I said, you want to meet up and settle this? You just name a time and place."

"The time will be soon," he said. "As for the place, just pay close attention and I'm pretty sure you'll figure it out before long. Things are about to get lively, Cassie."

The line went dead and I instantly dialed Alfie. He answered sleepily.

"I need you to check my phone," I said. "The bomber just called me, see if you can figure out his number."

"Give me five minutes," he said.

It actually took him almost ten minutes to call me back, but the news wasn't good. "I got the number he called from, but it's a typical burner phone. One of those cheap ones that you can activate with a credit card, and he only activated it an hour ago. The credit card he used belongs to somebody in Oregon, so it's probably stolen. I'm sending the report to your email, anyway, so you can give it to the police. Facial recognition is still running, so I'm going back to bed."

He hung up. I looked at Dex and saw the worry in his eyes.

"You are not going to meet this guy alone," he said. "Not as long as I'm alive."

I smiled and reached out to touch his face. "Of course not," I said. "We're partners, right?"

He grabbed me and pulled me down, kissing me and holding me close. I surrendered to it, because I suddenly just needed to feel alive.

Thirty minutes later, I realized that it was not quite eight o'clock yet. Alfie was probably going to charge me double for waking him up, but it was worth it. I let Dex go take the first shower while I waited for eight and the chance to call Pennington.

"Why did I just know I was going to hear from you first thing this morning?" Pennington asked.

"I don't know, are you psychic?" I told him about the call from the bomber, and the veiled hint that he was about to do something more. I also forwarded him the email Alfie had sent me, with the report on the number and credit card.

"One of these days," he said, "you've got to introduce me to your computer guy."

"No way," I said. "He's pretty private, I think he's got PTSD or something. Never comes out of his cave."

"Yeah, whatever. Keep me posted if you learn anything more." He hung up, and I went to take my own shower as Dex was coming out.

When I came out of the shower, I went ahead and got dressed before I went to the kitchen. Dex had bacon and egg sandwiches waiting for me along with a fresh pot of coffee, and I happily sat down to enjoy them.

"What's on your agenda for the day?" Dex asked.

"Going to the office, I guess," I said. "I need to put out some advertising, let people know I'm there."

"What if I had a better idea?"

"I'm listening," I said. "What are you thinking?"

"I just called Lonnie Beals. He's the deputy sheriff who runs the concealed carry course here. It's only a three hour course, and he and I have actually done some shooting before, so he knows I can handle a gun. He says if I'll come by this morning, I can have a permit before lunch."

I broke into a smile. "Thank you, Dex," I said. "I can't tell you how much better I'll feel knowing you can defend yourself."

We finished breakfast and went out to Lonnie's place, which was out near Sand Springs. When I had come to Oklahoma, I had to pass the CCW test even though I already had a Missouri permit. I had met Lonnie then, and found him to be a pretty great guy.

"About time you did this," he said to Dex. "Especially if you're going to be with this gal. From what I'm hearing, she has a tendency to attract some pretty crazy people."

I stuck my tongue out at him, and he chuckled.

I sat beside Dex while he listened to the things Lonnie was telling him, and took the written part of the test. He passed, of course, and then we went out to the firing range behind Lonnie's house. Dex had brought along a Colt .45, and had to demonstrate that he knew how to use it properly. That was really nothing but a formality, so that Lonnie could sign his paperwork. We actually left with his permit at ten after eleven.

"Let's celebrate," I said. "I want to buy you a new holster. Heck, I'll buy you a whole new gun if you want."

Dex laughed. "I like my old forty-five," he said. "It's been a good gun for a long time. I bought it surplus, after I got back from Afghanistan, and it's probably my favorite."

He let me take him to a local gun store, and I convinced him that a shoulder holster would just look good on him. Of course, that required something to cover it up, so I bought him a black leather vest. That served a dual purpose, because it was actually a concealed carry vest; it had a pocket hidden on the inside that was big enough to hold his pistol. If he didn't feel like putting on the shoulder holster, the vest was good enough.

While we were there, I spotted a beautiful little Kimber Ultra "Crimson Carry" forty-five that I liked. My own pistol was a nine millimeter, but I'd heard horror stories about people shot with a nine and not even slowing down. The dealer was willing to let me test fire the Kimber, and I was able to put every round exactly where I wanted it. I bought it, along with two boxes of hollowpoint ammunition and the new holster that would let me carry it the same way I had been doing with my nine millimeter.

We were in my car, because Dex said he had another errand he wanted to run that day, but would need a ride for it. When we finished up at the gun shop, I looked at him and asked, "Okay, where to next?"

He directed me back into Tulsa, and to a used car dealership called "Less Is More." I think I must've looked at him a little funny when he told me to pull in, but he grinned and I decided to wait and see what was up. We parked in front of the little building and got out of the car, and a large, round moon pie of a man stepped out with a big smile on his face.

"Dex," he said. "Good to see you, man. How long has it been, anyway?"

"Couple of years, anyway," Dex said. "Lester Moore, this is Cassie McGraw, my girlfriend. Cassie, meet Les Moore."

I shook hands with him, and grinned. "Nice name," I said. "Did your parents do that to you?"

He laughed. "Actually, it was Mom. Dad said he was dead set against it, but mom just liked the way it sounded." He let go of my hand and turned back to Dex. "It's around back, come on."

We walked around to the back of the office building, and I suddenly realized what we were doing there. Dex was staring at a truck, one of those big ones that has the flatbed that slides back and tilts down, so you can load a car on it.

"It's only got sixty thousand miles on it," Lester was saying, "but I just don't really need it. I don't do any repair work, anymore, and when I buy cars at the auction, I just have them delivered."

Dex was crawling all over the truck, looking underneath it, raising the hood and crawling over the engine, giving it a thorough inspection. He started it up and worked the bed, making sure everything was operating properly, and then he and I took it for a test drive.

"Equipment?" I asked with a smile.

"One of the most important pieces," Dex said. "With this, I can go pick up the cars I buy all by myself. It seems like a big expense right now, but it'll save a fortune in hauling and towing bills."

"I'm not objecting," I said. "I kinda like the way it rides. How much does he want for it?"

"Well, it's in great shape, but it's still ten years old. He's asking eleven thousand, but I was going to offer him eight thousand cash. He'll probably haggle, but I should get it for about ninety-five hundred."

I shrugged. "I don't know what it's really worth," I said, "but that doesn't sound all that bad, to me."

We took it back to the car lot and the haggling began. Lester didn't want to come under ten thousand, and Dex refused to go over nine. I waited until it looked like they were both about to get angry, then stuck my own two cents' worth in.

"Dex," I said, "forget about this one. Let's just go buy a brand-new one. That way you get the warranty and everything."

Dex looked at me, a huge smile spreading across his face. "Really?"

"Okay, okay, okay," Lester said. "Nine grand. But that's only if you take it today."

I smiled at Dex. "Write the man a check," I said.

EIGHTEEN

IT TOOK A FEW MINUTES to finish up the paperwork and get insurance on it, and then we took the truck and my car to the house. I decided the office could wait another day or so, so I parked the car in the driveway and locked it up. I climbed up in the truck with Dex, and we went off in search of antique cars.

Dex had called the ads he had seen on Craigslist, so the first one we bought was the Cadillac convertible. To me, the car looked like it was almost perfect already, but Dex pointed out little flaws that most people, he said, would never notice. There were tiny little cracks in the paint, for instance, and a couple of little bubbly spots that he said meant there was rust underneath it. In order to make it worth the kind of money he planned to get out of it, he would have to take the car completely apart and strip off all the paint. Most likely, he said, he would have to replace a number of the body panels.

I waited until he wasn't looking and googled "automobile body panels." I never knew you could buy whole sections of a car body to replace parts that were rusted or dented, but you can.

The guy selling the car wasn't thrilled about taking a check, but I got him to call my bank and speak to David. David assured him that any check written on any account connected to me would be honored, and could not possibly bounce. By the time he got off the phone, he was smiling from ear to ear.

We got back in the truck and drove away, but we didn't head back into Tulsa as I had expected. Instead, Dex went further south and followed GPS directions from his phone to get another car. It was the Plymouth Cuda I had liked, and we got out and walked around it.

This car was actually in better shape than the Cadillac, but it was what Dex called a "hemi clone." It was designed to look like something called a Hemi Cuda, which was worth an awful lot of money, but it didn't have a Hemi engine in it. It was just painted and marked like one, but the engine under the hood, Dex said, was just a standard 383.

He bought the car anyway, and that's when I found out that the truck could handle two cars at once. There was something under the bed at the back called a "stinger," and it extended out and picked up the front end of the second car by the wheels. Dex made sure the four speed manual transmission was in neutral, and then we were back in the truck and gone again.

"I didn't think to ask," Dex said, "but can you drive a stick shift?"

"How many times have I told you," I asked, "I'm a farm girl? Of course I can drive a stick shift, I had to drive tractors and trucks and all kinds of things back home."

He smiled. "Good," he said. "I'm thinking about building that Cuda for you."

I looked at the car in the rearview mirror on my side, and then turned back to Dex. "But I just bought a new Mustang," I said. "Why do I need another car?"

"Because I want to do something for you," he said. "Cassie, you've made my dream come true with this shop. I want to do something nice for you, and I know you like that car. Let me build it for you, turn into a show quality car that you'll be proud of."

Dammit. There was that overwhelming feeling again. I kept my mouth shut and just smiled.

We took the cars to the shop and put them inside the building, then spent the rest of the day working there. I went to the building supplies store and bought things Dex wanted, including thick, shatterproof Plexiglas for the broken windows, a new steel door for the main entrance, twelve gallons of paint, assorted lumber and plywood, and twenty gallons of something called rubberized roof cement. I took the truck, which was actually a lot of fun.

Of course, I also bought paint rollers and lots of other things, and by the time we were ready to quit for the day, the building was solid and secure. All of the broken windows had been replaced with the Plexiglas, the steel door was in place and had new locks on it, and the first coat of paint was on the interior walls. It was going to take a second coat to cover up all the graffiti, but I was looking forward to coming back the next day to help paint again.

"So," I asked as we were cleaning up and getting ready to leave, "have you decided what to call this place?"

Dex grinned, and turned a little red in the face. "I had an idea," he said. "I'm not sure what you're going to think of it, though."

"Oh, come on, spit it out. What is it?"

"Well, we're partners, right? I thought about calling it Tate and McGraw Custom Automotive."

I couldn't help it, I kissed him.

We went home and took it easy the rest of the night. Dex found us a movie on Netflix, and Critter was happy to lie on his lap and purr while we watched it. It was a nice way to spend an evening, though I did have a tendency to pick my phone up and check it from time to time.

"Alfie never called," Dex said, about eight o'clock. "Think we ought to check in with him?"

I dialed the number and put it on speaker.

"Have I ever mentioned that you drive me absolutely nuts?" Alfie said as he answered.

"I think you might've said that once or twice," I said. "Why this time?"

"Because I can't find a real match to that face anywhere around us. I can try running it through the FBI database, but that would probably take a couple of days."

"Okay," I said. "Don't worry, you know I'm good for the bill."

"I'm not worried about that, I've got one of your credit card numbers, remember? I'll tell you something weird, though. I got a match off that picture that really surprised me, but it isn't him."

The back of my neck suddenly started to crawl. "How can you be sure it isn't him?"

"Because the one that came up as a preliminary match was for a guy who's dead," Alfie said. "The weird thing is the fact that the dead guy that was almost a match? I'm talking about your dead ex-fiancé, Michael Kendall."

The room started spinning, and it seemed like I was somehow being transported through time. I was back in the house I shared with Mike, and it was spinning around me, as well. I saw the living room, exactly the way it had been the last time I saw it, and suddenly one thing jumped out at me.

One day, while Mike had been at work, I had gotten tired of all the boxes of his stuff that he had never even bothered unpacking when he moved into the place. I started in the living room, pulling everything out and finding places to put it. This was actually what ended up leading to me learning about his past, but that day I was just having fun playing home decorator.

I put out his football trophies, lots of knickknacks and such that he seemed to have collected over the years, and a lot of pictures. There were pictures of him and his buddies from the force, but there were also pictures of his family. Some of them were of Mike and his brothers, Danny and John.

The one that jumped out at me in this mental virtual-reality was the picture of Mike, Danny, and John, all holding fishing poles. Mike was in the center, with Danny on his left and John on his right.

The bomber was staring out of that picture at me. It was Mike's brother Danny.

I snapped back to reality and shook my head as I sat up. I moved so fast that Critter jumped off Dex's lap and hissed at me, but I didn't care.

"Alfie, I know who it is," I said. "I never met him, because he was gone the one time I went with Mike to meet his family, but it's his brother Danny. Danny Kendall, and the last I knew he was somewhere in California."

I could hear the keyboard clacking as Alfie's fingers flew over it. "Danny Kendall, I'm assuming that's a Daniel?"

"Yeah, I think so," I said. "I'm trying to remember where he lived, I think it was Palm Springs, somewhere around there."

"Found him, last known address was in Coronado. Looking at his photo, and I'm going to say we have a winner. There are some slight differences, but it's the same guy. No doubt in my mind, it's the same guy. How did you figure it out?"

"I've been thinking all day that there was something familiar about him, but I couldn't place it. I knew it wasn't a face I had seen before, at least not up close and personal, but it was definitely familiar looking. When you said you got a partial match to Mike, I suddenly remembered a picture I saw of Mike and his brothers, and it hit me then. Danny was the tallest of the three of them, so he wasn't as beefy as his brothers. That's why I wasn't connecting Mike to him just from his face, because overall, they don't look that much alike."

"Okay, well, I just ran Danny Kendall's background, and you need to be extremely careful. Five years as a Navy SEAL, a demolitions expert, a crack shot with just about any weapon you can imagine. He made a small fortune from an investment in a buddy's startup tech company in Silicon Valley, but he's been in and out of trouble since discharged from the Navy two years ago. He was at least picked up and questioned back in California on everything from traffic offenses to attempted murder, but only a couple of misdemeanors ever stuck. Last record of him in California was about two months ago."

"Wait a minute," I said. "He was just discharged two years ago? But he was living in California back when I was with Mike, and nobody ever said anything about him being in the Navy SEALs."

"SEAL team members keep their identities very secret," Dex said beside me. "Nobody outside their own little community really knows much about what they do. Most of the time, they even ask their families to keep it a secret. There's always the fear that a member of a SEAL team can be compromised by threatening a family member, or someone they love."

I thought about what he said for a moment, and it made sense. "Alfie? Can you see anything about why he left the Navy?"

"He actually got kicked out," Alfie said. "Bad conduct discharge, stemming from emotional instability after—after the death of his brother."

I nodded. "So that's why he blames me," I said. "I exposed Mike's crimes, Mike got killed, and Danny went off the deep end and got kicked out of the Navy."

"I'd say that's the way it looks to me," Alfie said, "but you're the one with the psych degree. I'm emailing you everything I got on him, right now."

"Okay," I said. "I've got to call Detective Pennington."

I cut off the call with Alfie as my phone chimed to tell me I'd gotten an email. I glanced at it long enough to know it was the information about Danny, then thumbed Pennington's number.

"Detective Pennington," he said. "Cassie?"

"I know who it is," I said. It took me only a few minutes to explain how I had figured it out, and then I forwarded the email directly to him. He went to a computer and opened it up, then told me he was going to put an alert out for Danny immediately.

I hung up the phone and looked at Dex. "Am I ever going to be free of Mike?" I asked.

"You already are," Dex said. "This guy Danny is a nutcase, and he's trying to hurt innocent people in ways that he thinks will hurt you. You can't blame yourself, Cassie."

"I don't," I said. "Like Alfie said, I'm the one with the psych degree. I know how it all works, and I'm not going to let myself fall into that trap." I looked at him and smiled, letting Freda out. "I'm going to make the bastard pay for what he's done."

Pennington called me back a few minutes later to tell me that the alert was out, and that they had already started checking every motel and hotel. We both knew it wasn't likely Danny was operating under his own name, but they had to try.

A search of California motor vehicle records showed that Danny owned a white Ford pickup truck, and an all points bulletin was put out for that, as well. While it was unlikely that he was actually driving that truck around Tulsa, Pennington refused to leave any possibility unexplored.

Unfortunately, I didn't know Danny personally, so I didn't have any insight to offer. When I got off the phone with Pennington, I sat back on the couch again and tried to think of anything else that might help.

One idea struck me. About six months after I got out of the hospital, I got a phone call from Mike's mother. She called to tell me how sorry she was for what had happened, both to me and to Mike. I didn't really want to talk to her, but I could hear the genuine sorrow and regret in her voice, so I managed to be polite. I listened to her telling me what a good boy Mike had been growing up, and how she couldn't understand what could have driven him to the things they now knew he had done.

I knew that family had suffered a lot because of Mike, and I knew they were going to suffer a lot more over what Danny was doing. I hated to be the one to tell them, but if there was even the slightest possibility that she might be able to help me find a way to stop Danny, I had to try.

I googled the number and stared at it for several seconds before I finally hit the button to dial. I put the phone to my ear, holding up a finger to tell Dex to be very quiet.

"Hello?" I had been lucky, and it was Mike's mother Bernice who answered the phone.

"Bernice? Bernice, this is Cassie McGraw."

There was silence on the line for a couple of seconds, and then she cleared her throat. "Cassie," she said. "How are you doing? I think about you now and then, and I hope you're doing okay."

"I moved on," I said. "I actually went back to school about a year after—after everything happened, and finished getting my degree in psychology. I work as a counselor for abused women, now, in Tulsa."

"Oh," she said. "Well, that's good. Are you—I mean, how are you doing yourself? I know you were pretty traumatized."

"I'm doing okay, Bernice," I said. "Like I said, I've moved on. I actually have a boyfriend, can you believe that?"

"Oh, that's—well, that's wonderful," she said. "Is he, you know, good to you?"

"Yes, he is," I said. "He's pretty wonderful, to be honest. Bernice, I'm afraid there's a reason I'm calling you, and to be honest, I need your help."

"My help? How? How can I help, I mean?"

NINETEEN

I TOOK A DEEP BREATH and mentally gritted my teeth. "Bernice, have you heard any news about Tulsa the last few days?"

"Oh! Oh, yes, now that you mention it. They had some bombings up there, isn't that right?"

"Yes, that's right. The first one was in the counseling center where I was working, and we just had another one, yesterday, in a shelter where we put women and children when they have to get out of an abusive situation."

"Oh, that's terrible," she said. "Was—was anyone hurt?"

"There were a lot of injuries, and some fatalities," I said. "Bernice, the reason I'm calling you is because—it's because we have reason to believe the bomber is your son Danny."

There was absolute silence on the line for almost a minute. I kept waiting for her to simply hang up, but the line didn't go dead and I could hear her ragged breathing. I was just about to speak again when she said, very softly, "Cassie, are you sure?"

"We got a picture of the bomber from a security camera," I said. "I'm afraid it's him."

"Oh, my God," she said, and I could hear her sobbing. "Danny just hasn't been the same since everything happened. He was the youngest, you know? He just about idolized Michael, and when everything happened, and everything came out, he just refused to believe any of it. He tried to convince the police in St. Louis that they were wrong, even after it came out that there were videotapes. He kept insisting it couldn't have been Michael, and—oh, Cassie, he kept saying you were lying. We told him over and over that it was true, and we even told him what Michael and his friend did to you, but he just wouldn't listen. He started getting in trouble, and he got—he lost his job, and that just about ruined him. He came back here a few months ago, to Dallas, but he just couldn't—he just couldn't get along with his dad or his brother. We finally had to ask him to leave."

I took a deep breath. "Bernice, I'm truly sorry about all of this," I said. "I hate being the one to tell you what's going on, but is there anything you could tell me that might help us find him? I'm actually working with the police on this, and we need to find him before he can hurt anyone else."

She was quiet again for a few seconds, except for an occasional sob. "He—he called me last week. He said that he figured out how to come to grips with everything, and that he was going to be all right. I asked him where he was, but he said he was just visiting an old friend. He wouldn't say where."

My ear had perked up. "Bernice, did he call you from his own phone?"

"Well, yes," she said. "It was the same number he's had for years."

"A cell phone, right? Bernice, can you give me that number?"

She stopped talking yet again for a moment, and then I could hear her genuinely weeping. "If I do," she said, "can you stop him without hurting him?"

"We're going to try," I said. "I promise you, Bernice, we don't want to hurt him. We just have to stop him from hurting anyone else. The bomb yesterday? A little boy was killed."

"Oh my God," she wailed. "Oh, my God! Cassie, I don't understand what happened to my boys. I just don't understand it at all."

"I know, Bernice," I said. "And you can't blame yourself. Both of them were adults, and they made their own choices. Don't fall for people trying to tell you that it goes back to the way they were raised, because I know you did the best you could for your family."

I could hear her forcing herself to get her emotions under control. It took a moment, but finally she read off the number to me. Dex had been listening, and already had a pencil and paper in his hand. As I repeated the number back to her, he wrote it down.

"Cassie, please," Bernice said, "please try not to let him get hurt."

"I promise you, Bernice, I'll do my best. Thank you."

She hung up without saying anything else, and I dialed Alfie immediately.

"Gimme something hot," Alfie said when he answered. He often had some kind of weird line that he used when he answered the phone.

I rattled off the phone number to him. "That's Danny Kendall's cell number. Can you find it?"

"Does a duck go putt-putt-putt across the lake when he farts? Hang on, this will only take a few minutes. Okay, I found the carrier, now I'm getting the electronic identification number for the phone. With that, I can turn on its GPS without him even knowing it. Okay, three, two, one, bingo! GPS is on, getting the location..."

He was quiet for about ten seconds, and then he came back on the line.

"Cassie?"

"Yeah?" The back of my neck started crawling again.

"Do you have your gun on you?"

"Ye-es," I said slowly. "Why?"

"Because that phone is inside your house. I'm looking at a Google Earth map showing where it's located, and the pin is right smack on your house."

"Okay, thanks, Alfie," I said as calmly as possible. "I'll talk to you later." I ended the call and leaned closer to Dex.

"Danny's phone," I whispered in his ear, "is inside this house right now."

Dex was cool. He pretended I had said something sexy and chuckled, kissed me, then raised his arms and stretched. "I don't know about you," he said, "but I'm ready for something to drink. Want anything from the kitchen?"

"Sure," I said. "I'll come with you."

We both got up off the couch and started toward the kitchen, and I suddenly spun, drew my new Kimber, and started going through the hallway. Dex checked the kitchen and the bathroom, then the garage, and then came hurrying down the hall to catch me as I got to our bedroom.

There was no sign of Danny anywhere in the house, but we went through it again, just to be sure. When we still didn't find him, I took out my phone and started to dial his number, hoping to make the phone ring so we could find it.

Dex snatched it out of my hand. "I know what you're doing," he said, "and I think it might be a really bad idea. What we need to do is grab the cat and get out of this house, now."

It suddenly hit me what he was saying. Cell phones can be used as detonators on bombs, and I was just about to dial that very number. I spun, ran for the living room and grabbed Critter, and then both of us were out the front door and into the yard.

I called Pennington as soon as we were out behind our cars. It took a few seconds to tell him what was going on, and there were sirens splitting the air only a minute later.

Five squad cars showed up, along with a fire truck and an ambulance. A few minutes later, the bomb squad arrived with that weird truck of theirs. Pennington pulled in right behind them and walked over to where Dex and I were standing behind the fire engine.

"You're absolutely certain his phone is in your house?" Pennington asked.

I nodded. "My computer guy is," I said, "and that's good enough for me."

He nodded. "Well, if he's put it inside your house, I'd almost bet it's rigged to a bomb. You are one lucky lady, do you know that? It's a miracle he hasn't set it off already."

The bomb squad guys were putting on their armored suits, and then they took a weird-looking device and started toward the house. The thing looked like a large portable radio, almost like a boombox, but it had a long rod that was attached to it by a cord.

"What's that thing?" I asked Pennington.

"Electronic bomb sniffer," he replied. "If there is a bomb in there, that thing will find it."

We stood back and watched, and the minutes dragged by. I was as nervous as could be, constantly afraid that Danny would call his phone and set off the bomb while those cops were inside. I know they were wearing armor, but I'm just not that confident it would have actually protected them.

Twenty minutes went by, and then thirty. They were still inside, still going through the house and trying to find the bomb. After forty-five minutes, they came outside again, and took off their helmets as soon as they stepped out the door.

"No bomb in there," one of them called out. Everybody started to relax, but I was still a wreck.

"Did they find the phone?" I asked. "The phone is in there, and I can't imagine why it would be there if it doesn't have a bomb attached to it."

Pennington motioned for the bomb squad to come closer. "Guys, is there any chance you missed it?"

"Oh, sure," the first guy said. "We can only detect the most common explosives, so if there's a bomb using something really weird, we might miss it. On the other hand, the explosives we can't detect are so unusual that they'd be almost impossible to get."

Pennington chewed on his bottom lip for a moment, then turned to me. "You got that number?" He asked.

"Yeah," I said. "I was going to call it to try to find the phone, when Dex pointed out that it might've been a bad idea."

"Try it now," Pennington said.

I stared at him for a moment, but then I took my phone and finished punching in the number. My thumb hovered over the dial button for about five seconds, and then I pushed.

Nothing happened. Pennington looked at me for a second, then said, "Wait here." He started walking toward the house, and went right through the front door.

The phone rang about eight times, then went to voicemail, which said the mailbox was full. I hung up, and Pennington shouted out, "Try it again."

I rolled my eye, but I hit redial. I could hear the phone ringing on my end, and then suddenly it stopped.

"I found it," said Pennington's voice. "No bomb. It was hidden behind your toilet tank, stuck to it with duct tape."

He came walking out of the house, holding the phone. Dex and I met him at the front steps.

"What the hell is he trying to do?" I asked. "Is he just trying to tell me he can get into my house?"

"I'd say he's trying to tell you more than that," Pennington said. "He expected you to figure out who he was, Cassie. He figured you were going to get his number and try to call him, so he planted the phone in your house to scare you. He wants you to know he can get to you anywhere, and that for whatever reason, he has no intention of actually killing you at this point."

I looked at him and thought about what he had just said. "He's going to bomb another shelter," I said. "We need to evacuate all of them, now."

"Good Lord," Pennington said, "how many people are we talking about?"

I shook my head. "I honestly don't know, but I guess probably a hundred or so. I've got all of their phone numbers, but I don't know how they'll get everybody out of them. Any idea where we could put them?"

He grimaced. "Only place I could think of would be the gymnasium at one of the schools," he said. "You start calling them, tell them to just get everybody outside and away from the buildings, and I'll see what I can do about transportation and emergency shelter."

He walked away and took out his own phone, while I started calling all the shelter numbers in my contacts. I had them all, because sometimes I needed to reach them after hours or on weekends.

It took almost two hours to get through to all of them, and convince them to get everybody outside. We were lucky that it was a warm night with no rain, but a lot of the guests in the shelters were pretty upset about having to evacuate, anyway.

Pennington had hit the jackpot. He had called somebody at City Hall, who pointed out that the National Guard Armory had plenty of room and all the cots and such that could be needed. He got hold of whoever was on night duty there, and that person managed to reach his commanding officer. Arrangements were quickly made, and then someone else came up with the idea of commandeering school buses.

By midnight, every shelter in the county was empty. The bomb squad was going from one to the other, searching through the buildings with their electronic dog nose. Dex and I finally got to bed around one, and we just laid there holding each other for an hour before either of us got to sleep.

My phone woke me at a few minutes before six, and I snatched it up to my ear.

"Cassie McGraw," I said.

"You were right," Pennington said. "They found a bomb in the Broken Arrow Family Refuge. If it had gone off with everyone there, it probably would've killed more than a dozen. Most of those would've been kids."

"Wow," I said. "We got lucky."

"If we got lucky," Pennington said, "then luck must be spelled C-A-S-S-I-E. We never would have thought to check the other shelters last night if you hadn't tracked down that phone. A lot of people in this city owe you a debt of gratitude."

"Bull," I said. "We just have to catch this guy and put him away."

"We've got every cop looking for him, called in all the reserves, everything. The news shows are running everything we know about him, his picture, his name, everything. We're playing out the reward angle as hard as we can, but I'm still looking for anything more we can do. You come up with any ideas, you better call me."

"I will," I promised. "I will."

TWENTY

I PUT THE PHONE BACK on my nightstand and rolled over closer to Dex. I told him what Pennington had said, that we had actually saved lives, and he wrapped his arms around me and held me tight. We laid there for quite some time, but neither of us could get back to sleep.

We finally got up around eight and went through the motions of showers and breakfast. I really didn't have much of an appetite, but Dex insisted I eat at least a waffle. The last thing I needed was to let my blood sugar get low, which happened to me now and then.

I called the hospital to check on Marsha and Angie, but since I was not family, they wouldn't tell me anything. I called Nicole a few minutes later, she told me that Marsha seemed to be doing fairly well. She was talking more, even though her jaw was still braced the way it had been, and seemed to be in better spirits.

"You ought to stop out and see her," she said. "She doesn't really blame you, Cassie. I think she was still in shock that day, because she's asked about you several times since then."

"I might," I said. "Maybe I should give her a little more time, though. The last thing I want to do is make her feel worse. What about Angie? Any news there?"

"No," Nicole said with a sigh. "She's still in a coma. The doctors are worried, they expected her to wake up by now.

One of the nurses told me they're thinking it's psychological, that she's refusing to wake up because she's afraid of what's waiting."

We talked for a few more minutes, and I told her that we knew who the bomber was, now. I didn't go into a lot of detail, and thankfully she didn't ask. She promised to call me if there was any change with Angie, and I said I'd let her know of any new developments with the case. We said goodbye, and promised to call each other later.

Dex and I went to the shop building and started working again. I went back to painting, while Dex climbed up on the roof and started spreading the coating he'd had me buy. It turned out the roof was pretty solid structurally, but it hadn't had a new application of roof coating in many years. He was putting it on thick enough, he said, that it should last at least another decade before it needed any serious repair work.

I finished painting around noon, but Dex was still up on the roof. I called up to him that I was going to get lunch, then got in the truck and drove away. I glanced in the rearview mirror and saw him staring at me, and I halfway expected him to call and ask what I was doing.

He didn't, though. He told me later he just figured I liked driving the truck, which might have had a small grain of truth hidden in it somewhere.

The real reason I took it, though, was because I wanted to go by the office supply store. I went in and picked him out a desk and chair, got him a computer and printer and various other office supplies and gadgets, and then I happened to spot a video security system. It worked through the Internet with a cloud storage account that could hold up to a month's worth of video, and you could log in from any computer and see what was going on in real time. When it ran out of space, it simply started over at the beginning, slowly erasing what it already had.

It came with six cameras, and I added that to my purchase. When I got done, I stopped by McDonald's and grabbed us burgers and fries, then drove back to the shop.

Dex was down off the roof by then, and he looked a little like a kid at Christmas. He loved the desk and chair, really liked the computer system, but the video security system absolutely lit his fire. We sat down and ate lunch, and then he carried everything in. He started putting up the security system while I put the desk together.

By the end of the day, Dex said he was ready to move his tools in. He called up Jimmy and arranged for him and Nicole to come join us for dinner, so Jimmy could help load the tools onto our truck. They said they would be delighted, so we made a stop at the grocery store on the way home.

Dex is one of those men who is just an absolute genius on the grill. We had one, a nice gas grill that we had brought from his house when he moved in with me, so we bought steaks and potatoes and corn, and I grabbed a coconut cream pie for dessert. Dex added a case of beer and we headed for the checkout line.

Once again, since we now knew that Danny had been in the house at least once, Dex insisted on checking it out before letting me go inside. He didn't find any sign that anyone had been there, so he helped me carry the bags in and then went to get the grill out of the garage and set it up on my back deck.

"I'm going to need to clean it," he said. "You might stick some of those beers in the freezer, so they get nice and cold in a hurry."

"Already beat you to it," I said. "They'll be nice and chilled by the time Jimmy and Nicole get here."

Oh, I spoke too soon. Jimmy and Nicole showed up about twenty minutes later, and the beers weren't quite as cold as I like them. The guys each took one, anyway, but Nicole and I decided to wait.

Dex had the grill fired up, and he started cooking as soon as they arrived. The corn and potatoes got buttered and wrapped in foil, then went on the grill for twenty minutes. Dex had to keep rolling them over, using his big grill spatula like a maestro waving a baton. When he figured they were ready, he moved them to the edges of the grill and tossed on the steaks.

Nicole went into the house and came out with a couple of cans of beer, then handed me one. "I think they're good, now," she said. She opened hers and took a drink, then smacked her lips and moaned in delight. "Oh, yeah."

I popped open my own, but I decided to drink slowly. With everything going on, with Danny out there somewhere, I didn't want to find myself impaired. I can handle a couple of beers in a single night without any noticeable effects, so I sipped at it.

Dinner was delicious, and it was nice to have company. Dex and I didn't entertain very often, because we both tend to be loners, but Jimmy was Dex's best friend, and Nicole and I had grown kind of close over the last few months. We talked about having them over more often, especially since they announced they were moving in together, themselves. I couldn't help feeling a little pride in that, since it was Dex and me who introduced them.

After dinner, Nicole and I sat on a couple of folding chairs in the front yard, and watched the hilarity as the boys tried to load up all of Dex's tools. As I mentioned before, he had several big toolboxes on wheels, and they were far too heavy to pick up. He backed the truck in front of the garage, then slid the bed back and tilted it down. That way, he could hook the winch cable onto the toolboxes and pull them up onto the truck.

Each time, he had to tilt the bed back up level so they could move the toolboxes around and strap them down. Getting everything loaded up took almost an hour and a half, so it was getting close to nine o'clock by the time they were done. Dex and Jimmy drove off with the truck, and Nicole and I got into my car to follow them.

"Jimmy's excited about coming to work for Dex," Nicole said. "It's all he's been talking about the last few days, how they're going to build these fantastic cars, like you see on TV." She looked over at me and raised her eyebrows. "I know you're not hurting for money, Cassie, but isn't this going to cost quite a fortune?"

"Not nearly as much as I thought," I said. "I know that Dex is a fantastic mechanic, and this is something he's apparently always wanted to do. I consider it an investment. He's already explained to me how the shop will make money, and it ought to do pretty well."

"Okay, I'm sure you know best," she said. "I just can't help but wonder what will happen if you decide things aren't working out between the two of you. The last I knew, you weren't ready to make this any kind of long-term commitment. Has anything changed?"

I glanced at her and grinned. "Are you asking as my friend, or as my counselor?"

"I'm asking as your friend," she said, sticking her tongue out at me. "I don't think you need a counselor, and if you do, you need to find somebody besides me. No, I'm just thinking of all you've been through. When you guys moved in together, you made it real plain that this was sort of an experiment. Now you're going to be some kind of business partners on top of everything else. It makes me wonder if you reevaluated your position."

I licked my lips and thought about it for a moment. "Maybe you're not my counselor," I said, "but I wouldn't want you repeating what I'm about to say. You okay with that?"

She pretended to zip her lips shut. "Stays between you and me, I promise."

"Okay, then," I said. "There are occasional private moments when it dawns on me that the last thing I would ever want is to not be with Dex. Am I in love with him? I really don't know how to answer that, but I definitely care a great deal about him. He gives me a sense of—I guess I'd call it a sense of completeness, know what I mean?"

She smiled. "I understand exactly what that means," she said. "I don't know if that has anything to do with being in love or not, but if you know you want to be with him, then that's half the battle most couples end up dealing with. I've seen far too many of them who rushed together, then spend the next few years wondering why."

"Well, I know why I'm with him," I said. "It's because I smile and laugh more since I've known him than I have since the fire. I don't know if I ever told you, but until I met Dex, I thought I was a genuine man hater. I couldn't stand the thought of dating, I wouldn't even let myself have male friends, because as far as I was concerned they were all vicious, abusive bastards. Since I started letting Dex into my life, however, I've come to the conclusion that it wasn't that I hated men; it was just that I was afraid of them. Once I realized that, everything shifted into a whole different perspective. Fear isn't something I am going to put up with, so it was necessary to let some of my guard down." I shrugged. "Dex got past it. What else is there to say?"

She giggled. "And is there any possibility that this thing might evolve into something more?"

I rolled my eye. "Okay, again, this between you and me. I strongly suspect that, if I would even hint that I was willing, Dex would be dragging me down to the jewelry store to buy an engagement ring. Do I think about it? Sure, every once in a while I do. Am I ready for it? Not even close. When I do let myself think about what it would be like to be Mrs. Cassie Tate, it starts off with a smile and a warm feeling, but then this nervousness sets in. I'm not really sure what about it makes me nervous, but something does. Until I can get past that, I'm not willing to stick my neck out any further. That make any sense?"

"Yeah, it does. On the other hand, I think I've gotten to know you fairly well. Are you sure the nervousness doesn't come from feelings of inadequacy?"

"Inadequacy? Where did that question come from?" I asked.

"Cassie, you're always making comments about your scars, about the way you look. Most people take it as you having a good sense of humor, but you and I both know that it's a form of self-deprecation. You consider your scars a handicap. Are you sure you're not just thinking that it would be wrong to saddle a man with a wife who looked like Freda Krueger?"

I think that was the first time I've ever heard anyone else use Freda's name, and it came as something of a shock. I mean, for me to talk about her is one thing, but nobody else had the right to say something like...

She got you, Abby said. *She hit the nail right on the head, didn't she?*

I pushed her back, and caught myself biting my bottom lip. That's something I do when I don't like what I'm about to say.

"There might be some of that in there," I said. "I mean, think about it. Dex is a pretty good looking guy, in a Marlboro Man kind of way. Why should he be stuck with something that looks like me? I mean, do I really have the right to do that to anybody?"

"You're asking the wrong question," Nicole said. "What you should be asking is what gives you the right to decide what Dex wants, or what he deserves? Isn't that his call?"

I made a face that said she was right, but I wasn't ready to give up. "Maybe it is," I said, "but how long would it be before he gets tired of looking at me? I'm not blind, Nicole. There are millions of women out there who don't look like Frankenstein. Looking at this face every day, maybe for years and years? I can't help thinking that would eventually take a toll on a man."

"Do you honestly think so? Do you think that anybody who cares about you gets tired of looking at your face? Cassie, Dex didn't know you before you were burned, so to him, the way you look is just the way you look. Now, I can be blunt enough to say that it probably wasn't your appearance that attracted him in the first place, but something did. Why do you think that's going to change?"

I didn't answer, because we were pulling up at the shop about then. I glanced at her as I got out of the car, and she pulled the zipper across her lips once more.

The tools got unloaded into the shop, and we all headed for home. It was close to eleven by the time Dex and I got back to the house, and we were both tired enough to not even bother with the TV. Critter had been fed and was content that we had returned, so we went to the bedroom and dropped clothes on the floor like we usually did.

TWENTY-ONE

I DON'T KNOW ABOUT Dex, but I slept like a rock. I remember opening my eye once, noticing the sun shining through the window, then realizing it was a Saturday. I rolled over and went back to sleep, cuddled up against Dex.

It wasn't going to last long, though. My phone rang just a few minutes later, and I felt that now familiar crawling on the back of my neck when I reached to pick it up.

It was a number I didn't know, of course. I hit the answer button and put it to my ear.

"Cassie McGraw."

"Good morning, bitch," Danny Kendall said. "You think you're pretty hot shit, right now, don't you? You think you really accomplished something, clearing out all the shelters?"

"Kept you from raising your body count," I said. "That strikes me as a win." Dex rolled over and looked at me, but I held up a hand for him to be quiet.

"Yeah, you think you're cool. What you don't realize is, you're making your own job harder. You're supposed to be finding me, stopping me. How are you going to do that if you're not letting me do anything?"

Suddenly he laughed. "Oh, but wait a minute," he said. "You're still working on the assumption that you're smarter than I am. Okay, yeah, that explains a lot."

"What the hell are you going on about?" I asked. "Do you know that you sound absolutely crazy right now?"

"Oh, is that an official diagnosis? Should I be making an appointment with a psychiatrist? Of course I'm crazy, you stupid bitch, because you took away the only thing in this world that really mattered to me. Did Mike ever tell you how close we were?"

"Mike? If you want to know the truth, he hardly ever mentioned you. Hell, I didn't even know you were in the Navy until now. Maybe you weren't as close as you seem to think you were."

"Shut up! Just shut your mouth, bitch, you don't know what you're talking about! Mike and me, we were more than just brothers, a lot more. John, he was the oldest, so he was always off doing his own thing, but Mike was always right there with me." He was breathing hard, like he was on the verge of losing control. "And you, you're the one who took him away."

"Danny, I didn't take him away," I said. "His partner in rape and murder is the one who killed him, not me."

"But it was your fault! You knew what a fantastic guy Mike was, you should have just kept your mouth shut about what you found out. I read everything about that case, those things happened long before he ever met you. You had no right to tell anyone about that stuff."

He was shouting loudly enough that Dex could hear every word, and the look in his eyes told me that he knew the same thing I did: Danny Kendall was out of his mind.

"Danny," I said, "I wasn't trying to get Mike killed. I wanted him to get help, because that need he had to hurt and kill people, that's a sign of a badly warped personality.

If he hadn't called that other guy, Stuart, he might even still be alive. I was talking to him the whole time, trying to get him to see that he needed help, but Stuart insisted that they had to kill me. When Mike said he didn't want to do it, that's when Stuart killed him."

"Liar," Danny said. "That's all you ever did, you lied. You know why Mike came after you? Because he knew the truth, that you never really loved him at all, that you were just there to try to find the proof about the things he did. That's your whole thing, isn't it? You like to pretend you're some kind of super detective, and make yourself out to be some big hero."

"Danny, what is it you really want? Do you want to kill me? Is that it?"

"Kill you? Oh, hell, no! I don't want you dead, because then you won't be suffering anymore. What I want from you is for you to know that all these people are dying, and it's all your fault. You took away the only person in the world I cared about. Well, guess what, bitch, I'm taking away everybody you care about. *Everybody*!"

"But you said you want me to stop you. If that's what you want, then let's figure out where we can meet. Just tell me, I'll come right now."

There was silence on the line for couple of seconds, and then he laughed again. His personality was flip-flopping back and forth, one second in a rage, and calm and collected in the next.

"Yeah, you'd like that," he said calmly. "I'm not quite ready, yet. Got a few more people to take out, a few more pins to push into that voodoo doll I use you for. I'm going to hurt you, Cassie, the same way you hurt me, only a hundred times worse."

"Danny, there's no point to this," I said desperately. "You've already killed several people I care about, you already hurt me. The trouble is, you're not thinking about everybody else you're hurting. What about your mother? I talked to her the other night, and she's so torn up over..."

"Don't talk to my mother! She never understood anything about us, nothing. All she ever cared about was John, what a great athlete John was, what a great student John was, how John was going to accomplish so much in the world. You know what John did? John got his high school girlfriend pregnant, and he works in a factory. That's what Johnny accomplished. Me and Mike, though? We actually went out into the world and made something of ourselves." There was a banging noise, like he was slamming the phone against something. "And you had to screw it all up."

"Danny..."

"Shut up, I'm not done," he said. "I told you the last time we talked. If you want to stop me, you've got to pay attention. Watch the things I do, and you will figure out where to find me. Just remember this: if you don't come alone when you figure it out, an awful lot of people are going to die."

The phone went dead. I dropped it on the bed and looked up at Dex.

"He's completely lost it," I said. "He's not making any sense at all."

Dex shook his head. "You better call Pennington," he said. "I'll go put on coffee."

I called Pennington as Dex was climbing out of bed, and gave him a quick rundown of the call. I told him we were putting on coffee, and he said he'd be right over.

I got up and pulled on the same clothes I had worn the day before, then made my way out to the kitchen. The coffee pot was just beginning to burp and gurgle, so I sat down at the table with Dex.

"He keeps saying he wants me to figure out how to find him," I said. "I wish I could figure out what he means by that."

"I heard him," Dex said. "He said pay attention and you'll figure it out. Pay attention to what?"

"To what he's doing, I guess," I said. "I just don't see how that makes any sense. I mean, he blew up the outreach and took Marsha and Angie, but he killed Brenda and Leanne right there. That was the first thing. The second thing he did was beat Marsha and leave her in my dumpster. After that, he tried to blow up my car, which doesn't make any sense at all when he claims he doesn't want to kill me. Then he beat up Angie and threw her out on the street in front of my office. Next, he put a bomb in New Beginnings and blew it up, and tried to plant another bomb on my new car while we were there dealing with the injuries he caused there. He planted his phone inside our house, but didn't bother to put a bomb with it. Then he put a bomb out at Broken Arrow, but we managed to avoid anybody getting hurt on that one." I shook my head and threw my hands in the air. "I don't see it adding up, do you?"

He shook his head. "Not to me," he said. "Maybe we should try looking at it from another direction. Let's look at the places where he's attacked. You've got the outreach, then the parking garage at the hospital. After that was New Beginnings, and then Broken Arrow. Is there any kind of pattern there that you can see?"

I thought about it, but I couldn't see anything that connected those places, other than the obvious. I shook my head.

"Okay," he said, "then let's look at the people. He killed Brenda and that lady, Leanne, right? Then he thought he killed Marsha, or at least that's what we believe. Angie? I'm pretty sure he knew she wasn't dead when he tossed her out of his car..."

"Wait a minute," I said. "We've forgotten about the fact that he has an accomplice. When he dumped Angie, the witnesses said she was pushed out the back door of a sedan. That means there was somebody else in that back seat with her while he drove, or somebody else was driving while he pushed her out."

"Yeah, but I don't see where that has any bearing on what we're trying to figure out."

"It might not," I said. "On the other hand, if we could figure out who the accomplice was, they might be easier to find than Danny is."

We continued kicking ideas around, but nothing seemed to make any sense. Whatever it was Danny wanted me to figure out, I wasn't reading the clues properly.

My doorbell rang, and Dex went to let the detective in. He joined us at the table and Dex poured each of us a cup of coffee.

I went over the phone call again, giving it to him with all the detail I could remember. He used an app on his phone to record it all, but he was writing notes at the same time.

"He's taunting you," Pennington said. "He's trying to make you worry about who he's going to hurt next."

"Yeah, well, guess what?" I asked. "It's working."

"I know that," he said gently. "I just wish I knew how to stop this bastard so that you could get back to doing what you do."

"Yeah," I said. "You and me both."

"We've been going over the things he's done so far," Dex said. "He told her twice now that he wants her to pay attention in order to figure out how to stop him. Can you see any kind of pattern in his actions up to now?"

Pennington shook his head. "Other than the fact that he's obviously targeting people that will upset Cassie, no. I don't see anything that could point to a specific place or time or anything like that."

"Neither could we," I said. "What about the accomplice? Have we got anything on who that could be?"

"Nothing. Other than the witness statement that Angie was pushed out the back of a car, we don't have anything that indicates there was a second person involved anywhere else. It could have been another patsy, like Richard Long. I still think he was only killed to try to throw us off for a little while."

"But you said he had gunshot residue on his hands," I said. "Doesn't that mean he fired a gun recently?"

He grimaced. "Not necessarily. Gunshot residue sticks to skin, no matter where it comes from. It could mean he fired a gun, or it could mean he shook hands with somebody who had fired a gun. There was a study done a few years ago where they tested the hands of school kids under ten years old, and more than half of them tested positive for GSR. You can literally just pick it up in the environment."

I shook my head. I was just about to ask another question when Pennington's phone rang. He pulled it out and answered it quickly.

"Detective Pennington." He listened for a moment, and then his eyes suddenly went wide. "Secure the scene, I'll be right there."

He looked at me as he put the phone in his pocket. "Do you know an Antoinette Denham?"

"Oh, God, no," I said. "She was one of my clients at the Outreach. What happened?"

"She just walked into the hospital with a bomb wrapped around her. She told the security guards that only you can save her life, and if they try to take her out or evacuate the building, the bomb would blow up."

All three of us were up instantly and out the door. Pennington yelled something about meeting us there, jumped in his car, and roared out onto the street. Dex and I got into my Mustang, and I fired it up and followed.

With Pennington running his siren and lights, we made it to the hospital in less than ten minutes. I slid to a stop right behind him and the three of us rushed up to the emergency entrance. There were other police cars around the area, and the bomb squad truck was sitting at the end of the ER driveway.

I spotted her from the entrance. Toni Denham was sitting on a small chair off to the side of the ER lobby, in an area that looked like it was set up for kids. There were little tables with toys built into them scattered around, and the wall behind her had a mural of kids playing in a grassy field, with big, fluffy clouds overhead.

"There's nobody around her," I said. "That's good..."

"Security guards got everybody out of the area and back into the hallway behind the ER. She said that if the bomber sees people running out, he'll detonate the bomb, so they're keeping everyone inside but as far away from her as possible."

"Makes sense," I said. I took a deep breath. "Okay, let me go find out why I'm the lucky girl he chose for this."

Dex grabbed my arm. "Cassie, wait..."

I pushed his hand gently away. "I can't, Dex," I said. "We don't how much time we've got, and she's scared."

Toni looked up at me with tears streaming down her face as I walked toward her, and started blubbering. "I'm sorry, I'm sorry, Cassie," she said. "He said he can blow this up from anywhere, if I don't do exactly what he tells me."

I looked her over quickly, and saw that she had some kind of headset hooked onto her right ear.

"It's okay," I said. "Is he talking to you right now?"

She nodded. "Yeah," she said. "He grabbed me as I was leaving my house, and put me in a van. He had a gun, Cassie. He pointed it at me and made me put this on, then he buckled the straps and said if I tried to take it off, it would explode. He put this thing on my ear and dropped me in the street outside, and then he told me to come in here and say that only you could save me."

"Hey, I don't suppose he might have mentioned exactly how I could do that, did he?" I had a smile on my face as I asked, but it didn't seem to be doing anything to relieve her fears.

"No. He just told me to say that and..." She stopped talking for a moment, and her eyes glazed over as she listened to some new instruction through the headset. "He says if you look closely, you'll figure out how to disarm the bomb and get this off me." She sobbed. "He says you've only got fifteen minutes from right now, or it's going to blow."

TWENTY-TWO

I NODDED. "OKAY, THEN let me see what I can figure out." I finished crossing the distance to her, and knelt down right in front of where she was sitting.

This bomb didn't look like anything I had ever seen in movies, or anything I expected a bomb to look like. There were a lot of what looked like rectangular sticks, about two inches wide and maybe a foot long. There were probably a dozen of them attached to this vest-like thing she was wearing, and a lot of wires attached to all of them.

Right in the front, right on top of those things, was a box made of plastic. It had an LED display on it that was counting down from fifteen minutes. Apparently, I had already wasted thirty seconds.

There was also a cell phone attached to it, the kind with an actual little keyboard that slides out the back. It was open, and its display said, "ENTER PASSWORD." I stared at it for another thirty seconds, trying to figure out just what the password might be, but I didn't have a clue. The headset Toni was wearing was wired into it.

I looked at Toni. "Ask him if I can talk to him directly," I said.

She started to ask, but then she stopped and listened. A second later, she nodded, and I reached up to take the headset off her ear. It was on a cord that was attached to the cell phone, so I had to lean close to get it onto my own ear.

"Danny? It's Cassie."

"I'm watching the countdown," he said. "You got thirteen and a half minutes left. You sure you want to waste it talking to me?"

"Well, I'm kinda hoping you might give me some kind of clue about this password. I'm guessing that if I enter it right, it will turn off the bomb?"

"That's right. But I don't think you need my help; everything you need to figure out that password is right there with you."

I thought about what he said. Everything I needed was right there with me? I thought about what was there with me, but I was pretty sure he wouldn't have any clue what was in my pockets, so I didn't think he was talking about anything I brought with me.

So what else was there? Well, we were in the emergency room lobby, but it only held a lot of chairs, some tables with magazines, this kids area, all the usual stuff. Somehow, I didn't think any of that had anything to do with figuring out this password.

The only other thing was the bomb itself. I looked it over again, trying to see something about it that might trigger an idea, but absolutely nothing on it looked familiar in any way.

I glanced at the countdown display, and it was down to eleven minutes and twenty seconds.

"Hey, how about just a single hint? One little hint, okay?"

"Oh, no way," he said. "You're the great Cassie McGraw. You're a private investigator, it seems to me that figuring out clues ought to be right down your alley."

I gritted my teeth to keep from telling him exactly what I thought of him. I was pretty sure he really could set off the bomb, so I didn't want to set him off. I went back to looking it over, thinking again about what was there with me. Other than the bomb and the typical ER fixtures, though, I just couldn't see anything else.

Nine minutes, thirty-six seconds. Time was running out, and I was getting pretty frustrated. Still, I just couldn't see anything that gave me ideas about a password.

I had assumed he wouldn't know what I had in my pockets, but I decided to think about that, anyway. My phone, of course, but that didn't make me think about passwords. I had a case on my phone that held my ID, credit cards, that sort of thing. I had the little badge case that held my PI identification card. I had some money, but I don't usually carry a lot of cash, so I didn't think that would have any connection.

Seven minutes, twenty-nine seconds. Half my time was already up, and I didn't have a single clue.

What was it Dex always said? He claimed that what made me a good investigator was the fact that I looked at things from a different perspective, that I asked different questions. I thought about how to apply that to the situation, and suddenly imagined that I was out of my body, standing back by Dex and watching myself as I tried to figure out what to do.

What could I see from this new perspective? Well, I could see myself, and of course myself is something that is always with me. Could it be that simple? Was the password my own name? I started to try it, but I decided I ought to finish asking myself the questions, first.

What else could I see that was with me? I saw the chair Toni was sitting in, I saw the bomb wrapped around her, I saw all the signs and posters and the mural on the walls, I saw all the chairs and tables and magazines.

Four minutes, forty seconds. I softly growled in frustration, because I already looked at all of those things. I was just about to go ahead and try putting my own name in, but Abby suddenly spoke up.

What else is with you? He said everything you need is with you, so what else is with you right now?

I looked at the bomb once more, and then my eyes raised up to meet Toni's. I started to tell her I was going to try something, when it suddenly dawned on me that I had missed the obvious. I had gone over and over everything around me, but I had missed the fact that the main thing that was with me at that moment was Toni, herself.

Was it her name? Was that the password? No, that would be way too obvious. Danny wanted to be devious, and he wanted me to make a genuine deduction to solve this dilemma. I was certain I was on the right track, that it was the fact that Toni Denham was there with me that was the most important clue.

How the hell had he chosen her? Oh my gosh, the son of a bitch was able to get into my client files! Of course, he could have forced Angie to give him my password, to get into my files...

My password for my client files on the cloud server was 4Abby43v3r.

One minute, nine seconds. I looked Toni in the eye and smiled, then entered my own cloud password.

The timer went blank.

"Damn, you did it," Danny said. "You had me going for a minute there, Cassie, I wasn't sure you were going to make it. Would've been a shame if that thing had gone off, we couldn't have finished off this little game we're playing."

I swallowed hard, and reached up to touch Toni's face. "How do I get this thing off her?"

"Well, now that you disarmed it, you can just unbuckle it. There are two buckles on her left side. If you had tried to take them off before it was disarmed, it would've set off the bomb, but now it's perfectly safe."

"Okay." I wasn't sure that I believed him, but I leaned around her and found the buckles, quickly undid them and lifted the bomb off her. Once it was free, I jerked my head to tell her to get up and run, and she was off like a shot. "So you think this is a game? I'm not sure I really feel that way about it, but whatever. Have I learned whatever it was you wanted me to learn from this particular incident?"

"We shall see," he said. The line went dead, and I set the bomb on the chair and laid the headset down with it.

The bomb squad guys were there a second later, while Dex and Pennington grabbed my arms and dragged me out the door. Pennington demanded to know everything that had happened, so I had to explain it all.

"I knew you could do it," Dex said. "But I'll confess I was getting a little nervous, there, as time was running out."

I looked at him, my eye wide and bright. "You think you were getting nervous? I'm surprised my pants aren't wet. I'm pretty sure I darn near peed myself a couple of times."

The bomb squad picked up the vest and carried it out, not even being careful. They had done a more thorough job of disarming it than I had done, removing the plastic box, the phone, and the wires. Pennington waved at them, and one of them came over to talk to us.

"What did you find?" he asked.

"C4, enough to have done some serious damage to this part of the hospital. The whole thing was wired into that phone, programmed to go off on a timer or with a signal that could be entered from a remote phone. Once she put in the password, it turned off the countdown completely, but the phone was still on. He still could have set it off by sending a signal, probably a numeric code, from the phone he was on."

I understood completely. Danny Kendall could have killed me even after Toni ran away.

The only reason he hadn't was because he wanted to finish the game.

Pennington said that Toni seemed to be okay, other than being terrified. He asked me if I thought she was in any further danger, and I shook my head.

"I don't think so," I said. "He used her to make a point he wanted me to learn. I'm not real sure what it was, yet, but he got all the mileage out of her he needs. I'm pretty sure he won't bother her again."

He nodded. He told one of the uniformed officers to get her full statement, then go ahead and drive her home. She broke loose from the cops that were talking to her for a minute, and came running over to me. She almost knocked me down when she threw both arms around my neck, but Dex put a hand on my back and helped me stay on my feet.

"I don't how to thank you," she said, still crying. "Oh, Cassie, I was so scared."

"Shhh," I said, squeezing her in a hug. "It's okay, now. You'll be all right. You've got my number, you can call me anytime you need to. Okay?"

She nodded her head, and I could feel it against the side of my own. I hugged her again and let her go, and she started to pull away, but then she stopped and kissed me on my cheek. On the burned side.

She let go, then, and walked away. The officers took her somewhere to sit down and talk, and Pennington told me that I could leave anytime I wanted.

"I'm already here at the hospital," I said. "I might as well go up and see Marsha."

Dex went with me, and we rode the elevator up to her floor. There were different police officers on duty, but I think most of the Tulsa cops know my face. One of them nodded to me and opened the door to let us in.

Marsha was sitting up in the bed, and her eyes lit up when she saw me. The IV was out of her arm, and she held both hands out to me with her fingers beckoning me closer. I stepped up to the bed and she grabbed me and pulled me into a hug.

"I'm sorry," she said through her clenched teeth. "I didn't mean it, Cassie, I didn't mean it."

"It's okay, Marsha," I said. "Believe me, I understood completely. How are you feeling?"

"My stinking jaw hurts, and I'm still pretty sore, but I'm getting better. Hey, what's this I hear about you opening your own office?"

I smiled. "I just felt like it was time, like it was the right thing to do."

"I'm proud of you," she said. "I got a visit from Bishop McGuire, and he said we're not going to reopen. He said the Outreach has been good, but there are too many other places in the city, now."

"That figures," I said. "It's probably too much of a financial burden on the church. What are you going to do now?"

She shrugged, but it looked a little painful. "I don't know. I'm pretty sure one of the other places would take me on, but I might want to just go part-time. After this, I suddenly feel the need to spend more time with my children and grandkids."

I smiled. "I'm sure I can understand that," I said. "And if you're only interested in part-time, give me a call. Nicole is planning to work with me a couple days a week, so I'm setting up an extra office. I'd be happy to hire you."

We talked for a few more minutes, and I could tell she was getting tired. I gave her another hug and a promise to visit again soon, and then she surprised me by holding out her arms to Dex. He leaned down and let her hug him, being gentle so that he wouldn't accidentally lean any weight on her, and I heard her say to him, "You're one of the best things that could ever have happened to Cassie."

He grinned and looked up at me. "I'm glad you think so," he said, "but I think I got the better end of the deal."

We started to walk away, but I suddenly turned and looked at Marsha. "Marsha, one more thing. We are pretty sure the guy who did this has somebody working with him. When he had you, did you see anyone else?"

She narrowed her eyes and looked at me for a moment, started to shake her head, and then stopped. "I didn't actually see anyone," she said. "But I heard somebody. He was outside our room at one point, and I heard him talking to someone. I never saw them, but it was a woman's voice."

"A woman's voice? Have the police asked you about this yet?"

"No. They asked me if there was another man with him, but I had forgotten about hearing the woman until just now."

"Thank you," I said. "I think that might be a very big help."

We left Marsha's room, and I went to check on Angie. Unfortunately, she was still not responding. I spoke to a nurse who said that the doctor was becoming concerned. They were already talking about the possibility of long-term coma care, but they hadn't quite given up hope yet.

Dex and I left the room and made our way out of the hospital. Neither one of us really had any plans for that day, but we didn't particularly want to go back home.

"How would you feel," Dex asked, "about just escaping for a day or two? Let's just go somewhere, put all of this behind us for a little while."

I looked at him, and a part of me wanted to say that we couldn't do that, that I needed to stay close in case Danny were to strike again. I almost said it, but then a flash of anger made me refuse to let Danny rule my life.

“Let me ask you a question,” I said. “How would you feel about a trip to Illinois?”

“Illinois? Are you talking about meeting your parents?” He was grinning from ear to ear.

I nodded. “Yeah. I think it’s about time.”

TWENTY-THREE

WE WENT BACK HOME AND packed a couple of overnight bags, put down extra food and water for Critter, and got back into my car. I let Dex drive as we headed out, and I called Pennington.

"Jim," I said, "I've got to get away for a day or so. I think maybe I can think a little better if I put some distance between myself and what's going on. I don't think Danny is going to try another stunt like the one today in the next forty-eight hours, so we're taking an overnight trip to visit my folks back in Illinois."

He let out a sigh. "I don't know that the timing is great," he said, "but I don't blame you. Keep your phone handy, in case I need you, okay?"

"I've got it charging now, so it'll be ready and working all the time. If something happens, give me a call."

Google Maps says it's a seven hour drive, but Dex and I are both the kind who like to push the speed limit, so we made it in five and a half, arriving at just after two. We followed I-44 to St. Louis, then took I-64 over to US 51. I didn't bother to call ahead until we were just getting off the interstate, and Mom went into happy fits when I told her we were only ten minutes away.

I had told them about Dex several months earlier, but I had described him as just a good friend that I could hang out with sometimes. When we decided just before Christmas to move in together, I had been a little too chicken to tell them until the middle of January. They were both nervously supportive, remembering what happened the last time I moved in with a guy, but they also knew I was never going to let myself get into that kind of a situation again. I was the girl who campaigned against any kind of abusive relationship; Daddy said once that he pitied any man who ever tried to abuse me again.

They knew that I was a private investigator, and it was actually Daddy who gave me my first gun and convinced me to get my concealed carry permit. He knew darn well that I could handle a gun, and he said he hadn't been a bit surprised when he heard that I had shot Roger McCoy. Of course, I had explained the circumstances around the shooting, but Daddy said he was proud that I didn't hesitate when the time came.

We pulled up in front of the house and both of my parents came running out the front door. I was driving at that point, so they hurried around to my side to give me welcoming hugs and kisses, and then we all walked around the car together so I could introduce them to Dex.

That was a moment of revelation. Seeing Dex and my dad standing face-to-face, it suddenly hit me that my boyfriend bore a strong resemblance to my father. I couldn't believe that I had never noticed that before, but I've read many articles about how a girl will tend to be attracted to men that remind them of dear old dad. Maybe there was some truth to it, after all.

"Dex," Daddy said as he shook hands. "Cassie has told us quite a bit about you. I understand you are a veteran, sir."

"I am," Dex said. "I was an Army mechanic, which was really just a cheap way to get an education in automotive repair and maintenance."

"Don't let him snow you, Dad," I said. "Dex got two medals for bravery while he was in Afghanistan."

"Cassie," Dex whined, but I saw the look of respect he suddenly got from my father.

"I served in Desert Storm," Daddy said. "I was with the Corps of Engineers, but I only got to take care of building maintenance at one of our bases. It isn't just the infantry that serves, because without the engineers and the mechanics, the infantry can't do what they have to do."

"I agree with you, sir," Dex said. "I just hate it when she brags about it."

That got both my parents to laugh, and broke the ice the rest of the way. We went inside where Mom had a big lunch laid out on the table. Since we'd known we were going to get there in the early afternoon, Dex and I had skipped stopping for lunch, so the big platter of left over roast beef and microwaved bowls of veggies were a welcome sight. Tell Mom the president is going to drop by for lunch in ten minutes, and she can produce a five course meal out of leftovers.

Of course, Mom knows that I need to eat more than most girls my size, due to the burns, but I had never gotten around to mentioning that Dex had also been touched by fire. Mom just figured he had a wonderfully healthy appetite, as he put away two full plates without even slowing down.

After lunch, Mom took me upstairs to my old room for a private talk, while Daddy and Dex went out onto the big front porch. Daddy likes an occasional cigar, and Dex happily accepted when Daddy offered him one. Of course, that meant the front porch, because mom doesn't allow smoking in the house.

"So," Mom said as we were sitting on my bed. "You brought him to meet us. Does that mean it's getting serious?"

"Well, I think the fact that we're living together means it's already pretty serious," I said. "But if you're looking for wedding plans, you need to slow down. I'll admit that I'm a little bit crazy about Dex, but I'm just not ready to take any real permanent steps." I gave her a sheepish smile. "I know you'd rather hear something else, but..."

"Cassie," Mom said, cutting me off. "After what you've been through, I wasn't sure you'd ever even have a boyfriend again. I know how hard it must be for you to trust another man at all. I'm very, very proud of you, Cassie."

"Oh, I trust Dex," I said. "To be honest, I trust him completely. If there's one thing I know for sure, it's that he would never, ever do anything to hurt me, not on purpose. He actually saved my life once, already, you know."

Her eyes got wide. "He did? How?"

I had told her about the recent case involving the abductions of abused women, and she knew that I had even been involved in the investigation. I hadn't quite mentioned the fact that I had gone undercover, or that I had actually killed one of the perpetrators myself, but they found that out when they were reading the news stories about it. Those stories, however, left everyone thinking that it was the police who had saved me at the last minute. I had to explain that, in truth, it was Dex who had come crashing through an overhead door and plowed a car into the man who was trying to kill me.

"Well," she said when she got her head wrapped around it. "Sounds to me like he's pretty determined to keep you safe, then."

"I'll say," I said with a laugh. "He went and got his own concealed carry permit, so that he can pretend to be my bodyguard. He really is quite a guy, mom. And, oh my goodness, I hadn't noticed it before today, but did you see how much he looks like Daddy?"

She smiled. "I saw that the first time you showed us a picture of him. I always used to tease you that your daddy was your very first crush. Do you remember telling me, I think you were about six years old, that you were going to marry him when you grew up?"

I giggled. "Oh, my gosh, hush," I said. "I was just a little girl, that was normal."

She reached over and stroked my hair. "Yes, it was."

Out on the porch, however, an entirely different conversation was taking place.

"So, Dex," my dad had said. "You and Cassie are living together."

"Yes, sir, we are," Dex said. "I'm hoping we'll change that, someday, though."

"Yeah? You that fond of her, are you?"

Dex looked him in the eye. "Yes, sir," he said. " I love her, and Cassie is fully aware of my feelings, but she doesn't like me to say it out loud."

"Well, you know what she's been through, right? I'd imagine hearing those words is a little difficult for her sometimes."

"Yes, sir, I agree. I generally keep them to myself, but I am afraid they slip out now and then."

They sat quietly for a couple of minutes, puffing on the cigars and trying to see who could blow a bigger smoke ring.

"So, how did you come to be so close to Cassie?"

"Well, it started out because neither one of us really cared much for the dating scene, but we both liked to go out and have some fun once in a while. We had gotten to be friends when she handled a situation for me, tracking down an old friend of mine who had gotten into some trouble and helping her get out of it. We talked it over and decided that having a friend we could talk to, go out to dinner with, have a few beers or even do a little dancing with, seemed like a good idea. We started out just once in a while, then it turned into a Friday night habit, and then I realized one day that I was thinking about her all through the week. Back in December, she asked me to help her with her case she was working on, and we had to pretend we were a married couple for a few days. That meant staying together in an apartment, and when it was over, neither one of us wanted that part to end. We sat down and talked, and she asked me to move in with her."

Daddy nodded. "I guess that sounds about right," he said. "I guess her having a few million dollars in the bank didn't really have anything to do with it, did it?"

Dex looked him in the eye. "Of course it did," he said. "That was the reason I had to move in with her, instead of her moving in with me. She bought her house, I was just renting mine."

"Uh-huh," Daddy said. "Has she been spending a lot of that money on you?"

"Not until a couple days ago," Dex said, still meeting my dad eye to eye. "That's when she asked me if I'd like to have my own business, and bankrolled me so I could open my own shop."

"A repair shop? Is there really any money in that?"

"Oh, there can be," Dex said. "What we're doing, though, is starting a custom shop. I'll be building custom and restored antique cars. And before you ask, yes, sir, I'm very good at it."

"Well, that sounds pretty good," Daddy said. "And I guess that explains it pretty well, too."

Dex cocked his head to one side and narrowed his eyes. "Explains what, sir?"

Daddy glared at him. "It explains why a good-looking young fella like yourself decides to fall in love with a woman with such terrible scars as my daughter bears."

Dex told me later that he started to get angry, but then he forced himself to stop and think about it from my dad's point of view. He didn't doubt for a second that Daddy loved me, but Daddy also wasn't blind. He could see just what the fire had done to my face, just how disfigured I really was, and while he might always insist that I was still his beautiful little girl, the eyes don't lie.

The way Dex saw it, any man with a daughter who was so disfigured would naturally be suspicious of any guy who expressed interest in her. Add in the fact that I had a healthy bank account, and that suspicion turned to outright distrust.

"I can see," Dex said, "how you might think that. However, there is something else you need to know. You see, I've been with some absolutely beautiful women, and you know what I found out? I found out that beauty, that kind of beauty, really is only skin deep. Ugliness, on the other hand, can show right through the most beautiful exterior." He flicked the ashes off his cigar, took a big puff, and then went on. "Now the reverse of that is also true. Cassie has some really ugly stars. I see people all the time who can't bear to look at her, and it makes me ache for her, sometimes it even makes me angry. I don't say anything, I don't do anything, because Cassie doesn't need me to draw attention to the fact that somebody else thinks she's ugly. Instead, I make sure that when I tell her how I feel about her, she knows that it's because of the woman she is on the inside, not because of what I see on the outside. I make sure she understands that I'm in love with who she is, not what she looks like. When I reach for her, I don't flinch away if I happen to touch her scars. When I feel like kissing her face, I make sure to kiss all of it, not just the part on what she calls 'her pretty side.' When we go out together, I reach out to take her hand, but I don't care whether it's her right hand or her left hand. Now, you think you got me figured out, but I'm going to suggest that you ask Cassie what she thinks about all this. You can ask her without me being in the room, I won't mind a bit."

Daddy just looked at him for a long moment, then nodded. "Fizzed you off, didn't I? I challenged you to convince me that you're not just using my daughter, and it made you mad. Am I right?"

"Yes, sir, you're right," Dex said. "But then I put myself in your shoes for a minute, and I could see things the way you might see them. If I were in your position, if that were my daughter and I was talking to her boyfriend, I might feel exactly the same way you do. I'm trying to tell you that I'm not out to use Cassie in any way. I don't want her money, I want her. I want her in my life for as long as I can have her there, and I'll even confess to you right now that that is one of the reasons I agreed to this business deal. See, sometimes she gets to feeling like she's not good enough for me, and that really breaks my heart. She might decide, someday, that living with me isn't going to work for her anymore. I don't know how I would handle that if it ever happened, but I do know this. I couldn't stand to go through life without seeing her, without talking to her, I just couldn't stand it. Well, now we're also business partners. If there's one thing about being business partners, is that you have to talk to each other. This whole auto shop is just my way of getting a little extra insurance on being able to see her for a long time to come."

Dex said Daddy stared at him for almost a minute without saying a word, and then broke out in a big smile.

"Damnation," he said. "You really do love my daughter, don't you?"

"Yes, sir, I do." Dex said he sat for a moment, then returned the smile. "And just for the record," he said, "I understand Cassie a whole lot better than just about anybody else could."

He stood up out of his chair, and suddenly peeled his T-shirt up over his head. Daddy gasped.

"I was burned when I was a kid," Dex said. "Car accident, got gasoline all over me from here down and it got lit up. I was just lucky enough that my scars can be covered up with my usual clothes."

"Put your shirt back on," Daddy said. "My wife don't need to see that. And I want to thank you, for sitting here and talking man-to-man with me about this. My wife, she reads the emails Cassie sends her and she's pretty convinced that Cassie is in love with you, too, but too scared to admit it. Me? I just needed to get the measure of the man who's going to be protecting my daughter when I'm dead and gone." He flicked his own ashes, then blew a smoke ring straight at Dex. "I don't think I could ask for a better one than you."

TWENTY-FOUR

BECAUSE WE HAD EATEN a late lunch, we had an even later dinner. Mom and I worked together in the kitchen, making fried chicken with mashed potatoes and gravy, green beans, corn, and pumpkin pie, and I found myself remembering some wonderful times when I was growing up. I had always loved cooking with my mother, and especially on the big weekend dinners.

It was a wonderful evening. We all sat around talking through most of the afternoon, and then sat down to that fantastic dinner. We followed that up by playing Monopoly, something I hadn't done since high school, and Dex ended up winning.

On a farm, you go to bed at a reasonable hour and get up early. By ten o'clock we were all ready to get some sleep, and Dex and I were cuddled up in the bed I had slept in all the way through high school. Luckily, it was a full size bed rather than a twin, but it wasn't nearly as roomy as the queen-size we had back home.

"It's fine," Dex said. "In case you never noticed, we only use about half of that big bed, anyway. Either you cuddle up on me, or I cuddle up on you, but we're always together on one side of it or the other. There's plenty of room in this one."

I giggled, thinking of the times my high school boyfriend, Scott, had snuck in through my window and complained about how small my bed was. Somehow, I didn't think I wanted to explain to Dex what I found so funny, but I lucked out and he didn't ask.

Of course, that naughty thought reminded me of the times Scott and I had made love in this bed, being careful of the squeaky spot in the box spring so that Mom and Daddy wouldn't hear us. Since they were just down the hall, that might have been a bad thing.

I suddenly felt that insatiable, mischievous desire to re-create those moments with Dex, so I let him know I was in the mood to get frisky. He opened his eyes and looked at me, and a smile spread across his face as he reached for me.

Yep. Same spot still squeaks. Mom and Daddy were either ignoring us, or giggling.

Afterward, as we lay there cuddled together, Dex told me about the conversation with my dad. He has an excellent memory, so he probably repeated it word for word, but he went to great pains to make sure I understood that he was not offended. Oh, he admitted to getting a little irritated for a moment, but then it was like he told my dad. He put himself in Daddy's shoes and tried to see it from his point of view. When he did that, the irritation popped like a bubble.

"I'm sorry," I said. "I always was Daddy's girl, and he's always been very protective of me. I didn't think about the possibility he might give you a third-degree."

"Nothing to be sorry for," Dex said. "Be grateful that your father loves you that much. Besides, I told you when we first started getting together that girls' parents never seem to like me. I'm hoping I can win your dad over, but this is how it usually starts."

I poked him in the ribs. "From what you've told me, Daddy is already starting to like you," I said. "I'm pretty sure Mom thinks you might be the best thing that ever happened to me."

"Your mom might like me," he said, "but I think the best I can hope for out of your dad, for right now at least, is that we respect each other. I'm pretty sure he believes I care about you, and he seemed to think I would be adequate to take care of you once he's gone, but he never actually said he liked me. I'm just saying."

We cuddled ourselves to sleep, and woke early with the dawn. My room had east-facing windows, and the sheer curtains did nothing to cut down the sunlight coming in. That's probably why I wake up whenever sunlight manages to touch me in the mornings.

The smell of coffee was already coming up the stairs, so I let Dex get the first shower while I went down to see Mom in the kitchen. She broke out into a big smile when I walked in, and pointed to the coffee pot.

"Did you sleep okay?" Mom asked.

"Oh, yeah," I said. "We both did. Although, it did seem a little strange, sleeping with Dex in my old bed. When I brought Mike out to meet you, you made him sleep on the couch downstairs."

"That's because you were still pretending to be a virgin," Mom said, "so I kept pretending I believed it."

I'll bet my eye was as big as it's ever been. "Mom!"

She gave me the "mom look," the one that says I only thought I had her fooled. "Your bed springs squeak, Cassie," she said. "And your dad spotted Scott climbing out your window more than once. I'm just glad you never ended up pregnant."

I stuttered a couple of times, then finally managed to speak. "I was—careful," I said.

"I figured you would be," she said. "As for now, you've already been living with Dex for a few months. It would feel kind of silly to pretend we didn't know you were sleeping together at home, and you're an adult, now."

I gave her a wry grin. "Your grown-up daughter, who's living in sin?"

"I don't think sleeping together means you're living in sin," she said. "As long as you're happy, Cassie, that's what matters most."

Mom was making biscuits, but she had eggs and bacon cooking on the stove. I took over with the biscuits, beating the dough and rolling it out, then folding it over and doing it again. I hadn't made scratch biscuits in years, but making them that morning convinced me it was time to buy a rolling pin.

Dex came down a few minutes later, and I headed back out to get my own shower. We were only going to be staying for the morning, and planned on leaving shortly after lunch. I hurried through my shower so that I could spend as much time as possible just enjoying the peace and quiet of being at home on the farm.

Daddy had already been out working, turning over the south fields with the plow. It was already almost the end of March, and he would be planting corn in early April. I used to drive one of the tractors myself, sometimes, and I can clearly remember pulling the manure spreader, dumping tons and tons of cow shit onto the freshly plowed ground. Nowadays, Daddy had to plow the fields and then go spread the manure himself.

When he came in, he washed up at the kitchen sink like he always did, and then we sat down to eat. Mom poured Daddy a cup of coffee and set it by his plate, then fixed his plate for him. When that was done, she finally took her own chair.

We weren't a terribly religious family, because Mom and Daddy figured religion wasn't what got you into heaven, anyway. We were, however, a Christian family, and grace was said over every meal. The day before, Daddy had said grace at both lunch and dinner.

That morning, he looked over at Dex. "Would you mind to ask the blessing?"

Oh, boy. It didn't take a genius to figure out that Daddy was throwing out another test. Was Dex good enough for his little girl? I wasn't sure what was going to happen, because I'd never heard Dex say any kind of prayer out loud.

He looked at my dad with a grin. "It will be an honor, sir," he said. He bowed his head, reached over and took my hand as I sat beside him, and then began to pray.

"Father in Heaven," he said, "we give You our thanks for this beautiful day, and for the chance to be together and enjoy Your bounty. Thank you, Father, for these wonderful people I've had the chance to meet, and for their daughter, who has brightened my life in so many ways. We ask You to bless this food for our consumption, and for the nourishment of our bodies, but to impart also to us Your grace, Your love and Your wisdom. In Jesus' name we ask these things. Amen."

"Amen," we all echoed. Mom was looking at Dex and beaming with pride, and Daddy simply looked at him approvingly.

I whispered a little prayer of thanks of my own.

After breakfast, Daddy asked Dex if he'd ever done any farm work, and Dex admitted that he had not. I joked that it was good that he hadn't, since it meant there was something I could do that he couldn't.

That might've been a mistake. Ten minutes later, he followed my dad out the door and got a quick lesson in how to drive the old Oliver tractor. It wasn't hard to drive, since you basically just put it in one gear and let out the clutch. Ten minutes later, Dex pulled the manure spreader in under the big hopper and Daddy filled it up, and then they headed for the field together.

Mom and I were left alone in the house, and we knew that the menfolk would not be back until lunchtime. We got ourselves each a cup of coffee and went out onto the front porch, to enjoy the sunny Sunday morning.

"Your Daddy likes him," Mom said. "He said Dex is a good man, probably the best man you could have found."

I smiled. "I can't argue with that," I said.

Mom seemed to hesitate. "Your father said—he said Dex has burn scars, too? On his chest?"

I nodded. "Not just his chest," I said. "They go all the way down, from the middle of his chest to his ankles. It happened when he was a teenager."

She looked closely at my face. "Does it bother you that—that he can hide his scars?"

I laughed a bit. "No, not at all," I said. "I'm glad he can, because people don't shy away from him the way they do me. He confessed it to me once it's one of the reasons he asked me out the first time. He figured that, if we ever got to the point where it would matter, I wouldn't suddenly get all grossed out when he took his clothes off. I guess he's had that problem in the past."

I knew what the next question was going to be before she had the chance to ask it, but at least she had the good grace to turn pink. "Cassie, if he was burned all the way down, does he... I mean, is he able to... Does everything work okay?"

She turned even redder when she saw my smile. "Oh, yeah," I said. "A lot better than okay."

"I'm not trying to be naughty," she said. "I was just wondering if, you know, someday, if you decided to have children..."

I whipped my face around to look at her, my one eye big and wide. "Children? Mom, I guarantee you there won't be any children unless we decide to get married. As far as whether it's possible? I would think so, I mean, as far as I can tell everything seems to be intact. It isn't something we've ever talked about. For that matter, I don't even know for sure if I can have children. There are issues with burned skin having enough plasticity, not to mention the spots where the artificial skin was used. It might not stretch enough for me to carry a baby."

She nodded. "Yes, I thought about those things. I never mentioned it to you, but I asked your doctor once about it. He said you probably wouldn't have any trouble conceiving, but that burn victims sometimes miscarry. I guess they're not really sure why, but it seems to happen in a small percentage of cases. As far as being able to carry a baby, he said there's no way to know in advance, but there are things your doctors could do if you did run into a problem."

Actually, I knew those things, as well, and more. One of the things that is fairly common for women who suffer major burns is that we often stop having periods. I had one after I woke up from my initial coma, but then nothing. My doctors told me it was possible that I was going into early menopause because of the trauma, but I never showed any other signs of it. Then, about the time I finished college, they started up again. They were sporadic at first, but for the last year I've been as regular as clockwork, so when Dex and I decided to be "friends with benefits," I went straight to my doctor and asked for birth control. I had used Depo-Provera, the shot, when I was with Mike; it had worked, so I just went back on it.

The thing is, I also knew that my parents had always dreamed of the day my little ones would call them Grandma and Grandpa. A part of me wished I could give her hope that that day might still be coming, but I wasn't ready to make any kind of decisions like that.

Besides, I'd have to know how Dex felt about it. He was raised by his mother, with only occasional appearances from his deadbeat dad. He might have his own concerns about having children that would be completely unrelated to my scarring.

Luckily, Mom decided to move on to another topic.

"So, what are you going to do, now that the Outreach clinic is gone?"

I told her about opening my own office, and that I intended to keep right on doing it for free. She told me she was proud of me, but then she wanted to know about the investigation into the bombing itself. She'd heard about New Beginnings, and I had actually remembered to call her briefly when the Kia got blown up. I told her that the investigation was continuing, but she could tell I was holding something back.

"Cassie? What is it you're not saying?"

I sighed. "Well, we kinda know who the bomber is," I said. "It turns out that it's Mike's kid brother, Danny. I guess he went a little nuts back when everything happened, and instead of getting help, he's gotten worse and worse. He blames me for the fact that Mike ended up dead, and that's why he's doing things that seem to be connected to me."

I told her about the phone calls from Danny, and about what happened with Toni Denham the morning before. She did her best to stay calm, cool, and collected, but I could tell I was scaring her half to death.

"Oh, Cassie," she said finally. "Sometimes I wonder how you can be as strong as you are. You take things like this in stride, you just act like it's all part of your day. I pray, almost every day I pray that God will give you a normal life, but it seems like He must have designed you especially for some of the hardest things anybody could do."

"Mom," I said, "I get scared. Sometimes, when these things are going on, I think maybe I should just give up and stop working, stop trying to help people. The last case I worked on was dealing with people who felt women who chose to escape abuse should be punished. This guy, Danny, he just wants to hurt innocent people because he knows that will hurt me." I reached over and laid a hand on her arm. "The problem is, Mom, that there are so many women out there, women and kids, who need my help. They need to know that the abuse can actually become horrible, and I've already helped over a hundred women make that first, hard step. If I don't do it, who will?"

She nodded. "I know," she said. "I know."

TWENTY-FIVE

WE WENT INTO THE HOUSE a little later to start lunch, and Mom surprised me.

"I think we're going to just do a leftover spread," she said. "We put on the dog a bit yesterday, and we got a lot left from both lunch and dinner, so there's no point in cooking up a big Sunday meal. Let's go ahead and start getting it all set up, so we can sit down to eat when the men get cleaned up."

I could hear the tractors coming back toward us, so I knew it was getting close to lunchtime. Mom and I got out the roast beef, chicken, all the veggies, potatoes, gravy, and everything, and started heating it up. It would take Dad and Dex at least an hour to clean and put away all the equipment, so there was still plenty of time.

Heck, I've seen my mother put on a meal for twenty people in no more than an hour. Heating up leftovers was nothing!

And then my phone rang. I didn't know the number, so I stepped out on the porch while Mom was busy reheating the mashed potatoes.

"Cassie McGraw."

"Where the hell are you?" It was Danny Kendall.

"That's none of your business," I said calmly. "I decided to take a break from you for a day or two."

"You don't get to do that, Cassie! The game is running, you don't get to just check out and not play."

"Hey, Danny, you know what? This isn't a game. Games are not something you play with people's lives. Like I told you more than once, you want me? Then you bring it to me."

He laughed. "Little late for that, isn't it? Well, your little vacation came at a really bad time. Have you even heard the news today?"

A sinking feeling hit the pit of my stomach. It hadn't occurred to me to look at any of the news websites, and since nobody had called, I simply assumed everything was okay back home.

"Danny? What have you done?"

"Me? I just left you another chance to be a hero. Too bad you're not going to be there to save the day."

The line went dead suddenly, and I quickly went to my news app and scanned through the headlines. I saw the usual stuff about local politics, headlines about problems in certain neighborhoods, a dozen other topics that didn't seem to be related to anything important at all, and then I spotted the one that had to be what he was talking about.

Local Women Reported Missing

Three Tulsa area women have been reported missing by their families, and police are calling the disappearances suspicious. Connie Kirby, Wanda Sparks and Candace Lawson all failed to come home yesterday, but this isn't the first time. A few months ago, all three of these women were among those who were abducted by Frank and Michael Rawlings. They were found alive by a Tulsa private investigator, Cassie McGraw, and both Frank Rawlings and his son Michael were killed dur-

ing the rescue. Currently, police do not believe there is a connection to the previous case, but anyone with any information is urged to call the Tulsa Police Department.

I dialed Jim Pennington and put the phone to my ear. "It's Cassie. Danny just called me and said something about setting up a chance for me to be a hero again, and I just saw that some of the women from the last case seem to have disappeared. That's got to be what he is talking about, Jim."

"Whoa, whoa, what? Who's disappeared?"

"Wanda Sparks, Candy Lawson, and Connie Kirby. I worked with Detective Niles on that case, but they were three of the women who were abducted by the Rawlings. That case was all over the news, so Danny would have no trouble getting their names. Apparently he's tracked them down and decided to use them to set me up again. You didn't even know about this?"

"No, I hadn't heard anything about it. If it is missing persons, that's another whole department. Let me check into it, and I'll get back to you."

The line went dead and I turned to go back into the house. Mom was standing in the doorway, just looking at me.

"Cassie? What's wrong?"

I told her quickly what had happened, and followed her back into the kitchen. I was trembling with a combination of fear and rage. If those women died because I wasn't there to do whatever Danny wanted, I was going to feel like a monster.

Mom fixed me a cup of coffee and I sat down at the table. I was trying to guess just what it might've been that Danny was after from me, trying to figure out what he would've wanted me to do to try to save them. Unfortunately, without knowing any of the circumstances, I was flying blind.

My phone rang just as Dad and Dex were coming into the house. I snatched it up and saw that it was Pennington.

"Jim? What did you find out?"

"Not a whole lot," he said. "All three of those women went out sometime yesterday and never came back home. Their families reported them missing, but it wasn't until this morning that anyone put it together with what happened with Rawlings and his son. Cassie, I think you're probably right about Danny being behind this, but I don't have any idea what he meant about giving you a chance to be a hero. So far, we don't have any leads on them at all."

"Damn, damn, damn," I said. "I really didn't think he would do anything again this quickly. Jim, we're going to be on the way back within the hour. Call me if you find out anything else, okay?"

"You got it. But drive safe, okay?"

I promised we would, and then explained to Dex what was going on. He sat down beside me and put an arm around me, and I leaned against him.

"Cassie, we can grab something to eat on the way," he said. "If you think we need to get started back now "

"At this point, I don't think saving half an hour would make any difference. Get cleaned up so we can eat, and then we can go. I already packed our stuff up this morning."

He gave me a squeeze, then went and washed up. I noticed that he had an earthy smell, the same kind of smell my dad always had after a day in the fields. It was different, on him, and it made him smell masculine and strong.

Lunch was ready, so we sat down to eat. I'll confess that we hurried a bit, despite my insistence that we didn't need to, but we still managed to enjoy that last half-hour with my folks. Both Dex and I ate heartily, because we knew we weren't likely to stop again before we got back to Tulsa.

Mom must have figured that out, too. As Dex and I carried our bags out to the car, Mom came out with an old picnic basket and handed it to me. I opened it up to find roast beef sandwiches and several pieces of chicken inside, and I hugged her tight.

Daddy was standing on the other side of the car, shaking hands with Dex. The two of them were smiling at each other, and I got the impression that something had happened out in the field that bonded them together, somehow.

I let go of Mom and she hurried around the car to throw both arms around Dex. He returned her hug with a big smile, and even leaned his face down so she could give him a kiss on the cheek. She let go, then, and stepped back. Dex and I got into the car, and Mom and Daddy waved as we drove away.

We got back to the interstate and headed toward home. We were just crossing the bridge over the Mississippi, passing the famous Gateway Arch in St. Louis, when my phone rang again. I had it connected to the car stereo, some Bluetooth thing that Dex figured out, and the display on the dash told me it was Pennington calling.

I poked the answer button. "Go ahead," I said.

"Cassie, we found all three of them. They're okay, just a little shook up."

I looked at Dex, shaking my head. "What in the world? Was it Danny?"

"Yeah, it definitely was. He approached each of them yesterday with some line about not knowing how to get a little kid out of a car seat, then stuck them each with a needle that knocked them out cold and took them to someplace similar to the one he kept Marsha and Angie in. Just like them, he fed them and treated them decent, and he told them that you were going to come and save them again. A couple of hours ago, apparently, he went back and put hoods over their faces so they couldn't see anything, loaded them up in some kind of a van and took them out to Mohawk Park and let them go."

My mind was racing, trying to figure out just what Danny was up to. "Jim, you should probably take them to the hospital to get checked out. Make sure they haven't been drugged or given some kind of infection or something."

"That's where they're at now," he said. "Don't worry, I'm just as suspicious as you are. There was one more thing, though. He told them to tell you that this is the only reprieve you're going to get. He says you better be ready to play tomorrow. Any idea what that's supposed to mean?"

"Yeah," I growled. "He thinks this is some kind of game, and he wants me to play by his rules. The only problem is, I don't know what they are."

"Okay. Listen, I'll let you know if anything more comes out of this, but I have a feeling he's being straight on this. He let them go because you weren't available to do whatever he wanted, almost like he's trying to show you there's still something good in him. I'm not sure that's true, but I'd take him at his word that you won't get another break."

"Thanks, Jim," I said. "Believe me, I won't be taking any more vacations until this is over. He wants to bring this game to its end, and so do I."

I hit the button to cut off the call and continued driving through St. Louis. Dex was quiet, but he was just looking at me.

"What?" I asked.

"I was just thinking," he said. "I remember you said he told you that he wanted you to figure out how to find him, right?"

"Yeah. He said he wants me to stop him, but I had to figure out how."

"And there is supposed to be clues for you in the things he's doing, right?"

"That's the way I understand it, yeah. You got an idea?"

He shook his head. "I'm just trying to look at everything he's done so far and find something that could be called a common denominator. The only thing I'm seeing, though, is that it's all tied to your work as an abuse counselor. I mean, he blew up the Outreach; left Marsha, who you work for, in your dumpster, probably thought she was dead; he blew up your car while you were visiting her at the hospital; he beat up Angie and threw her out in a way that was designed to get your attention; he blew up New Beginnings, a shelter where you put people before; how did the Denham girl fit into it?"

"She's a client," I said. "She's been coming to see me for about a month, once or twice a week. Her husband likes to slap her around a lot, and he's the kind that threatens to kill her if she leaves. I've been trying to help her get up the courage."

"Okay, so she's part of it, too. Then we got this latest escapade, with some of the women from the Rawlings case. The only common thread in all of it is your work as an abuse counselor." He shook his head. "I'm just not seeing the clues he's talking about."

I shrugged. "Me neither," I said. "I guess we just have to wait and see what he does next."

We drove on through the afternoon, and finally got back into Tulsa at about six thirty. I called Pennington to let him know we were back, but he didn't have anything new to report. The women had checked out okay at the hospital, and had been allowed to go home.

We got to the house and went through it together, but found no sign that anyone had been there. I jokingly suggested that we should buy one of the security systems like we had for the shop and install it in the house. That way, we could literally look through the house from our phones before ever going inside.

"That's a great idea," Dex said. "I know I'd feel a lot better about you being home alone, that way."

I laughed. "Yeah? We'd just have to be sure to go in and erase all the video from the bedroom pretty often."

He grinned. "I'll handle that part," he said. I smacked him on the shoulder and told him he was a naughty boy, which only made him laugh harder.

We had snacked on the picnic basket as we drove, and we finished off what was left in it for dinner. Critter was happy to take a few of the leftovers, and then we all curled up on the couch together to watch a movie.

The movie was called "Courageous," and it struck me that it was actually about fatherhood. In the story, a police officer and his family are devastated by the death of their little daughter, who was killed in a car accident while riding with some friends. His son, who was older, begins to question what life is all about, and starts to rebel, which leads the officer to discover a local movement to guide men into becoming better fathers. It was an awesome movie, and it had some incredible themes, along with a couple of absolutely hilarious scenes.

Of course, watching the movie made me remember my conversation with Mom, and my thoughts about whether Dex would even want to be a father. It all sort of rolled around the back of my mind while the movie was playing, and I decided that it might be time to find out his thoughts on it.

I waited until the movie was finished, and we were getting ready for bed. We had locked up the house and gone to the bedroom, and I turned to him as I slid under the covers.

"I want to ask you an off-the-wall question," I began, "but I don't want you to read too much into it. Do you think you can manage that?"

"Off-the-wall? I guess I can try. Go ahead, what's the question?"

"You hardly ever talk about your childhood. You mentioned your mom a few times, but the only thing you've ever said about your dad is that he was never there. I was just wondering—this is the part I don't want you to read too much into—but did you ever think about having kids of your own?"

I'm not entirely sure what I expected. I thought he might freeze and stare at me, or he might bust out laughing, and I even considered the possibility that he would get upset. What I got was a chuckle as he went right ahead taking off his clothes and getting into bed beside me.

"Mom put a little pressure on you for grandkids?"

"No," I said, "not really. I mean, I know they would love the idea, but she's fully aware that we are not at that point in our relationship, so relax. Now, I really just wondered if you'd ever given it any thought."

"Of course I have," he said. "And someday, under the right circumstances, I think it could be great. I used to worry that I might not be a very good dad, because I didn't have an example to learn from. I got over that, though, when I realized that I had a perfect example of the kind of father I wouldn't want to be. I'm not just talking about my own dad, who ran out when I was little and only dropped by once in a while until I was in my early teens, but I've watched other men. Some of them were my buddies' fathers, and there have been others that I've seen who didn't do a very good job. I figure I know enough things to avoid to let me do at least a halfway decent job of raising a kid."

Now, I heard everything he said. It's not my fault that the only part that really stuck in my ear was that one little phrase.

"And what would be the right circumstances? Hypothetically, I mean."

He got himself settled in the bed and rolled onto his side so that he was facing me. "Right circumstances? That would involve you deciding you wanted to be a mother." He kissed me, then rolled over and turned his back to me.

I lay there for a long moment without saying anything, and then I reached out and put my hand against his back.

"You know, there's always the possibility that I couldn't even have a baby. Some women can't, after massive burns."

"That's true," he said. "In which case, there's always adoption. If, and I stress if, we ever got to that point."

TWENTY-SIX

MONDAY MORNING. DEX and I had agreed that, even with everything going on with Danny Kendall, it was time to get busy with our respective businesses. We rolled out of bed at six thirty, took a quick shower together, and then got dressed and went out for breakfast. The Denny's on North Sheridan was on the way, since the shop was just around the corner from my office, and I've always enjoyed having breakfast there.

When we were finished, I drove us to the shop and Dex pointed out that one corner of the big storage lot, inside the fence, was directly behind my office. The dumpster where I had found Marsha was right there, next to the fence. We decided to put a gate in so that I could keep my car parked there on our property.

For that morning, I simply walked around the block. I got to work at just a couple of minutes after eight, locked the door behind me and went into my office. I needed to get started on advertising, to let the women who needed me know that I was there.

I took out ads in all of the local newspapers, from the big dailies to the weekly shopper variety. When that was done, I called two or three of the radio stations and arranged for commercials. I decided to use a "public service announcement" style, talking about the dangers of abuse and then listing my name and phone number.

At about ten o'clock, my phone rang, and I looked at the display. It was Nicole calling, so I answered it quickly.

"Hey, girl," I said. "How are you doing?"

"I'm okay," she said. "I just thought you'd like to know that Angie woke up. I'm up here at the hospital now, and I was just stopping in to see how she was doing when I saw the nurses were getting all excited. She just woke up about twenty minutes ago, but..."

"But?" I asked.

"Cassie, she doesn't remember anything. I mean, she doesn't even know who she is."

"Oh, my God," I said. "What did the doctor say?"

"All I've heard is that amnesia is not uncommon after major trauma like she had. They say her memory might come back on its own, or it may not. I've actually read a lot about amnesia, and usually the patient will get back at least some memories, even if they don't get them all."

"So, she doesn't know who you are?"

"No. Like I said, she doesn't even know who she is. We told her, but nothing seems to be registering."

"Well, I'd like to come and see her, but I'm afraid I might be a shock. If she doesn't remember me, then we might be back to her being afraid of the way I look."

"Well, actually," Nicole said slowly, "I was thinking that, out of everyone she knows, you might be the one person whose appearance could trigger a memory. I mean, I know it's possible she won't remember you, and she might even freak out a bit, but I think it might be worth a try. If you're willing."

I thought about it for a moment. As a psychologist myself, I also knew a bit about amnesia, and her idea could possibly have some merit.

"Yeah, it's worth a try. I'll be there in a bit, I just need to finish up a couple things at my office."

"Okay, great. I'll see you when you get here."

Of course, what I really needed to finish up in my office was to lock up and go let Dex know that I was headed for the hospital. I had planned on calling more of my clients and trying to get appointments set for that week, but that could wait until the afternoon. Right now, Angie might need me more than any of my clients.

I locked up the building and walked around the block, and found Dex talking to the Snap-On man. There was a really big step van sitting beside the building, but the two of them were in the office, going through a catalog.

"Hey," I said as I stuck my head in the door. "I don't want to interrupt, but I wanted to let you know that Angie woke up. Nicole called, so I'm going up to the hospital to see her."

Dex nodded. "Okay, babe," he said. "Real quick, this is Tom Hardy, our Snap-On dealer. I'm going another fifty or sixty grand in debt."

Tom turned around with a smile, and I have to give him credit. It barely even faltered when he saw me, and then he was up and holding his hand out. I shook hands with him, then looked at Dex and said, "Okay. Have fun."

Tom chuckled, and I turned around and walked out the door. I had to go right back in, though, because the truck was blocking the exit through the fence. Tom came out and moved it, and I got my car and took off for the hospital.

When I got there, I went straight to Angie's room. I was surprised to see that the police guards were gone, but I knew they couldn't keep them there forever. Danny seemed to be focusing his efforts elsewhere, nowadays, so I guess they decided Angie was safe.

Nicole was waiting in the hallway for me, and smiled when she saw me coming from the elevator. We stopped just out of sight from Angie's open door, and Nicole brought me up to date.

"She's a little bit combative," she said. "I think it's because she doesn't understand how she ended up in the hospital, and she's obviously terrified that she can't remember anything about her life. I can imagine how scary that would be, so I can't say that I blame her. Anyway, I just thought I'd give you a heads up before you go in. I really don't have a clue how she's going to react, but if she's gonna recognize anybody, I think it might be you."

I took a deep breath. "Okay, then," I said. "Wish me luck, here goes."

I stepped into the room and looked at Angie. She was laying back on the bed, the head end tilted up somewhat, and her face was turned slightly away as she watched television. There was some sort of talk show on, but I'd never been a big fan of them and didn't recognize this one. I walked to within a couple of feet of the bed before she noticed me and turned to look my way.

"Holy God," she said. "Who are you?"

"Hi, Angie," I said. "My name is Cassie, Cassie McGraw. You and I used to work together. Nicole called and told me you were awake, and I just wanted to come down and see how you're doing."

She was staring at my face, and while she didn't look as terrified as when she first met me almost nine months earlier, there was definitely an aura of revulsion.

"I don't remember you," Angie said. "I don't remember anything."

"Yeah, that's what I heard. I came to work at the Outreach about nine months ago, and I'm afraid the way I look seemed to have scared you pretty badly, back then. It took a while, but you finally got used to it. Ever since then, we were pretty good friends. You've even been to my house for dinner a couple of times."

She stared at me for several seconds, and then she cocked her head to one side. "Do you have a cat?"

I smiled. "Yes. Her name is Critter, and she loved you to pieces. Each time you came over, she'd climb up in your lap, lay down, and purr. I remember you stroking her and smiling a lot."

"I remember a cat," Angie said, "but they tell me I don't have any pets. You wouldn't have a picture of her, would you?"

I took out my phone and scrolled through my pictures. I had a couple pictures of Critter, but then I found the perfect one. It was actually a picture of Critter curled up in Angie's lap. I opened it up and handed her the phone.

"Wow," she said. "Yeah, that's the cat I remember." She looked at the picture for a long moment, then handed the phone back. "I wish I could remember more than just that."

"Well, as it happens, I happen to have a degree in psychology. The fact that you've remembered something is a very good sign. It means that your memories are intact, you're just having trouble reaching them."

"So, you think they'll come back, then?"

"I think some of them will," I said. "I can't make any promises, but you should at least start to remember things about your life before long, I think."

She was staring at me again, but the revulsion wasn't there anymore. It was more like she was trying to analyze or quantify what she was seeing, the damage to my face.

"You wear an eye patch. Did you lose your eye?"

I nodded. "Yeah, I was in a bad fire, and that's what happened to me. I lost my eyeball and my left ear, and ended up looking like this."

"Oh wow," she said suddenly. "You have a lot of eye patches, right? You put, like, rhinestones on them, that kind of stuff?"

I smiled brightly. "Yes! Yes, I like to decorate them. I put a heart made of rhinestones on one, and you told me that it actually looked nice."

She nodded her head. "Yeah, that's what I'm remembering. It was a heart, with lots of rhinestones. Red ones and white ones and blue ones, right?"

"Exactly. See? I think you'll remember things."

She reached down and picked up the call button, and pressed it for the nurse. When the nurse came in, she glanced at me for a second, then looked at Angie.

"Hey, honey, everything okay?"

"Yeah," Angie said. "This is Cassie, and I kind of remember her. Well, I remember her eyepatch, and she's the one who has the cat that I remembered."

The nurse looked at me, her eyes wide. "Really? That's very good." She turned back to Angie. "Let me go and get the doctor, he's going to want to hear about this." She turned and hurried out the door, and Angie looked back at me.

"They said I worked at some kind of counseling center," she said. "You worked there, too?"

"I did, yes. I was a counselor there, for women in abusive relationships."

"Then I guess you're out of a job, too, right? They said the place got blown up, and the guy who did it is the one who hurt me."

"Yes," I said. "I decided to open my own office, because I have a lot of clients who need me. When you get out of here, if you're still looking for a job, I could always use a receptionist. That's what you did at the Outreach."

"Yeah, they told me that. It's just that I—I don't think I remember how to do it."

"I think it would come back to you," I said. "And it isn't really a hard job, anyway. I could show you everything you need to know."

She smiled at me, then, for the first time since I'd come in. "That's really nice," she said. "I still don't really remember you, but there's something about you that just makes me feel comfortable. You think maybe that's just kind of a memory of the fact we were friends?"

"I'm sure that's what it is. I'm just glad to hear you say it, because back when we first met, you were absolutely terrified of me."

She giggled. "Oh, come on, you're not that scary looking. And I can tell you're really a nice person. Maybe, if you're serious, we can talk about that job when I get out."

I dug in my purse and found one of my business cards, the old one from the outreach, and handed it to her. "I don't have my new business cards yet, but that's my cell number on the back of this one. You call me anytime, and I mean that. This doesn't have to be just about a job, you can call me for any reason at all."

The doctor came in just then and asked Angie a series of questions. He was definitely encouraged that she was able to remember Critter; he confessed he hadn't been sure there really was a cat that she remembered, or that it might've been a cat she had when she was a child. Knowing that it was a more recent memory made him feel better.

He was even more encouraged when she told him about my eye patches. The one I was wearing that day was plain, just a simple black patch with an elastic band. Most of my patches are made of leather, but they have a tendency to start to smell after a while. All of my nice ones were currently sitting in a plastic tub full of baking soda, which would leave them smelling clean and fresh again.

The one she remembered, though, was the one I had made only a few weeks earlier, for Valentine's Day. The fact that she could describe it perfectly, even down to the colors, convinced the doctor that her memory loss was not permanent, after all.

Nicole came back in after the doctor left, and we stayed and visited with Angie for an hour or so. She was still in some pain from the surgery she'd undergone, but she insisted it really wasn't very bad. I could tell she was getting tired, though, so we finally left her to rest and went up to visit Marsha.

The police guards were gone from her room, as well. We walked in to find her sitting up and watching television, and she broke into a smile when she saw us.

"My two favorite girls," she said. "How is Angie?"

Nicole looked over at me with a smile. "I came up earlier and told her that Angie woke up. I figured it might brighten her day."

"And it did," Marsha said. "I was getting pretty worried about her."

Marsha had gotten so accustomed to talking with her teeth clamped shut that she was actually very easy to understand, now. I had actually tried talking with my own teeth clamped together, just to see what it was like, and I hope and pray I never have to do it for real. I sounded like a robot, and it wasn't nice.

"I think we all were," I said. "She's doing pretty good. Apparently she has some amnesia, but she remembers my cat, Critter, and she remembers some of my rhinestone eye patches. The doctor thinks it's pretty likely that she'll get her memory back."

"Oh, I'm so glad. That poor kid. I don't know what she'll do for a job, now."

"I offered her one," I said. "I'm planning to hire a receptionist, anyway. The doctor said she'll be able to go home in a few days, so I offered her the job."

Marsha just looked at me for a moment. "You're going to go broke, if you keep hiring all of us. You need to go ahead and file for tax-exempt status. Even though the bishop doesn't want to keep the Outreach going, I'm sure I could get him to donate some money to help cover your costs."

"We'll see," I said. "Somebody once told me that charities are really just a way to hide money. I don't ever want anyone thinking that about me. I'd rather spend the money out of my own pocket. Besides, I'm not planning to get any bigger. I can afford to support a small office, with just the four of us."

"And I'm not going to cost her anything, anyway," Nicole said. "I go back to work on my regular job next week, so I'm just going to donate my time, like I did at St. Mary's."

"See?" I said. "It's not gonna cost me that much to keep us all together."

My phone suddenly buzzed, and I looked at it. It showed me an image from inside my car, as someone stuck a piece of paper under my windshield wiper. The lettering on it was facing inward, and I could read it easily, because it was written in thick red letters.

Ready for the next round?

TWENTY-SEVEN

I CALLED PENNINGTON as I hurried out to the parking garage, and there were two squad cars at my car by the time I got to it. There was no sign of Danny anywhere, but there was no doubt in my mind that it was he who put the paper on my windshield.

I had to wait for the crime scene guys to get there, and they took the paper off with a pair of tweezers. It was dropped into a plastic bag that was sealed, and taken away to be checked for fingerprints. I couldn't really see the sense, since we knew exactly who had done it, but Pennington explained that it was necessary to have a recorded chain of custody for every piece of evidence. If Danny's fingerprints were on it, it would be the first piece of physical evidence that connected him to the crimes.

"He's about to do something," I said to Pennington. "We need to get ready for whatever it is."

"Well, I hope it's not like the last one. I kept waiting for you to blow yourself to hell and back, that time."

"Yeah, well, believe me when I say that's not on my list of things to do today. That poor girl was terrified, though, and I couldn't just walk away and leave her in that situation."

He scowled at me. "I think you just have a hero complex," he said. "You want to save everybody."

"Says the guy wearing the badge," I said. "Are you gonna tell me you don't feel the same way?"

"Of course I do," he replied. "But at least I get paid for it. All you would've gotten is a nice obituary."

I shook my head. "Jim, you're such a pessimist."

"Wrong. I'm a realist. Alicia keeps telling me you're the luckiest person she's ever known, but luck don't hold out forever. One of these days, you're going to find yourself in a really bad situation. Don't count on lucky saving you then."

He turned and walked away, and I got into my car to head back to my office. It was lunchtime, so I picked up some tacos to take with me, then parked at the shop again and went in to tell Dex about Angie, and then of course, I told him about the note on the windshield. We ate lunch while we talked.

He grunted. "At least he's warned us," he said. "I've been thinking about what we talked about yesterday, in the car. Everything he does is connected to your work, so I've been trying to guess at what he might do next."

"Any luck?" I asked.

He shook his head. "The only thing I can think of is that he's gotten into your client files, so all of your clients are potential targets. I just can't see any way we can watch all of them, all the time."

I frowned, because he was right. Any one of my clients could be Danny's next target, but there was no way I could imagine to guess which one. Besides, I hadn't placed anybody in New Beginnings in a couple of months, so he wasn't after anyone I knew. Maybe my clients were actually safe, for the most part.

While I couldn't watch my clients, though, there was something else I could do. I kissed Dex and went back to my office, then sat down and started calling all of them again. This time, I told them all about Danny and the fact that he was trying to hurt me with his attacks. I told them all to be extremely careful, and not to trust anyone they didn't know. He had gotten Wanda, Connie, and Candace by using a ruse, and I told them all about it.

I half expected most of them to tell me they were finished with me, but only a couple of them even said they wanted to take a break from our meetings. By the time I got finished with all of them, I had ten appointments scheduled, scattered over the next four days.

It was almost three o'clock by then, and I was sitting there trying to think of something else to do when my phone rang once again. I didn't know the number, so I answered it cautiously.

"Cassie McGraw," I said.

"Okay, so are you starting to figure out any of the clues I'm giving you?" Danny asked.

I sighed. "Danny, nothing you do is making any sense at all. Why don't we just meet up somewhere? I'm all alone right now, you tell me where you want to meet, and I'll come."

"That's not how the game is going to be played," he said. "You just don't know how to listen, do you? I'm trying to tell you what you need to know in order to stop me, but you have to be smart enough to understand it. I studied you, Cassie, so I know you've got the brains. All you need to do is turn them on and use them. Now, are you ready for the next round?"

I leaned back in my chair, exasperated. "Go ahead," I said.

"Okay, this one might point you in the right direction. If you can figure it out in time, you'll not only save lives, you'll probably start to get an idea of how to find me. Listen closely. You need to be able to hear your own voice, better than anyone else can, while no one else can hear it at all. Now, if you figure out what that means, then you'll know what you have to do to disarm the next bomb."

"Do what? Danny, do you have any idea how crazy that sounds?"

He didn't answer, and I realized he had hung up. I sat there, staring at my phone, and trying to figure out what in the world he had just said.

I played it back in my mind. He said I needed to hear my own voice better than anyone else could, but it had to be while no one else could hear it at all. It made no sense, none. No matter how I tried to understand it, it just didn't add up.

I got up from my desk and left the office, locking the door behind me and walking around the block to the shop. When I got inside, Dex was already well into taking apart the antique Cadillac convertible we had bought. He had the seats out of it and was taking off the panels on the inside of the doors.

Something in my face must've told him that I got another call. He put down his tools and looked at me, then got to his feet and walked over to stand in front of me.

"What's he up to now?"

"I really wish I knew," I said. "He called me a few minutes ago, and said that if I can figure this thing out, I can disarm his next bomb and save lives, but what he said doesn't make any sense."

He walked me over to the office and set me down in one of the chairs, then took the one beside me.

"Tell me what he said, word for word," he said. "As close as you can remember."

I blew air out of my mouth in frustration. "He said I need to be able to hear my own voice better than anyone else can, while nobody else can hear me at all. Does that make any sense to you?"

Dex looked into my eye for a second, and then he started to smile. "Maybe," he said. "Cassie, have you ever been to the Center of the Universe?"

I stared at him. "What? Now you're sounding as crazy as he does. And just what the hell is that supposed to mean?"

"Did you get any kind of time limit on this? Are you supposed to solve it by a certain deadline?"

I shook my head. "He didn't give me a particular time. He just said if I figure it out 'in time,' then I'd know how to disarm the next bomb and save lives."

Dex got to his feet and held out a hand. I took it and he lifted me up out of my chair.

"Let's go," he said. "There might not be any time to waste."

We left the shop and he locked it up, then we got into my car with Dex driving.

"The Center of the Universe is this really weird landmark here in Tulsa," he said. "It's a small circle of concrete surrounded by a circle of bricks, and it's got some really strange acoustical properties. If you stand exactly in the center and say something, you can suddenly hear your own voice a lot louder than normal. If you make any other kind of sound, it's also a lot louder than it would normally be. Some people think it's an echo from this round planter that surrounds the area, but there's no delay like you get with an echo. Nobody really has any idea how it works, but one of the other interesting features about it is that anybody standing outside the circle of bricks can't hear what you say at all."

I think my eyeball was trying to pop out of its socket. "You're kidding, right? There really is such a place?"

"Yep. It's down by the Jazz Hall of Fame, which was the old Union Train Depot, near the corner of West Archer Street and North Boston Avenue. It's the only thing in the world I can think of that would make it possible for you to hear your voice better than anyone else while nobody else can hear it at all."

It took a few minutes to make it through traffic, but we finally got to the area he was talking about. We had to get out of the car and walk across a footbridge over the tracks, and there was the insane place he was telling me about.

"Go ahead," Dex said. "Go right to the center of it and say something."

I looked at him like he was a crazy man, but I walked across the circle of bricks to the little concrete circle in the middle. I stood right on top of it and looked back at Dex, who was standing outside the circle of bricks, and tried to think of something to say.

According to Dex, whatever I said would be amplified as far as I was concerned, but he wouldn't be able to hear anything. I could only think of one thing I could say that would absolutely tell me if that was true or not, because there was no way he could fail to react if he heard me. I looked directly at him, and then I said, "I love you."

I heard it perfectly, and with some indefinable quality I couldn't explain. And he was right, it was definitely louder. I could certainly hear my voice better than anyone else as long as I stood in that spot.

And Dex's face didn't change at all. Had he heard me say that, there was no doubt in my mind that I would've seen some kind of reaction, but there was nothing. I was almost certain I was standing exactly where I was supposed to be, but I had no idea how this was supposed to tell me anything about how to disarm a bomb.

I looked around where I was standing, down on the ground. There was nothing on the circle of bricks that I could see that could possibly have anything to do with the situation, so I looked around the area even further. I slowly turned in a circle while standing in that same spot, and suddenly I spotted something really weird.

It was some kind of sculpture or something, a tall, strange-looking tower with a weird shape on top. As I looked at it, I noticed something fluttering on it, about eight feet off the ground. I walked out of the circle toward it, and Dex came to join me.

"Well?" he asked. "What did you think?"

"I think it's really weird," I said. "But you're right, I could hear myself amplified. You really couldn't hear what I said?"

"Nope. I tried to read your lips, but I was never all that good at it. It sort of looked like you said something about an idiot, but I hope you weren't talking to me."

I couldn't help it, I grinned. "No, I didn't say that. I just made some noises, that's all. What is this thing?" I pointed at the sculpture.

He looked up at it and shrugged. "That's called the Artificial Cloud Statute. I don't know if anybody really knows what it's supposed to mean, but it's got all these weird symbols all over it. On one side it's got what looks like airplanes diving toward the ground and crashing, and on the other side is a bunch of people who seem to have their arms or legs cut off."

We got up to it, and I looked up at the thing I had seen fluttering. There was a piece of paper stuck to it, and I pointed it out to Dex. "Can you get that?"

It was just a little out of his reach, but he managed to grab onto the sculpture and jump enough to snag it. He brought it down, looked at it, and then handed it to me. It was a sheet of notebook paper, like you find in some kids' school notebooks, and there was a single word written on it: DESIDERATA. It had been stuck to the sculpture with a wad of chewing gum.

It was written in the same thick, red ink as the note that had been on my windshield.

"Desiderata," I said. "Any idea what that's supposed to mean?"

"I know it was something some guy wrote, a long time ago. My mom used to have a recording of it, and she listened to it every once in a while. I can't remember all of it, but it seemed to me that it always boiled down to the fact that the world turns the way it wants to, and you really can't do much about it."

I googled it.

Go placidly amid the noise and the haste, and remember what peace there may be in silence. As far as possible, without surrender, be on good terms with all persons.

Speak your truth quietly and clearly; and listen to others, even to the dull and the ignorant; they too have their story.

Avoid loud and aggressive persons; they are vexatious to the spirit. If you compare yourself with others, you may become vain or bitter, for always there will be greater and lesser persons than yourself.

Enjoy your achievements as well as your plans. Keep interested in your own career, however humble; it is a real possession in the changing fortunes of time.

Exercise caution in your business affairs, for the world is full of trickery. But let this not blind you to what virtue there is; many persons strive for high ideals, and everywhere life is full of heroism.

Be yourself. Especially, do not feign affection. Neither be cynical about love; for in the face of all aridity and disenchantment it is as perennial as the grass.

Take kindly the counsel of the years, gracefully surrendering the things of youth.

Nurture strength of spirit to shield you in sudden misfortune. But do not distress yourself with dark imaginings. Many fears are born of fatigue and loneliness.

Beyond a wholesome discipline, be gentle with yourself. You are a child of the universe no less than the trees and the stars; you have a right to be here.

And whether or not it is clear to you, no doubt the universe is unfolding as it should. Therefore be at peace with God, what-

ever you conceive Him to be. And whatever your labors and aspirations, in the noisy confusion of life, keep peace in your soul. With all its sham, drudgery and broken dreams, it is still a beautiful world. Be cheerful. Strive to be happy.

I guess it could be considered some good advice, but Dex was right. More than anything else, it basically just said that life is going to happen however it happens. Other than watching what other people are up to, there just isn't much you can do about it.

"Okay," I said. "Somehow, this is supposed to tell me how to disarm a bomb. Now, if only I knew where that bomb might be, I might have a chance. I'm calling Pennington."

I took out my phone and hit the button, and Pennington answered on the first ring. It took me a moment to explain to him what was going on, but he didn't have any idea what I should do next, either.

"I don't know anything new," he said. "If he's planted another bomb somewhere, it hasn't turned up yet. I guess the only thing you can do right now is wait. But, Cassie, if he calls you to tell you where the bomb is, I want to know about it. Understand me?"

"Yes, sir," I said sarcastically. "I'll call you immediately, I promise."

I put my phone back in my pocket and looked up at Dex. "Nothing to do but wait," I said.

TWENTY-EIGHT

AS IT TURNED OUT, WE didn't have to wait long. We hadn't even made it back to the shop building when my phone rang again, and I looked to see that it was Pennington calling.

"Okay, you're on," he said. "A woman just walked into the lobby of the Mayo Hotel with a bomb strapped to her, just like the other day. She told the front desk that neither she nor anyone else can leave the building or the bomb will be detonated, and that they were to call the police and say that only you could disarm the bomb."

"Okay," I said. "We're on the way."

I looked at Dex. "Mayo Hotel," I said. "We've got another bomb like the one Toni Denham was wearing the other day."

"You think 'desiderata' is the password, this time?"

"I don't know," I said. "This is supposed to be some kind of clue, though."

We arrived at the hotel a few minutes later. I saw Pennington standing just outside, and the bomb squad truck was parked in the street out front. Dex and I walked up to Pennington, and he gave me a wry grin.

"Her name is Beverly Walker," he said, and I gasped. "I take it you know her?"

I nodded. "She was just in my office a few days ago," I said. "She was the very first client in my new office."

"Well, according to her, Danny says if the bomb squad gets near her, if we try to evacuate the building, or if she tries to leave, he'll set it off. He's got to be watching from somewhere around here, but if we start searching, that's liable to be another trigger." He put a hand on my shoulder. "You don't absolutely have to do this, you know."

I made a face at him. "Yeah, right," I said. "The other day, after I got done, the bomb squad just pulled the wires out and said it was harmless. Can I do that?"

He shook his head. "No, I'm afraid not. If you try to disconnect anything before it's disarmed, they say it will trigger what's called an interrupt circuit and make the bomb go off."

"Oh, ducky," I said sarcastically. "So be it. Let me see what I can do."

I walked into the building and saw Beverly sitting on a couch in the lobby. There were a couple of cops inside, but they were staying away from her. I wondered if that was because they were scared, or because they were afraid Danny was watching and didn't want him to get the wrong idea.

I went straight to Beverly and knelt down in front of her.

"Fancy meeting you here," I said. I saw that she had a headset on, just like Toni had worn. "Is he on the line?"

"Yes," she said nervously. "He says you should be able to get me out of this thing."

"That's the idea," I said. "Can I talk to him?"

She reached up and took off the headset, and passed it to me. Like the other one, it was attached to a cell phone on the front of the bomb. I put it on my ear.

"Hey, Danny," I said conversationally. "So, I think giving me the password would be just a little too easy, so I'm guessing that it's not desiderata. Am I right?"

"Well, you can type it in and see," he said. "You might want to bear in mind that you only get three tries. If you haven't got it right by the third try, the bomb goes off."

"Yeah, I kinda figured it'd be something like that. I'm pretty sure you didn't hand it to me as a freebie, though, so I'm going to save my guesses for a minute. How much time have I got?"

"I haven't started the countdown yet," he said. "How about we start it—now. Fifteen minutes."

The cell phone was just like the one before, one of those cheap, non-smart phone types with the slide-out keyboard. The headset I was wearing had a wire that was running right into it, rather than one that plugged in. That told me that Danny was capable of messing with the electronics, so there was no telling what kind of gizmos and gadgets were actually involved in this thing. I looked at the wires, but didn't dare try to touch them. No matter how I figured it, the only hope I had was getting the password right.

I was quite certain it wouldn't be the same password he had used before, but I really didn't believe that it was going to be 'desiderata,' either. On the other hand, he said I had three tries. If time started getting short, I would probably type it in just to see.

I took out my phone and looked at the poem again. If the title was a clue, then the password might be in the poem, itself. I scanned through it looking for particular words that jumped out at me.

Nothing. There were a few odd words in it, but nothing that struck me as what I would choose for a password, not even for my email. I read through it again, just to be sure, but it still didn't shake any ideas loose.

Twelve minutes, twenty seconds. I needed to try something, but I didn't actually trust Danny on whether there were three chances or not. I closed my eye and tried to put myself into his mind for a moment, see if maybe trying to think like him would give me any insights.

For some reason, he had chosen this poem. I didn't think he was trying to gain any wisdom from it, and I didn't believe that he was even capable of following its advice about peace and wisdom. Danny Kendall was a man full of hate, and this poem spoke of love and compassion and goodness. Still, there had to be something about it that he connected to his feelings about me.

When I thought about it that way, it dawned on me that there might be words in it that he would use to describe those feelings. I opened my eye and read through it one more time.

What words in the poem might Danny ascribe to me? He didn't want to be on good terms with me, I was sure of that. And while he might consider me dull and ignorant, I didn't think that was anything important to him. He would undoubtedly consider me aggressive, though.

Nine minutes, twenty-six seconds. There was one word in the poem that I suddenly realized would probably describe me perfectly to Danny. I slowly reached out and punched it into the keyboard.

That word was *vexatious*. I hesitated before I typed the final S, but then I did it and pressed the enter key.

The countdown display went blank, and I suddenly realized I had been holding my breath.

"Damn, Cassie," Danny said in my ear. "You're two for two. It's all clear, you can unbuckle her now. I think you ought to go out and celebrate tonight. Maybe if you let your hair down a bit, you might start to figure out the puzzle."

The phone line went dead, and I reached for the straps and began unbuckling them.

"It's all done, Beverly," I said. "It's disarmed, and I'll have you out of it in just a minute."

She started crying. I lifted the vest off her and set it down gently on the couch, then got to my feet and took her hand. We walked out together, with my arm around her as she wept on my shoulder. The bomb squad guys passed us on the way.

A couple of police officers took Beverly to where an ambulance and paramedics were waiting, and they started checking her over. Dex and Pennington grabbed hold of my arms and yanked me out of the way as people came flooding out of the hotel. I guess the word spread that the bomb was disarmed, and people were checking out as fast as they could.

"You did it again," Dex said. He wrapped his arms around me and held me close for a moment, then kissed me quickly before letting me go.

"I got lucky again," I said, "but we both know that's not gonna last much longer." I turned to Pennington. "We've got to stop this guy. It just hit me, has anybody been tracing the cell phones? He was talking to me through that phone that was hooked up to the bomb; isn't there a way to trace the call? Find out where he was?"

"We had people working on it," Pennington said, "but the call was through a VoIP server. He bounced it through a lot of proxy servers, so there was no way to get a trace. He could literally have been sitting inside the hotel or in one of the buildings around us, but the call seemed to be coming from Latvia."

I grimaced. "Okay, it was just a thought. Any other bright ideas?"

"Not any that would make sense. Our tip line is going crazy with calls, people hoping to collect the reward, but nothing has panned out." An officer ran up and handed him a sheet of paper, and he looked it over. "We did have someone monitoring the call, while you were talking to Danny. This is the transcript they just printed out. Any idea what he means about figuring out the puzzle?"

"I told you," I said. "Every time he talks to me, he says I have to figure out some clues he's leaving about where to find him. I don't have the slightest idea what clues they might be, though. Dex and I have both gone over and over it, and I can't see any kind of pattern going on, other than the fact that he's targeting my clients and people like them."

The detective just looked at me for a moment. "Yeah, I don't see any particular pattern, either. I'll have CSI look over each incident, see if they can spot anything. If they come up with any ideas, I'll let you know."

I nodded. "You done with us for now?" I asked. "It's almost 5 o'clock, and I need to eat something soon. The one thing Danny said that made any sense is that I should go out and celebrate tonight, and I think that's exactly what I'm going to do."

Pennington nodded. "We're done for now," he said. "Let me know if you get any other contacts from Danny Kendall."

I turned to Dex. "I need food, and then I need to go get plastered. You game?"

He broke into a big smile. "I'll be your designated driver," he said. "Come on, babe." He took my hand and we started walking toward my car.

We went to a little place we had discovered a month or so back, a tavern called Gray's Roadhouse. It was hidden in the back of a small shopping center, and had a fantastic kitchen that offered everything from hot wings to T-bones. It had a small dance floor, and seemed to be the place where local bands could get started.

The place wasn't very big. There was a dozen tables, a long bar that could seat about twenty, and ledges on two walls where patrons could set their drinks while they stand. There were times when it was so packed that there was a line outside, waiting for tables or barstools to clear, but that was usually after seven. When we got there at five thirty, the place wasn't even half-full.

We grabbed a table near where the band was setting up. Dex struck up a quick conversation with the bandleader, and found out they were a country group known as Scarecrow. We'd never heard of them, which always makes me wonder if they're going to be any good, but a couple of people at neighboring tables told us we were likely to enjoy them.

I, of course, am always easily recognized. The barmaid, whose name was Reagan, came out of the kitchen and broke into a big smile when she saw us. She was the reason we had found the place; Reagan was one of my clients from the Outreach, and I had helped her get herself and her kids away from her drug addict husband.

"Cassie, I'm glad to see you," she said. "I heard what happened, and I was scared to death until I heard you were okay."

"I'm fine, Reagan," I said. "How are you doing?"

"Pretty good," she said. "I don't know if you heard, but my ex got busted for dealing meth a couple weeks ago. I guess he tried to run from the cops and hit one of them with his car. He's going away for a long, long time."

I jumped up and gave her a hug. Her ex, Bart, had been stalking her at one point, and had threatened violence against her and her children. A long jail sentence for him would give her a chance to really start over.

We ordered wings, because Dex and I both love them. I can't handle the really hot buffalo wings, but they serve a Thai sauce that's absolutely wonderful. I could put away a dozen by myself, and sometimes ordered more. Dex always went for two dozen, and occasionally he'd get the second dozen in Thai sauce, so I could steal one or two if I was still hungry.

I had learned the hard way not to drink at all until I had food in my stomach, so I settled for a Doctor Pepper while I was eating. Dex ordered a beer, but I knew him well enough to know he'd sip on that one for quite a while. When he decided to be designated driver, he never allowed himself more than two beers for the whole night.

The band was all set up, and they were scheduled to start at six thirty, but they decided to do what they called an "on-site rehearsal." What that meant was that they were going to play through a couple of songs before their actual start time, just to be sure everything was tuned up and ready.

Dex and I were just finishing up our dinner, so I went ahead and ordered my first beer as the band members were taking their positions. There were three men and two women up there, and I was sort of surprised to see that the girls were playing electric guitar and bass. The drummer was a big guy, there was a skinny fellow who looked like he couldn't possibly be more than fifteen on keyboards, and the singer reminded me of Jack Black. He played rhythm guitar, and he and both of the girls had microphone stands in front of them. There was another microphone hanging over the drummer, and one more mounted to the keyboard.

"Looks like all of them sing," Dex said. "You don't see that very often anymore."

"I just hope they're good," I said. "I feel like dancing tonight."

The lead strummed a chord on his guitar, and then the rest of them started playing. It didn't take five seconds for us to realize that they definitely knew how to play, and then the singer stepped up to his microphone.

"This old day's been dragging on, I've been working since the crack of dawn,

Thank God that clock is moving on and soon I'll be with you,

I punch my card and run out the door, can't stand to be without you anymore,

Feeling you move when we're on the floor, oh, babe, those things you do,

"When you dance with me baby, you know you drive me crazy,

Everything gets perfect when you start to shake that thing,

Ain't nothing else that matters, the world could be in tatters,

Life can't get no better than it does—when you dance!"

It took me a moment to pick my jaw up off the table, and then I noticed that Dex was staring at the band just as hard as I was. He turned and looked at me, his eyes wide and his smile wider.

"They're good," he said, the surprise evident in his voice. He was absolutely right, too, because the music we were hearing was every bit as good as anything coming out of the radio lately.

The couple at the next table leaned over toward us, and the lady patted my shoulder. "We told you," she said. "These guys are going somewhere."

"I'll say," I said. "Do they write their own music?"

She grinned. "Actually, they write the music, but I write the lyrics." She held out a hand. "I'm Donna Fenton. The girl on electric guitar is my daughter, Shannon, and that's her brother Shane singing lead."

"They really are incredible," I said. "I'm Cassie McGraw, by the way."

Donna nodded. "I recognize you from your picture in the paper. I understand you're having some rough times lately."

I grimaced. "It seems to come with the territory. This maniac is blaming me for something that happened a long time ago, and we're trying to put a stop to him."

"You will," Donna said. "You've got that grit, and it shows. I hope you enjoy the band, and please tell your friends about them."

I promised I would, and Dex and I went back to listening to the music. When they started the second song, he reached over and grabbed my hand and I followed him out onto the dance floor.

"We should've danced to the first song," he said in my ear. "It fit, because I do love to watch you dance."

I laughed. "Everybody does," I said. "It's not often you get to see a monster shake her booty."

And shake it I did! The music was fast and hot, and I desperately needed to feel alive, especially after coming so close to death so many times lately. Dex held onto me and met me move for move, and I'm sure some people might have been shocked at some of the things we did on the dance floor.

I didn't care. I was celebrating the fact that I was alive, and that Beverly Walker was alive. I didn't want to think about riddles or clues or games; I didn't want to think about Danny Kendall, or just how insane he really had to be. I just wanted to be alive and with Dex.

TWENTY-NINE

MY PHONE WAS RINGING, and I flailed out with my hand to find it on the nightstand. I managed to get my eye open and looked at it, and it was another number I didn't recognize. I groaned as I put it to my ear.

"Cassie McGraw," I said sleepily. "What is it now?"

"Ms. McGraw?" It was a voice I didn't recognize, a woman's voice. "I'm sorry to be calling so early, but I think I may have some information that you need."

I shook my head to clear it, and tried to focus on what she was saying. "Who is this?" I asked.

"Look, I don't want to give my name. I got your number from somebody you know, and I promise I wouldn't bother you if I didn't think it was really important."

I pushed myself up to a sitting position, and Dex rolled over on his side to look up at me.

"Okay," I said. "What is it?"

"I think I may know where the bomber is staying. I'm not really sure about this, but somebody has been staying in a house down the road from me, and it's a house that I know is supposed to be empty. Whoever it is drives a van and doesn't use the regular driveway. They've been cutting across a field beside the house and parking the van inside a barn."

"Have you seen the driver?" I asked.

"Yeah, a couple of times. I haven't gotten up close, or got a real good look, but he's tall and fairly young. I saw the picture on the news of the guy you're looking for, and it could be him. I just don't know for sure, and I didn't want to call the police."

"That's fine, I'll take care of them," I said. I grabbed a pen and notepad out of my nightstand drawer. "Where is the house? How do I get to it?"

"It's outside of Sapulpa," she said. "If you take Route 66 out past Kellyville, you'll come to Slick Road. Turn south on Slick Road and follow that for about two miles till you come to 181st Street, then go a quarter-mile past that. There's an unmarked county road on the right, and if you follow that to the end you'll find the house. It's a big yellow house with two barns. He parks the van in the one closest to the house."

"Okay, I've got it. Listen, you know there is a reward out, right? If we get this guy, you call me back and I'll make sure you get to collect it."

"I don't want any reward," the woman said. "I—I stayed in the New Beginnings shelter once. If this is him, I hope you can put him away forever." She hung up, and the line was dead.

I looked at my phone and saw that it was just after seven. Dex and I had stayed out dancing until almost one, and I vaguely remember him dragging me out of the Roadhouse. We both should have been up already, but I guess neither of us thought to set an alarm.

"What was that?" Dex asked, and I explained quickly. "Then you better call Detective Pennington."

I looked at him for a moment and licked my lips. "Yeah," I said. I called up Pennington's cell number in my contacts and hit the button.

"Cassie? Another call?"

"A different one," I said. I told him about the woman who called, and gave him the directions I had written down. "I want to go along. If he's there, I want to be there when you arrest him."

"That's out in Creek County," Pennington said. "I'll have to coordinate this with the sheriff's office out there, and that'll take a little time."

"How much time? We need to nail this guy."

"I agree, but there are still channels I have to go through when we cross jurisdictional lines. It shouldn't take long, give me an hour at most."

I huffed. "Fine, call me." I hung up and got out of bed.

"Cassie?" Dex said. "Where you going?"

"I'm going out to that house," I said. "As a private investigator, I can work anywhere in the state of Oklahoma. I don't have to," I used finger quotes, "wait till I 'coordinate' with anybody." I picked up the pants I'd been wearing the day before and sniffed them, then tossed them at the laundry basket we kept in our room and went to my dresser. I pulled out clean clothes and tossed them on the bed, then started getting dressed.

Dex was on his feet and putting on a pair of jeans. "Then I'm going with you," he said.

I didn't say anything, which he obviously took as my acceptance. A part of me wanted to be strong and independent, and tell him to stay home, but another part admitted that

I would feel better with him along. We were both dressed within ten minutes, and went out the door without even thinking about Critter.

From my house, it took only twenty-five minutes to get to Kellyville, and we found Slick Road just a short distance beyond it. I turned left and watched my odometer, but Dex spotted the sign for 181st Street before we'd gone the full two miles. A minute later, we turned onto the unmarked county road.

It was gravel, and it was rough. My new Mustang sat low enough to drag in a few spots, but I didn't care. I drove slowly and kept to the high spots when I could, and we had gone about a mile by the time the house came into view.

I stopped the car, and then backed up a bit. I had seen an entrance into a wooded area, and I pulled the car in far enough that it would be out of sight from the house.

We got out of the car and started walking back toward the road, but Dex spotted a path in the woods. "Maybe we should try this," he said. It seemed to parallel the road, so I agreed.

We were still about a half mile from the house, and it sat in the middle of a large clearing. We wouldn't be able to get all the way up to it and stay in the cover of the trees, but I wanted to avoid being seen as long as possible. When we came to the edge of the woods nearest to the house, we stopped and squatted down.

"I wish I grabbed the binoculars," Dex said. I looked at him for a moment, then took out my phone and turned on its video camera. I zoomed in as tight as it would go on the house, and panned it around to try to see any signs of occupancy.

We were facing the front of the house, which was across the gravel road from where we were in the woods. The windows appeared to be dark, and I couldn't see anything that indicated somebody was living in the house. I turned the phone toward the barn, which happened to be sitting on the side closest to us and had a big open doorway.

It was hard to make out, but I was sure I saw the front end of a van in the dark interior. I held my phone out for Dex to see, and he nodded.

"That looks like a van," he said. "Any word yet from Pennington or the sheriff?"

I shook my head. "Nothing yet."

No sooner had I spoken than we heard vehicles approaching. We stayed back out of sight and watched as two Creek County Sheriff's cars pulled up and turned in the driveway of the house. Two deputies got out of each one, and the four of them walked together toward the front door.

"What are they doing?" I asked. "Shouldn't a couple of them hang back?"

"I would think so," Dex said. "Maybe they know whoever owns this place. It's possible whoever is there is supposed to be there."

The deputies stepped onto the front porch and one of them knocked on the door. They stood there for a moment, but there was no answer so he knocked again, louder.

I still had the video app on my phone, and I raised it up and pointed at the house again. I could see the deputies clearly, as they talked to one another, but then they started down the steps off the porch. I was still watching the front of the house, and I saw the curtain at the front window move.

There was a muffled sound, like a gunshot but not as loud as I would expect, and the window shattered. One of the deputies pitched forward and landed on his face, and all three of the others were down only a second later.

"Oh, my God," I said, "oh, my God! Dex, he just shot them!"

"I know, I saw," Dex said. "Come on!"

He grabbed my hand and we took off running back down the path. "Where are we going? We can't just leave them..."

"He was a Navy SEAL," Dex said. "They're almost certainly dead, but there's nothing we can do for them. Call 911, now, and tell them what you saw. What we're doing is getting back to the car, and I'm getting you out of here."

The path was fairly clear, so I let Dex lead me by the hand while I tried to punch 911, but my phone rang at that moment. It was Pennington, and I answered instantly.

"Jim! They sent deputies to check the house, and he killed them all!"

"What? Cassie, are you out there?"

"Yes, we came out because I wanted to be close, but the deputies just knocked on the door and he shot them all dead. I was about to call 911 when you rang through!"

"Get out of there," Pennington said. "I'll handle it." The line went dead, and I kept running.

We got to the car a moment later, and were just about to get in when we heard a vehicle. It was coming from the direction of the house, and Dex yanked me back into the tree line. He had his gun in his hand, and I drew my own.

It was the van, of course, and it sailed past our little hiding spot without slowing down. I jumped up and ran for the car, with Dex on my heels. I got behind the wheel and started it as he was climbing in, then threw it into reverse and backed out of the wooded driveway. When I hit the gravel road, I spun the car around, threw it into drive, and floored it.

That was a mistake, on gravel. The car slid sideways, and it took me a second to get it back under control. When I did, I gave it gas carefully and we bounced and bumped all the way down the road.

We caught up with the van just as it turned onto Slick Road, turning south instead of north. I didn't even bother to stop, but cut the wheels and let the car fishtail onto the blacktop. Danny had his foot in the carburetor as far as it would go, and the van was accelerating rapidly. I was up to eighty miles per hour and he was still pulling away from me.

I tossed my phone to Dex. "Call Pennington back, tell him where we are and what's happening."

Dex didn't argue, or bat an eye. He hit the call back button and put the phone to his ear, but took it down a moment later and hit redial again. "Went to voicemail," he said. "I'm trying again."

An intersection loomed ahead, and Danny hit the brakes hard and fishtailed through a right turn onto Highway 16. I stayed on him, the Mustang taking the turn easily at forty miles an hour, and handling the curves a lot better than the big van could.

Beside me, Dex finally got through. "Pennington? This is Dex Tate. The guy took off in his van, and we're following him. Right now, we're on Highway 16, going west. It's a blue Chevy van, late nineties, license number 755-ADA." He listened for a moment, then nodded. "Okay, got it." He ended the call and turned to me, speaking loudly over the sound of my engine.

"This road leads into Bristow," he said. "Pennington is trying to get a roadblock set up there."

"If he gets into town," I said, "that puts more people at risk. We need to stop him, if we can."

Dex nodded and rolled down his window. I glanced over to see what he was doing, and saw that he had his gun out and was trying to aim ahead.

"I'm gonna try to get his tires," he said. He unbuckled his seatbelt and raised up on the seat, getting his head and shoulders out the window. He held the pistol in both hands, but it was almost impossible to hold it steady in the wind.

The back door of the van suddenly flew open, and there was Danny, kneeling on the floor and aiming a rifle. My heart leapt into my throat as I realized that Dex was presenting a perfect target, and I instinctively grabbed at him and pulled, trying to drag him back into the car before Danny could fire. It made me swerve to the right, and I felt the wheels on that side drop off the pavement for a second.

Everything went into slow motion. I saw the flash as the rifle went off, but I didn't hear the shot. I screamed as I felt Dex jerk, but then my windshield turned into an almost opaque sheet of cracks. Dex dropped into the seat beside me as I hit the brake pedal, and I turned to look at him, expecting to see blood everywhere.

He was looking at me, his eyes wide. "Watch the road!" he shouted, and I turned my eye forward again. It didn't help much, because I could barely make out the van ahead of us, let alone the road. I kept my foot on the brake and watched the van dwindle into the distance until I couldn't even make it out anymore through the shattered glass.

I got the car onto the side of the road and stopped, then slammed it into park and turned to Dex. I grabbed him and ran my hands over his body, looking for the bloody wound I knew had to be there, but there was nothing.

"Oh, God, I thought he shot you," I said. "Are you okay, were you hit?"

"I'm fine, Cassie," Dex said. "I thought he shot you!"

We both looked at the bullet hole through the windshield, and realized that it was almost dead center. We turned and looked behind us, and saw that the back window was also a spider web of cracks.

I looked at Dex again, and felt my heart trying its best to slow down and sink back into its proper position. That moment of terror when I thought he had to have been shot was replaying itself over and over in my mind, and I couldn't help thinking that my stubbornness had almost gotten him killed.

"Well," Dex said, "now we know for sure that he's not alone. Somebody else was driving."

THIRTY

IT TOOK ME A MOMENT to register what he'd said, but then I nodded. Obviously, someone else had to be driving while Danny was at the back of the vehicle aiming at us. I reached over and picked up my phone from where Dex had laid it on the console and dialed Pennington again.

"We're working on the roadblock," he said, but I cut him off.

"We lost him," I said. "He shot out the windshield of my car. He's definitely got somebody else with him, because someone else was driving."

"Do what? Are you okay?"

"We're fine," I said. "The last we saw of him, he was going straight ahead on 16, doing about eighty-five miles an hour."

"Geez," he said. "Let me see what's happening on the roadblock, and I'll get back to you."

I put the phone down and looked at Dex. "So," I said, "how much is the new glass going to cost?"

He looked at me for a second, and he burst out laughing. "Probably quite a bit," he said. "And somehow, I don't think you want to turn this in to your insurance company."

"Yeah, probably not. They're still upset about the Kia getting blown to smithereens. I had to explain what happened, and then they found out I'm a private eye, and my rates doubled. I can imagine what this would do."

A couple of sheriff's deputies showed up a few minutes later. Pennington had told them about us, but they actually seemed a little nervous when they approached the car. Dex and I were sitting on the hood at that point, and it turned out all they wanted to do was take our statement.

It was one of the most unfriendly interviews I've ever been involved in. They were justifiably upset and angry over the loss of their friends and coworkers, but I got the impression that, if it weren't for Pennington, they might have decided to take us in as accessories. The Creek County Sheriff's Office, I was informed, did not approve of private investigators being involved in police work.

"And if I hadn't been there," I said, "how long would it have been before you knew they got shot? At least now, you have a description and license number on the vehicle that was involved."

A burst of static came through the radio one of the deputies was holding, and he adjusted some control on it.

"Say again, dispatch," he said. There was an earpiece in his ear, and he listened for a moment. Suddenly, his face lit up, and he turned to his partner. "Jenkins, Palmer, and Story are all still alive," he said. "They're in the ambulances, on the way to the hospital."

"What about Ramirez?" his partner asked.

"He didn't make it," the first deputy said. "The other three still have a chance, though." He stopped, then turned and looked at me. "I guess we can thank you for that," he said. "By the way, we found the woman who called you. She lives right down the road, so it wasn't hard. Just a concerned citizen, I guess, but she should've called us." He sighed. "Is there anything we can do for you, Ms. McGraw?"

I reined Freda in a bit. "I think we'll be okay," I said. "We can call somebody to come get us."

He nodded, and his partner looked at me as if he was going to say something, then turned and walked away. They got back into their car and drove off, and I looked over at Dex.

"Well," I said. "Who do we call?"

He grinned and took out his phone, then called a towing service out of Bristow. All he told them was that our windshield was shattered so that we couldn't drive the car, and that we needed it taken all the way to Tulsa. The guy said he could be there in ten minutes, and he showed up just as Pennington found us.

They got the car loaded up—it was a rollback truck, like the one we had bought—and Dex climbed up in the truck with the driver while Pennington offered me a ride. I slid into the front seat of his unmarked car, noticing again how crowded it was.

"I'm gonna start calling you Lucky," he said. "It's a miracle Danny didn't aim directly at you, but that bullet hole is just to the right of dead center on your windshield."

I was quiet for a few seconds, but then the tears started to roll. Pennington looked over at me, concerned. "Cassie? What's the matter?"

"Dex was going to try to shoot out his tire," I said. "He climbed out the window, and he was trying to aim at the tire, but we were moving so fast the wind was blowing him all over. That's when the back door of the van opened up, and I saw Danny aiming a rifle. Jim, I swear he was aiming at Dex. I reached over to try to pull him back into the car, and I guess I swerved to the right, my wheels went off on the grass for a moment, and that's when the bullet hit the windshield."

He drove for a couple seconds while it sank in. "Sounds like your luck is rubbing off on Dex," he said. "If the gun was aimed at him, swerving off the road is what saved his life."

"Yeah," I said softly. "I figured that out."

We rode the rest of the way in silence, and Dex had the driver take the truck to our shop. He opened the overhead door as the car was unloaded, then climbed into it and drove it inside. Pennington followed me in and looked at the shattered glass once more.

"You're just going to change the glass yourself?"

"Yeah," Dex said. "I can do it a lot cheaper than a glass shop. We're not turning it in to the insurance, anyway."

We gave the detective a quick tour of the shop, and he drooled over the Cuda. Jim was probably in his early fifties, and talked about how he'd always wanted one of those cars when he was a teenager. The two of them were talking about something called a "crate engine" when my phone rang.

I didn't even think to look at the display, I just put it to my ear. "Cassie McGraw," I said.

"That was pretty crazy," Danny Kendall said. "I couldn't tell, did I hit your boyfriend?"

"No," I said. "But you owe me for a new front and back glass." Dex and Pennington heard me, and turned to stare at me.

"Well, good," Danny said. "I don't need you distracted right now. We're coming up on the last couple of rounds, are you starting to catch on yet?"

I thought for a second, and a grin came to my face. "You tell me," I said. "I came pretty close to catching your ass today, didn't I?"

He laughed. "Do you really think so? I don't. I don't know how you found me out there, but that was just one of several places I've had prepared. Don't worry, I'm not homeless. Unfortunately, that tells me you still haven't figured out the game. I guarantee you, I'll know when you do."

"And what happens then? You said when I figure it out, I'll know how to stop you. Is that still the plan?"

"Close enough," he said. "When you finally figure out the clues I've been giving you, it'll take you to your chance at the grand prize, but I hope you learned something today. Did you see what happened when you sent those cops to my door?"

"Yeah," I said bitterly. "I saw."

"That's what'll happen to any cops I see coming after me. Their deaths, Cassie, are on you. You should've come after me alone, and we could've jumped past everything else and gone straight to the end of the game."

"And what's the end of the game, Danny?" I demanded. "What happens then?"

"Oh, do you really want me to spoil the suspense? I know you have to be wondering, right? You wonder why I want this to end with you coming face-to-face with me?"

"Oh, hell, Danny," I said, exasperated. "I wonder what any of this is about. You blew up the place where I worked, killed two people but took two others hostage. You are nice to them for the first day, then you beat them both and left them for dead. You put a bomb on my car and blew it up, even though you say you don't want me dead. You blew up the shelter and killed a little kid, you rigged up suicide vests and made two of my clients wear them, just so you could make me figure out the password to disarm them. You put another bomb on my new car, and if you weren't trying to kill me, then that just makes no sense at all. I don't understand any of this, Danny. I don't have a clue what these clues are you're talking about, or what I'm supposed to figure out, or anything."

"Well, damn," he said. "I guess that's what I get for believing all your press. The newspapers make you out to be pretty damn smart, but maybe I'm going to have to make things a little more obvious. I'll tell you what, Cassie, here's a hint. Just look up. Okay? Just look up. And you might want to get ready. The next round begins in a little over an hour."

The line went dead. I took the phone down and looked at Dex and Pennington, and then I told them everything he had said.

"Look up?" Dex asked. "That could mean anything. Does it make any sense to you?"

I shook my head. "Absolutely nothing about this makes any sense," I said. "But I get the feeling it's all perfectly logical to him."

Pennington looked at me. "It may be," he said. "We finally got his military records yesterday afternoon, and this guy tested out as a bona fide genius. IQ over a hundred and fifty, and it turns out he's highly skilled with computers, electronics, all kinds of technology. He's an expert in demolitions, including improvised explosive devices, and with just about every kind of weapon they could train him for. In one of his evaluations, his commanding officer said that he viewed the world differently from everybody else. At the time, it made him a valuable member of his team. Later, they used the same comment against him when they kicked him out."

I shook my head. I don't care how smart he was supposed to be, the things he was doing still didn't add up to anything remotely logical. There was nothing at all that connected all of the different bombings and attempts that I could see.

"You said you were going to have the crime scene people look at everything," I said. "Did they come up with any ideas? See any clues?"

"Not yet, but they haven't given up. They're pretty smart, themselves, so they might come up with something."

"Well, something more is going to happen. Danny says the next round starts within an hour or so, but I haven't gotten any hints about passwords or anything. I guess the only thing we can do is wait and see."

Pennington nodded, and he left a few minutes later. Dex and I went into his office and sat there for a moment, and then I happened to glance at the clock. It was a little after ten, and I suddenly realized that I had an appointment coming in my office at eleven. I told Dex, gave him a kiss, and started walking around the block.

I unlocked the door and walked inside, turned on the lights in the reception area, and went into my own office for a few minutes, getting the computer online and making sure it wasn't too warm or cool. Everything seemed okay, so I went back out front and sat down at the reception desk.

My client that day was Annette Anderson. I had only seen her a couple of times before the bombing of the Outreach, but she was one that I was particularly concerned about. Her husband Randy was a micromanager, a man who makes every decision in the marriage, even down to telling her what she can wear, how her hair must be arranged, and who she's allowed to speak to. On those occasions when she had failed to do things exactly the way he wanted, he had beaten her severely. He had even broken a couple of her fingers and refused to allow her to have them seen by a doctor. As a result, they had grown crooked and caused her a lot of pain.

In our first meeting, she had responded to Freda quite well. Hearing my story, she said, made her even more determined to escape her situation, but when she returned for the second meeting—when we were supposed to arrange for her to go to a shelter—her own fears had overcome that determination. She had begged me to simply let her come and talk to me from time to time, until she could get up the courage to try again, and I had agreed.

To be honest, I had been surprised that she wanted to come to my new office at all. I had worried that the bombing might have made her afraid to even consider trying to escape again, but when I had called to tell her I was open for business, she had begged for an appointment right away. It had to be during the time when she knew her husband would be tied up on his job, and he was scheduled to be in Oklahoma City at ten thirty. That meant she had at least a couple of hours free, because he couldn't even take or make calls when he was in one of his corporate meetings.

A car stopped out front, and I looked through the window to see Annette step out of it. She stood beside the car for a moment, then turned and walked up to my door and pulled it open. I got to my feet and smiled as she stepped inside, and then I saw the tears streaming down her cheeks.

"Annette," I said, "what's the matter?"

She held out a hand to tell me to stay back, and the back of my neck started crawling again. I stopped where I was, and then she opened the light jacket she was wearing to show me the bomb vest that was underneath it. I stared at it for a second, then looked at the earpiece I knew I would see on her ear.

"He says if you call anyone," she said through her tears, "or if you try to leave the building, it goes off."

I nodded. "Come over here and sit down," I said. I pulled one of the chairs closer to the desk, and waited until she sat down on it, then knelt down in front of her. "Give me the earpiece."

She reached up slowly and took it off, then passed it over to me. I put it on my ear and said, "Hello, Danny."

"Cassie," he said, sounding as if he were delighted to speak to me again. "Are you ready? You're on your own with this one, no hints, no clues. If you've been paying any attention at all, you should be able to figure out what I'm trying to tell you. If you do, then you'll know what to do about this bomb."

"You are such an ass," I said. I looked closely at the bomb, which appeared to be identical to the last two. The phone with the keyboard was there, and the timer started at fifteen minutes while I watched. "So there's a password, right? Just like the others?"

"Of course there's a password," Danny replied. "All you got to do is think about the clues I've given you with almost everything I've done. Come on, Cassie, I've literally put it right in front of your eyes more than once. Turn on your brain, use it."

THIRTY-ONE

HE SAID NO HINTS, BUT he had just given me a big one. Something I had seen each time I had to deal with his insanity was supposed to tell me what I needed to know to save Annette, but also to stop Danny Kendall. The trouble was that I had been over and over those moments, and nothing was jumping out at me.

I looked into Annette's eyes. Danny had said that if I tried to leave the building, he would detonate the bomb. That might mean he was somewhere close by, watching to see if I left, but it was also possible that he was sitting all the way across the city watching through some sort of closed circuit cameras.

Of course, I had no intention of leaving Annette. I just wasn't sure how much he could see, and I was trying to think. I took hold of her hand and squeezed it, held up a finger to tell her to wait quietly, and then I closed my eye and tried to concentrate.

Back when I was still in the hospital after the fire, one of the nurses taught me some tricks that are supposed to help you pull yourself away from pain. The idea is to focus on a pleasant event from the past and explore every possible aspect of the memory. The idea is to occupy the mind to the point that pain can be ignored, but it also tends to develop the ability to recall details that you only noticed subconsciously. It's absolutely amazing how much you really see, but don't even realize that you see.

It was time to put that ability to use, and I went through the mental exercises I had learned back then to help me tune out the world around me. I took a deep breath through my nose and slowly let it out through my mouth, telling myself silently to remember the morning when St. Mary's had been destroyed.

I started with getting dressed that morning, when I thought of spring colors. I watched myself choosing the yellow skirt, the pink top and eyepatch, and then I was in the Kia, frustrated at all the red lights. I concentrated harder, trying to remember every inch of the journey from my house to the office. I saw not only the road ahead of me, but a number of cars that were on the road with me. There was a police car a couple of vehicles ahead of me, and it slowed me down when it stopped to make a left turn. I saw an older Corvette, and realized that I only knew what it was because Dex had shown me one.

None of this had registered on my conscious mind that day, but it was all there in my memories. I focused on the last couple of blocks before the office, and how I got stopped at each intersection. I remembered getting ready to turn to go to the alley, and having to stop so that van could pass in front of me. I noticed the big cloud design on the side of it, and realized that it was a service vehicle from Hamilton Pro-Cloud.

I saw the billowing smoke and heard the explosion again, and watched myself cut off the Lincoln SUV that was beside me as I aborted my turn and shot forward. I saw myself get out of the car and stand staring at what was left of the building. I remembered the police officer that arrived, the one that recognized me and asked if anyone was in the building. In a matter of seconds, I replayed the entire event in my mind.

What was next? It was the following morning, when I found Marsha at the dumpster. I went over every excruciating detail, looking for anything that connected to the events of the day before, but there was nothing.

Next was the bombing of my Kia. I played it over in my mind from the point where I emerged into the garage from the elevator. I remember standing there trying to think of where I had parked the car, and the blast that made me fall onto my rump. I remember the people who came rushing to check on me, and all the noise that I could barely hear because of the ringing in my ears. I remembered being surprised at the blue van that drove sedately down the spiral, and the way the driver glanced at me. And in that moment, even though I hadn't noticed it at the time, I saw the big cloud logo on the side of the van.

Cloud. Something about a cloud. The logo that Marsha drew, the one that Danny apparently was wearing when he abducted her, also had a cloud.

Was I on to something? I thought about New Beginnings, and suddenly remembered that Danny drove away in a blue van with a cloud on the side.

At the hospital, Danny had told Toni Denham to sit in the children's area of the waiting room, where the wall was done in a mural of clouds. The password that time had been my own password to my cloud storage account.

I thought about Beverly Walker and the Mayo Hotel; Danny had sent me on a treasure hunt for a clue to the password, and I found it on a weird sculpture called The Artificial Cloud.

Almost everything he had done had somehow involved a cloud, and the van he kept driving was actually from the cloud service that I used.

Maggie, the Hamilton Pro-Cloud sales rep, had told me that the company had recently been sold. And Alfie had told me that Danny Kendall had made a lot of money from some tech investment in Silicon Valley.

He'd said that I would know where to find him when I figured out the clues. I didn't know the address of Hamilton's office at that moment, but it wouldn't be hard to find. The question was what to do about this bomb.

I opened my eye and looked at the timer. Six minutes and twenty-one seconds, that's all I had left. The clue, I knew, was the clouds that I kept seeing, but what would he use for the password?

I typed in the word "cloud," and the timer didn't even hesitate. Apparently that wasn't it, but it looked like he was telling the truth will he said I had three tries.

What other word might be associated with clouds? I thought of Cumulus, Nimbus, thundercloud, rain cloud, and I don't know how many others, but none of them jumped out at me. There was something I was supposed to be seeing, and...

I looked at the password field on the phone. There were eight spaces this time, but I remembered that when I entered the other passwords, they each took all the available spaces. My cloud password, 4Abby43v3r, had ten characters. Vexatious had nine characters. This password had eight, then, but none of the things I had considered would fit.

Only eight letters, and connected somehow to the clouds I kept seeing. I racked my brain, watching the countdown timer go lower and lower. It was down to two minutes and seven seconds, but nothing was coming to mind.

Annette was crying, trembling. I needed to do something, even if it was wrong.

Eight freaking letters, and this would be over. Well, at least for the moment. The only problem was where to find them.

I close my eye again and tried to visualize the various clouds. Mostly, I had seen the one on the side of the van, so I focused on it...

I typed in 'Hamilton', and the countdown timer went blank.

"Bingo!" Danny said in my ear. "I knew you could do it. Now, are you ready for the final round? This one is for the prize, bitch, for all the marbles. Are you ready?"

I was reaching for the buckles, ready to let Annette out of that thing. "Soon as I let her go," I said. "That is just you and..."

"Don't touch the buckles! This one is a little different, Cassie. This one stays right where it is."

"Oh, come on, Danny," I said. "Are you changing the rules?"

"Oh, yes," he said. "I sure am. See, this lady is my insurance policy. I know you want to stop me, and I want us to come face-to-face. The trouble is, you're so tight with the police that the chance of getting you all alone was pretty slim.

I had to set up a situation that would give you a clear understanding of what's at stake, while motivating you to do things my way. You understand that, don't you?"

I sat back on my haunches, one hand stretched out to hold Annette's. "Fine," I said. "You want to be just you and me, that's what I want, too. I take it you're where I expect you to be?"

"I think you know where I am. Did you know that this company is housed in what used to be a hotel building? Old man Hamilton bought it for back taxes, but all he ever used was the ground floor. He put a bunch of servers in what used to be the ballroom, with all the fancy equipment to keep them running nice and cool. He just didn't have the savvy to turn it into a serious cloud storage business. He was content to work locally, but it really has a lot of potential."

"Yeah? Too bad you won't get to realize any of it. Now, tell me how we're going to play this out."

"Easy enough," he replied. "She's going to sit in your office, your own office, so nobody can look through the window and see her. I've already turned off your phones and Internet, so she can't contact anybody. You're going to lock her in, and explain to her that as long as you show up here, all alone, I won't punch in the code that will detonate the bomb. Now, what happens after that is still up in the air. That will all depend on whether or not you can finally put me down. If you do, you'll be able to turn off the device and let her go."

"And if not?" I asked. "What happens then?"

"Well, I guess that'll depend on how good a mood I'm in when it's over. You've got twenty minutes to be here."

The line went dead. I grabbed my phone and googled the address of Hamilton Pro-Cloud, and saw that it was seventeen minutes away according to Google Maps.

I grabbed Annette by the hand again. "You've got to do something for me," I said. I pulled her out of the chair and led her to my office, putting her in my chair. "You have to sit right here, and not move. He wants me to come to where he is, and I'm going to do my best to put a stop to him. When it's over, I'll come back and get you out of that thing, but if you try to take it off before then, it will explode. Do you understand?"

"Cassie, I can't..." The tears were flowing freely again.

"Annette, I am so sorry you got dragged into this, but I'm doing everything I possibly can to save your life. This is one time when you absolutely have to be strong. You have to sit here, do not leave this room. Do you understand me?"

She stared at me for a moment, her lips and jaw trembling, and then she nodded her head. "I'll stay right here," she said, sobbing.

I wrapped my arms around her neck and hugged her. "And I'll be back as fast as I possibly can."

I turned and hurried out the door, locking it behind me. I was sure he was genuinely watching, somehow, although now I was almost certain he was doing it through the Internet. I ran around the corner to the shop and hurried inside.

Dex looked up at me, and my face must have given it away. "Cassie? What's going on?"

"I can't tell you, and you can't help me." I pointed at the Cuda. "Does that run?"

He stared at me for three seconds, then nodded his head. He hurried to his little office and snatched up a set of keys, then tossed them to me as he ran and opened the overhead door in front of the car.

I got in and fumbled for a moment trying to get the key into the ignition, then shoved the clutch down and cranked it over. The engine sputtered once and then caught, and I grabbed the pistol grip shifter and pushed it into first gear, then gave it gas and let the clutch out.

The rear tires squealed as I left the garage, turning to the right and fishtailing. I got the car back under control and shot forward, and was impressed at how smoothly it shifted into second, then third. The light at the intersection ahead of me was red, but having to run to the shop had wasted a minute I couldn't afford.

I dropped it back to second gear and slowed the car down, but I could see a gap in the cross traffic. I pushed my foot to the floor and shot through it, right past the red lights and a half dozen drivers that were suddenly leaning on their horns.

The last thing I wanted to do was attract the attention of the police, however. I laid my phone in my lap and glanced down at it, and saw that I had just over fifteen minutes on my time limit, and sixteen minutes to go to my destination. No matter how I sliced it, I was going to have to break some speed limits to get there in time.

I made it through the next two intersections on green, but that told me that the next one would be red by the time I got there. I was running in third gear, not even up to fourth-gear speeds, but I decided it was time to change that.

I pressed the accelerator until the speedometer hit fifty, then shifted into high gear and started weaving through the traffic.

When I got to the next intersection, I slowed quickly down to forty and made it through on the green. A glance at my phone showed me that I had twelve minutes left on both the deadline and the trip.

I hit the gas again, this time making it up to sixty for half of the next mile. That would buy me an extra thirty seconds or so, I figured, but when I got to the intersection I shot through it on yellow. I had several more to go through before I got to my destination, so I kept the accelerator down almost all the way to the next one.

One by one I made it through them on either green or yellow, but I was sure somebody was probably calling the police to report that crazy lady in the hot rod car. For the last mile, I slowed down to the speed limit and tried to be as inconspicuous as possible.

That's not easy when you're driving a rare classic car, though. I heard a siren and glanced in the rearview mirror, just in time to see a squad car come fishtailing around a corner behind me.

I couldn't let a cop follow me to where I was going, so I had to lose him. I thought about where I was going and an alternate route, then dropped the shifter to second gear and drifted around the next corner to the right. I immediately took a left into an alley and shot through it, coming out on the next side street before the squad car even made it to the corner I had turned.

I went back to the street I had been on and stopped, looking back the way I had come. There was no sign of the squad car, so I eased the clutch out and turned the corner. My phone said I had three minutes left, and I knew I would make it with half a minute to spare.

Hamilton was in an old hotel, just as Danny had said. Beside it, abandoned and in disrepair, was an old drive-in restaurant. I whipped the car into its parking lot and around behind the building, shut it down, and jumped out. I jogged to the front of the Hamilton building, reached around behind and grabbed the grip of my Kimber, and yanked the door open.

The woman who was sitting at the reception desk looked up at me, and her eyes told me that she knew exactly who I was. This was undoubtedly Danny's female accomplice, and I fought back the urge to draw my pistol and put a bullet through her forehead.

"Where is he?" I asked menacingly, letting her see the gun in my hand.

She smirked. "He's waiting for you upstairs. You might want to leave that down here, though. He really doesn't like having guns pointed at him, but I think you found that out the hard way."

I took a step toward her, but she suddenly pointed a pistol of her own my way. "Just go upstairs," she said. "You mess with me, he blows up the lady you left behind."

I snarled at her, but turned toward the stairs.

THIRTY-TWO

AS SOON AS I STARTED up the stairs, that woman ditched out the front door. I didn't know if that was part of Danny's plan or not, but at least I would have a few minutes with nobody ready to sneak up behind me.

From the look of the stairs, I would guess that the building had been originally constructed sometime in the early part of the last century. The walls were old plaster, and it was cracked and falling off in some places. The stairs were wooden and worn down by what had probably been many thousands of feet going up and down the over the years.

All she had said was upstairs, but I had no idea just where Danny might be waiting. I made my way to the second floor, keeping my gun out ahead of me, and started going from room to room. Most of them were locked, and there was no sign of Danny Kendall. A part of me figured he would be on the top floor, but there was just no way to be sure.

Looking at these rooms, I was sure that this was where Marsha and Angie had been held. Each of the rooms had its own bathroom, and the doors were old, solid oak. I found a couple of rooms that had padlocks hanging on the outside, but they were open. I would guess those were where Danny had held his captives.

When I was sure there was no one on the second floor, I went back to the stairs and started up to the third. Looking up through the stairwell, it appeared to me that there were five floors. The third floor was just as empty as the second, and the rooms were in even worse repair. There was mold growing on some of the plastic, so I assumed that weather was getting in around some of the old windows.

It took me only about ten minutes to clear each floor, and I worried for a moment that Danny might not even know I was there, yet. I shook it off, because if he was capable of watching me in my office, he undoubtedly had some sort of system set up here, as well. When I got to the fourth floor and saw a video camera, I knew I was right.

The video camera made me wonder if Danny was on that floor.

"Danny? It's Cassie. Why don't you come on out and play?"

There was no answer, so I started looking through the rooms, being a bit more cautious than I had on the lower floors. Once again, I found no sign of him, so I went back to the stairs and started up one more time.

"That's far enough," Danny yelled. I was halfway up the last flight of stairs, and froze. "Put your gun down on the stairs, then come on up."

"Are you out of your freaking mind?" I yelled back. "I don't think so!"

"Oh, relax," he said. "I'm not going to shoot you. Just put it down and come on up here, there's something up here you need to see."

The back of my neck did its thing, and I carefully, slowly bent down and laid the Kimber on the step next to my foot.

If there was something up there he felt I needed to see, I was terrified that it was someone else in danger.

"Okay," I yelled. "I put it down. I'm coming up."

I kept my hands out in plain sight as I walked up the last eight steps. By then, I could see Danny standing in the hallway. He was holding a short automatic weapon, but the barrel was pointing down at the floor. He watched me coming toward him, and I was struck by the fact that he had an almost friendly-looking smile on his face.

And then it hit me that he really did look a lot like Mike, if the light was right and if I looked at his eyes. His eyes were so similar that I felt a massive shiver of fear, and I'll confess that I almost turned and ran down the stairs.

It was only the thought that he might have hostages that kept me from doing so. I made the last step and was on the floor with him, when he motioned for me to follow and turned his back to me. I almost dived back down the stairs for my gun, but he glanced over his shoulder to be sure I was coming. I lowered my hands and walked toward him.

"What is it I need to see, Danny?" I asked. "I thought we were just going to bring this to an end."

"We are," he said. "The only question is how. We'll get to that in a few minutes, though. Right now, I need you to see something."

He stepped into a room toward the back of the building and I cautiously made my way up to the door. He left it open, and I looked inside to see him standing in the middle of the room with his back to me.

That isn't what caught my attention, though.

The room was about fifteen feet wide and maybe twenty feet long, with the bathroom door on one side, just like all the others. I could see the top half of the bathroom door, but not the rest of it. The reason for that was because of the boxes that were stacked all the way around the room, leaving a space in the middle that was only about four feet wide.

Every one of the boxes was labeled "Block, Demolition, C4." There were numbers and dates as well, but I realized I was probably looking at enough explosive to level the building, and probably a few around it.

"Danny, what the... What is all this for?"

He spun and looked to me, his face split by a maniacal smile. "What's it for? Haven't you ever heard of going out in a blaze of glory? I'm going to show the whole world just what that really means."

I looked at the boxes, then looked back at his face. "So you brought me here to die with you?" I asked. "I thought you wanted me to stop you."

"Actually, you're the one who kept saying that," he said. "I just didn't argue with you. I figured, hey, if she thinks that's what it's all about, then she'll just be a little more cooperative at playing the game."

"Why do you keep calling it a game? Danny, just cut to the damn chase and tell me what this has all been about, would you?"

The smile vanished in a split second. "It's all been about Mike," he said. "Mike was my brother, Cassie, but he was a lot more than that, too. When we were growing up, Mike was the one who always made sure I was okay. When Mom and Dad were too busy enjoying their parties with their friends, it was Mike who made sure I got my homework done, who made sure I got a bath, who made sure I ate a decent meal before I went to bed. When we got a little older and our parents started taking trips and leaving us alone, Mike was the one who took me out and taught me to play ball, he was the one who taught me to drive, he was the one who did everything for me that your father is supposed to do. Because our father was just too busy."

There was a very different quality in him, at that point. The jocularity, the friendly competitiveness, that was all gone. I was looking at a man who had lost all touch with sanity, and I knew it.

"Danny," I said, keeping my voice calm. "I'm really sorry about Mike. You need to remember that I loved him, and I..."

He spun, then, and suddenly I was looking down the barrel of his M4.

"Shut up," he screamed. "You shut your mouth, you lying bitch!"

"Danny, I did. When I met Mike, I thought he was the most wonderful man in the world, but that was because I didn't know that he was sick. He wasn't bad, Danny, he was sick, and when everything happened I tried so hard to get him to get help. I didn't want him to die, Danny, I swear I didn't. It was his buddy that killed him, Danny, because Mike had decided that he didn't want me to die."

He stared at me for several seconds, and then he slowly lowered the gun. His face went through its transformation again, as the smile slowly oozed back into place.

"You think Mike was sick?" Danny asked. "Why? Because he killed some worthless whores that nobody gave a shit about, anyway? You don't know anything, do you realize that? You don't know a damn thing."

An anger started down in the pit of my stomach, and it was doing its best to crawl up to my mouth. "They were human beings, Danny, they were people. Nobody deserves to be raped and beaten and tortured and murdered. Nobody, I don't care who they are."

"When we were young," he said, "we used to go to this church all the time. I don't know if you knew it or not, but Mike could really sing. He had this beautiful voice, so we signed up for the youth choir. It was really cool, we traveled all over Texas and sang in different churches, and everywhere we went, people just raved about Mike's fantastic voice. He got so into the church, into being a good person, that we started going out in the street to tell people about God, me and him. Mike, he always said how Jesus didn't just go into the churches to find people; he went right out where the sinners were, because that's where he was needed the most. Mike said that's what he wanted to do, so we went into the worst parts of the city. We went to where the gangs hung out, and we told them about God. We went to where the druggies were, and we told them about God. Every time we went there, one or two of them would say they wanted to know more, and we'd take them to church. Sometimes, they'd even quit the gangs and the drugs and really become part of it all, you know?"

I smiled. This was a part of Mike I never would have dreamed on my own. "That's really beautiful, Danny," I said. "That's..."

"But then," he said, "then we went to where the prostitutes were. We went down to where they hung out on the street corners, and around the old motels, and we told them about God. And you know what happened? They laughed at us, Cassie. And then they teased us, and they flaunted themselves at us, and one night when we were trying so hard, when it seemed like God had abandoned us, we just couldn't take it anymore. They wanted to show us how they lived, and we let them. We went into the motel with them, and they turned us both into men that night."

My neck started crawling. Somehow, I knew what was going to come next.

"When it was over, when we were done, Mike said—he said, 'they can't live like this anymore.' He told me that the longer they stayed the way they were, the harder it would be for them to get into heaven, so it was up to us—it was up to us to make sure they got there. We knew what we had to do, because God showed us the way. We had to go into their world so that we could enter them into ours, because when they had congress with godly men, it made them worthy to enter heaven. And all we had to do was open the door."

I was staring at him, and my breathing was ragged. I had never dreamed that Mike's insanity had gone back so far, or that he had dragged his brother into it with him.

"And so you killed them," I said. It wasn't a question, it was a statement, and the smile that lit his face at that moment was radiant, almost beatific.

"We ushered them into heaven. They were lost sheep, and we were the shepherds. We were the ones who brought God's grace to them, and when we bestowed it upon them, they became worthy to enter heaven." He closed his eyes for just a second, as if relishing a special memory. "They didn't understand, of course. They were afraid, but we understood. They fought us, but we were so much stronger. Mike said that was the way it had to be, that we had to break them, the same way the potter has to break down the clay before he can make something of it. So we broke them, and we freed them from their sin and despair. We freed them from the guilt that they felt over the lives they were living, from the fear that permeated their lives because of the dangers around them, and we freed them from the despair they felt, because they believed they had no value. We told them they were forgiven, and that God loves them, and then we sent them home."

He jerked suddenly, like he had a quick, brief electric shock. His eyes lost the glow they held during his monologue, and the rage and anger and hate I'd seen before came back into them.

"Danny," I said, trying to think fast, "I never knew. I didn't realize that Mike was trying to save them..."

"You are such a liar," he said. "You said you loved Mike, but you didn't know anything about him. When stories of what we were doing started to get out, Mike was worried that something would happen to me. He said people wouldn't understand what we were trying to do for them, so I had to get away. He talked me into joining the Navy, because he said God wanted to protect me, and he waited until I left for basic training before he left Texas for good. While I was serving our country, Mike went to the police academy. He told me in his letters that God showed him that this was how he would continue his work, by being a missionary to another city."

He raised the barrel of the gun again and pointed at me. "One day he wrote to me and said he had to stop for a while, that things were getting too hot. He told me how God had led him to others who did the same kind of work, but there was danger they might get caught, so they had to stop for a while. He had to pretend that he was just a cop, put aside his real work and make himself fit in, and it was during that time that he wrote to me and said he met you. He said you were beautiful, and wonderful and that you were going to be his reward for all that he had done. I was so happy for him, because God had given him a woman that was truly worthy of such a powerful warrior for heaven."

He took four steps toward me, so that the barrel of the gun was only inches from my face. I was rooted to the spot, certain that I was about to die and suddenly all I could think of was Dex. It dawned on me that, if Danny pulled his trigger, or if he set off the explosives around us, Dex would never know that I loved him.

"But you weren't his reward," Danny said. "You are the emissary of Satan, sent to destroy the greatest man who ever lived. And now, because you betrayed Mike, God sent me here to deliver your punishment, your judgment."

I heard his words, but inside I was looking into Dex's eyes. I was thinking of that moment in the Center of the Universe when I had finally said those words aloud, but only because I knew he couldn't hear them.

And now, he never would.

Un-freaking-acceptable!

THIRTY-THREE

I SNAPPED MY LEFT HAND up and snatched the barrel, jerking my head hard to the left as I did so. Danny squeezed the trigger, and the bullet whizzed past my right ear, as I spun myself around and drove my right elbow into Danny's ribs. He grunted, and I put my back against the rifle and wrenched with all my strength on the barrel. I hit his ribs with my elbow again, and threw myself forward, and the gun went off once more as it came out of his hands.

I lost my grip on it, and it clattered out into the hallway. Danny screamed and lunged at me, and I tried to turn and face him but he was too fast. He wrapped his arms around me, pinning my own arms down to my sides as he pushed me forward toward the wall.

I knew what he was trying, to drive my face into the wall and stun me, so I kicked out with my feet and put them against the doorframe, then shoved back with everything I had. We went over backwards with me on top of him, and I heard the breath rush out of him. I brought my arms up hard and broke his grip, then rolled off of him as fast as I could.

He was down, but he wasn't out. He was rolling the other direction, trying to get onto his knees so that he could get to his feet, and I kicked as hard as I could. I caught him in the ribs on the other side, and he gasped again. I kicked again and got him in the head, and he hunkered down.

I turned and bolted out the door, my eyes on the M4 against the opposite wall. I dived for it, but Danny was on his feet and right behind me. I caught it by the strap just as he threw his arms around my legs, but there was no way I could turn it against him. He reached for it, and I flung it as far as I could, feeling a burst of satisfaction as it went over the railing of the stairs and fell all the way to the ground floor.

I was on the floor in the hallway, and Danny was crawling up me from my legs. He had me belly down, and suddenly I felt his hands go around my neck. He started to squeeze, and I knew that I couldn't take much of that without losing consciousness, and if I blacked out, I was dead.

He was sitting on me at that point, and he leaned down and put his face close to my good ear.

"You think you can get away from me?" he hissed. "You think you're going to escape your judgment? I am the messenger of Almighty God, sent to deliver the punishment you deserve for what you did to my brother! You're going to die, now, Cassie, and you're going to die knowing that everyone you care about blames you for the things that have happened these past few days. Everyone knows, they all know it's because of you that the judgment came to Tulsa. That is your punishment, and I am proud to be its deliverer."

His hands were strong, and they were making it hard to breathe. I could feel my lungs about to burst, and it looked like there were sparks exploding in my vision. I knew enough to realize that I was close to losing consciousness, but his face was right beside my own.

A year or so earlier, during one of the times when I was feeling sorry for myself, I had tried to paint my nails. The fingernails on my left hand, because the fingers are so warped, are misshapen and distorted. As a result, I keep them clipped very short, but the nails on my right hand I allowed to grow. When I painted them that night, I had liked the way they look, and so I had started using vitamin E and other products to help them grow strong. I let them grow long so that I could paint them and be proud of them, and it suddenly dawned on me that Danny's face was within their reach.

I let go of where I was trying to pull his hands off my throat and turned it over, and drove those nails straight into his eyes as hard as I could. I felt one of them snag in something, and curled my fingers and ripped with everything I had in me, and Danny's hands came off my throat as he screamed. I drew my knees up as hard as I could, put my hands against the floor and pushed with every bit of strength I had, bucking like a wild horse, and managed to flip him off of me. I rolled onto my back and saw him on the floor, one hand over his face, and there was blood running down it. I pulled back my legs as hard as I could and kicked at his face, and he screamed again. He fell backward until he was flat on the floor, and I jumped up and ran toward the stairs as hard as I could.

"*Cassieeee!*" He screamed out my name in rage, and I could hear him on his feet and running behind me. I dived just before I got to the stairs, slid over the edge and rolled down them, but I kept my eye on my Kimber and managed to snag it with my right hand as I rolled past. I hit the wall beside the stairs and caught the handrail with my left, jerking myself to a halt, and I raised the gun as I looked back up.

Danny was on the second to the top step, and he was holding a cell phone.

"Drop it," he screamed at me. "Drop it, or I blow us all to hell right now. That woman in your office? That bomb is on the same signal as the big one here, so you either drop your gun or I push the button. We can die together, if that's what you want, because I know that Mike is waiting for me in heaven right now. All you got waiting for you is a pit of fire and brimstone in hell."

I don't know how long we stayed frozen in that tableau, but it couldn't have been more than a few seconds. Danny was standing there, holding out the phone like it was a weapon, staring down at where I lay on the steps against the wall.

I thought about squeezing the trigger, but if I failed to hit his brain, he could drop his thumb on that button and I couldn't even guess how many people would die. With as much explosive as he had in that room, there was no doubt in my mind that this building would turn into shrapnel, and the shockwave would probably be enough to level buildings all around us. On the one side was the old drive-in restaurant, but there were two newer high-rise buildings on the other. In my mind, I imagined it looking a lot like 9/11 when everything started to collapse.

But if I didn't fire, if I surrendered and let him go, there was no doubt that I would die and he might still set the bombs off anyway. He wouldn't even have to be in the building, he was using a cell phone as a detonator, so all he would have to do is carry that phone out of range and then complete the call.

"Drop it, Cassie! Drop it now, or I'll..."

I shifted my aim and pulled the trigger.

When I had bought the Kimber, I had test fired it and found that I could hit whatever I was aiming at very well. I had also bought hollowpoint bullets, heavy lead bullets that are designed to expand when they hit something so that they do the maximum amount of damage possible. A regular forty-five caliber slug will make a half-inch hole going in and a three-inch hole going out; a hollowpoint makes a one-inch hole going in, but the one coming out could be as much as eight inches across. Every bit of tissue in between is basically turned to jelly.

Danny's wrist wasn't that wide. My shot struck his wrist dead center, and the flattening lead mass sheared his hand completely off. I watched, fascinated, as it fell away, still holding the phone, and rolled down the stairs toward me.

Danny screamed, and his eyes went wide as he stared at the stump of his wrist and the blood spurting out. He tried to step back up, but tripped over the top stair and fell onto his back, where he lay screaming. I twisted myself around to get my feet under me, let go of the rail and reached out carefully to pick up the phone. It was one of the old clamshell type, the kind that hangs up and cuts off when you close it, and I flipped it down and watched its lights go out.

I walked up the stairs again, keeping my gun out in front of me. Danny was laying on his back, staring at the empty space where his hand had been. Blood was still spurting out, and I tried to think of some way to stop it, but I didn't dare let down my guard.

I took out my own phone and called 911, told the operator that I needed police and paramedics on the top floor of the building immediately, and then I told her to notify Detective Pennington that it was Cassie McGraw calling. She tried to ask more questions but I cut her off.

Danny seemed to be getting weak, and when I looked at the copious amount of blood that was spreading around him on the floor, I wasn't a bit surprised. He looked up at me and tried to say something, but I couldn't make out what it was. Keeping my gun aimed directly at his face, I squatted down and reached out with my left hand and wrapped it around the stump of his wrist. I squeezed as hard as I could, and it seemed to slow the bleeding.

"If you fight me," I said, "I will let go. You'll bleed out, and save me a lot of headaches."

It was almost four minutes later when I finally heard people coming up the stairs. There were two police officers and two paramedics, and the officers instantly drew their guns and aimed them at me.

"Drop your weapon," one of them commanded, and I slowly put it behind me and laid it on the floor. I raised that hand high as I fell back onto my butt.

"I'm Cassie McGraw, private investigator," I said. "I've been working with Detective Jim Pennington on the bombing case, and this is Danny Kendall, the man who's been doing it all. He's bleeding badly, and I need the paramedics to take over here."

The paramedics didn't wait for the police to give permission, they swarmed up around me and one of them wrapped something around Danny's wrist and pulled it tight. He gently pushed my hand away, and it was all I could do to let go.

"What the hell did you do to him?" It was one of the officers who asked the question, and I pointed at Danny's hand, still laying on the stairs. They hadn't even noticed it as they were coming up, but one of the officers almost lost his dinner when he saw it.

"He was holding a cell phone that was rigged as a detonator," I said. "There's a woman wearing one of his bomb vests back in my office, and he said if I didn't come alone, he would blow her up. When I got here, I found out he had it rigged to do a lot more than that. If you let me get up, I'll show you what I mean."

The officer who had asked the question, whose name turned out to be Elders, actually came over and held out a hand to help me up. He had put his weapon back in his holster, but his partner was still keeping Danny covered.

"Come on," I said. "Believe me, you need to see this." I walked down the hall, limping slightly from the way my hips had been banged up rolling down the stairs, and walked right into the room with all the explosives. Elders stared at the boxes with his eyes wide, then put his finger to his lips and motioned for me to come back out of there. When we were thirty feet from the room, he stopped and looked me in the eye.

"Is that really C4 in there?"

"Considering he's been using a lot of it lately," I said, "I'm pretty sure it could be. I know I'd rather have somebody else deal with it than me."

Elders looked back at the room for a moment, then nodded his head as he turned back to me. "Yeah," he said. "Like the ATF, or somebody like that."

Pennington came up the stairs just then, with several more officers. Elders told them what I had just shown him, and then Pennington had me lead the way once again. Once they saw it for themselves, Pennington got on the phone to the FBI.

The paramedics decided they needed to get Danny to a hospital, and Pennington detailed three officers to follow and stand guard. All of them together rigged a blanket stretcher to carry him down, and then the paramedics loaded him onto their stretcher cart and took him out to the ambulance. It roared away a few moments later, and then Pennington turned to me.

"Cassie," he said. "Would you like to tell me just what the hell happened here?"

I told him the whole story, starting with Annette's arrival at my office. When I told him that I had figured out that the common denominator in all of the different events was a cloud, his jaw dropped and he slapped himself in the forehead.

Then we got to what happened when I arrived at Hamilton, and I gave him a description of the woman who had been downstairs when I got there. We were down in the lobby at this point, and I grinned as I pointed up at the security cameras. Somewhere in the building, I was sure, was a DVR that would have her picture on it.

What I hadn't figured out is why she took off. If I had been Danny, and had an accomplice with a gun down below,

I'm pretty sure I would've told her to stay put and shoot anybody but him who came back down the stairs. Pennington said he'd be sure to ask her about that, when he finally found her.

"You done good, Cassie," he said. "I understand why you couldn't call for backup, but you damn well managed to get your man."

My eye suddenly went wide and I stared at him. "Damn!" I said, and he looked startled. "Dammit, Jim, I forgot to tell the son of a bitch that I was making a citizen's arrest!"

He stared back at me for a couple of seconds, and then started chuckling. "Don't worry," he said. "I'll make absolutely certain everybody knows that this was your collar. And I need your gun, for ballistics, of course."

"Of course," I said, handing it over. "And can you send somebody to my office? There's a lady sitting there with a bomb wrapped around her, and I'm pretty sure she'd like to get out of it."

THIRTY-FOUR

THE PARAMEDICS WERE gone, so Pennington wanted to take me to the hospital to be checked out. I told him I was fine, but he insisted on walking me back to the Cuda. To be honest, I think he just wanted to drool over the car a bit more, because he did.

"Somebody called in a report that a car like this was racing through the city," he said after a moment. "It never even occurred to me that it was you. If it had, we might have gotten to you sooner, given you some backup."

"I'm glad you didn't," I said. "He was holding the phone, ready to hit whatever button would set off the bombs. He'd warned me before that if I didn't come alone, then a lot of people were going to die." I pointed to the top floor of the building. "How much of this block do you think that would take out?"

Pennington looked up, then turned back to me. "I don't know," he said, "and I don't want to find out. I'm going to have enough to do for the next few days, anyway. We'll have to check out every employee of this cloud company, see if any of them were aware of what he was doing, and maybe we'll find his accomplice while we're at it."

"That bitch is probably long gone," I said. "Just blows my mind that she took off the way she did..." I froze suddenly. "Oh, my God," I said. "Jim, Danny was planning to blow the building no matter what happened. That's the only reason he would've told her to get out, rather than stay there to back him up. He was planning his endgame, and he was going to take me out with him!"

Pennington stared at me for a few seconds, then nodded. "I think you're right," he said. "It definitely makes sense."

I shook my head. "Sometimes it blows my mind just how crazy people can be," I said. "Danny must have figured that taking me out while blowing himself to bits would get him some special reward in heaven. He had no intention of ever letting me stop him; he always planned for me and him to die together, I'm sure of it."

"Well, you beat him," Pennington said. "And, hey, you even managed to take him alive. From what I've read about you, that's almost a surprise. Most of your suspects end up dead, so you came out ahead of the game this time."

I flipped him the bird. "Smart ass," I said. "You need me for anything else right now?"

"We've got to get your official statement," he said. "Like I said, this was your collar. We need to get everything down on paper, so the prosecutor has plenty to work with. You might as well come on to the station now and get it over with. Save having to come back in tomorrow."

I nodded, then turned and opened the car door. I slipped in behind the wheel and dug the key out of my pocket, and Pennington grinned when I started it up.

"That is one sweet ride," he said. "If you ever decide to sell it, please let me know."

I grinned at him. "I'll see you at the station," I said. "I'm gonna swing through someplace and get some coffee on the way. I'll be there shortly."

He gave me a thumbs up sign, then turned and walked away. I put the shifter into reverse and backed up, then turned the car around and made my way around the little building to the driveway exit. I eased out into traffic, headed for the coffee shop that was only a couple of blocks away.

The back of my neck began to crawl, my own personal spidey-sense telling me that something was not right. I looked around quickly, then checked the mirrors. There was no one in sight that appeared to be any kind of threat, but I saw an SUV coming out of a parking lot and easing slowly up behind me. There was a car between me and it, and I couldn't see the driver, but the crawling sense wouldn't go away. Somehow, I just knew it was the woman who had been with Danny, so I guess I must have noticed her at the corner of my eye without realizing it as I passed that parking lot.

The light ahead of me turned green and I started forward, then suddenly turned to the right without bothering with a signal. I watched the rearview mirror, and saw the SUV make the turn behind me. There was no one between us, now, and I could barely make out enough of the driver to know that it definitely looked like the woman who had greeted me when I got to the cloud building.

I reached for my gun, then cursed under my breath. Anytime a weapon is used in a shooting during the investigation of a crime, the weapon has to be surrendered for ballistics verification. Pennington had taken my gun, telling me that I could pick it up the following day from the city ballistics lab.

I was completely unarmed, but if I was right about who was driving that SUV, she certainly wasn't.

The last thing I needed was to try to confront her alone, so I downshifted to second and pushed my foot down on the accelerator. The Cuda shot forward, and I saw the SUV accelerate behind me. I waited until the last possible second, then yanked the wheel and took the next left turn, fishtailing around the corner and fighting the car back to the straight and narrow. The SUV came around the corner behind me, but it couldn't take them the way the Cuda could. I had gained some distance between us, and I wasn't planning to give it up.

I was on a main thoroughfare, with two lanes going in each direction and a center turn lane. Traffic wasn't nearly as heavy as it could be, so I floored the gas pedal and shifted to high gear. I was up to almost seventy miles per hour, but that SUV was still back there, and finally starting to gain on me again.

What is it with crazy people, that they tend to find followers who will participate in their insanities? I didn't have a clue who this woman could be, but she was obviously attached to Danny Kendall. There wasn't much doubt in my mind that, if she caught me, she'd be planning on making sure I wasn't around to testify against him. That might not be the only reason she wanted me dead, but I'm sure it was in there, somewhere.

While traffic wasn't heavy, it wasn't light enough for me to really open up the car. I fumbled for my phone and got it out, then hit the button to call Pennington.

"I'll take mine black," he said as he answered, and I remembered that he thought I was at the coffee shop.

"Forget about coffee," I said. "Danny's accomplice is on my tail, and I don't think she wants to swap recipes. I'm on South Lewis, going south and about to pass 36th Street. She's driving a white SUV, I think it's a Ford."

"Take the turn, head for Harvard. I'll have officers waiting when you get there." The line went dead, and I dropped the phone on the passenger seat.

Making that turn wasn't easy, and I spun out. I came to a stop in the middle of the street, facing back toward Lewis, so I dropped the shifter to first gear and dumped the clutch while I yanked the wheel to the left. The rear tires screamed, but the car spun around and took off again.

Unfortunately, that gave the SUV the chance to catch up to me. It came around the corner just as I was starting to move again, and I saw a hand come out the driver side window holding a gun. It fired once, and the back window of the Cuda exploded into a million pieces.

"Geez, another window?" I shouted. "This has simply got to stop!" I rocked the wheel from side to side, keeping the car moving from one side of the road to the other. The idea was to make as hard a target as possible, but there's only so much you can do on a narrow city street. I couldn't get over about fifty miles an hour, because of so many cars parked along the side, but the crazy woman behind me didn't seem to care about them at all. She sideswiped at least two, but didn't even slow down when it happened.

There was still almost half a mile to go before I got to Harvard, and then my heart leapt into my throat as three kids ran out into the street in front of me. I yanked the wheel to the right, trying to avoid hitting them, but there was a pick-up truck parked at the curb. I cut the wheel back to the left, knowing I was just about out of time, and jumped right over the curb and into somebody's front yard.

I slammed on the brakes, but they just don't work well on grass. The car went into a slide and crashed through a fence between the yard I was in and the next one, and I tore the right front fender off on a tree. That made the car spin, and I slid sideways until the back end hit the corner of the house.

I was dazed, and shook my head to try to clear it quickly. When I got my eyes to focus again, the SUV was stopped in the street right in front of me and the driver was climbing out. Her gun was pointed straight at me, and I instinctively dived below the dashboard.

The windshield disintegrated as she fired, and some part of me flew into a rage. Dex and I had just paid a lot of money for this car, and it was being destroyed the first time I ever drove it! I thought about trying to open the passenger door and get out, but there was no cover out there. I was laying across the console, which was pretty doggone uncomfortable, and suddenly the crazy woman appeared at the driver's window.

The gun was pointed straight at me, and once again I thought I was going to die, but then I heard a scream and the woman looked back toward the street. I acted without even thinking, hooking my foot in the door handle and yanking with my toes, then kicking the door as hard as I could with both feet. The door struck the woman, the gun went off but the bullet flew right over me, and that enraged me even more.

I rolled up hard and my feet hit the ground, and I saw the woman sitting on the grass with a slightly stunned expression on her face, so I grabbed hold of the door and shoved it as hard as I could. It hit her again, knocking her over backwards, and then I was on my feet.

She still had the gun in her hand, and tried to raise it to aim at me, but I dived onto her like a wrestler. She was apparently left-handed, so my right hand grabbed hold of the gun and shoved it back, and I curled my left hand into a fist and started pounding on her as hard as I could. I struck her in the face several times, but then she reached up and jabbed me in the throat with her free hand, and I instinctively let go and put my hands up to my neck.

And that damned gun came back around toward my face. I slapped it away once again, but I couldn't catch at this time, and she tried to bring it back to bear on me, and that's when I lost it completely. I smacked her arm down, then raised both fists over my head and brought them down together into her face. Her nose shattered and blood flew everywhere, and then I grabbed the gun and twisted for all I was worth. I managed to wrench it out of her hand, then flipped it and pointed it at her as I climbed off.

"You so much as breathe wrong," I shouted, "and I will blow your ass away!"

Sirens were screaming, and it suddenly dawned on me that there were people standing in the yards around us. Squad cars came screeching up in front of the house, and a half-dozen officers were suddenly swarming around me, their own weapons aimed at both me and my attacker.

I laid the gun down on the ground and raised my hands. "I'm Cassie McGraw," I said. "Somebody call Detective Jim Pennington."

"I'm already here," Pennington said, as he forced his way through the crowd that was gathering around us. "Are you ever going to let the police do their jobs?"

I looked up at him, the remnants of my rage still simmering below the surface. "You weren't exactly here," I said. "I don't know about you, but when somebody's trying to kill me, I put up a fight!"

He broke into a grin. "Don't I know it. I'm not sure you even really need our help, but I'm holding out hope."

One of the officers had flipped the woman over and cuffed her, and they were dragging her to her feet. She managed to look at me, her busted nose still bleeding, and the hatred in her eyes caught my attention.

"Who are you?" I asked. "Why the hell were you helping Danny? Don't you know he's crazy?"

"He's not crazy," he said calmly. "He is God's warrior, just like his brother was. He brought me from the depths of my sin and raised me up to help him do God's work."

I stared at her for a moment, then turned to Pennington. "Why is it," I asked, "that all the loonies seem to be drawn to me?"

"I don't know," he said. "But at least you seem to be able to catch them."

"Oh, yeah," I said, "that reminds me." I turned to the crazy woman who was just about to be taken to the squad car and grabbed her face to make her look into my eye. "I hereby place you under citizen's arrest!"

EPILOGUE

I CALLED DEX THEN, to tell him all that had happened and let him know that I was okay.

"Are you sure? I mean, I've been—I've been worried, babe."

"I'm a little sore," I admitted. "I ended up tumbling down some stairs, which banged my hips up a bit, and I'm afraid I wrecked the Cuda."

"I can fix a car," he said. "I don't care about the car, I care about you. Are you really okay?"

"Yeah, I'll be fine. I could probably use one of your wonderful massages, later."

I could hear the smile come into his voice. "That will be no problem," he said. "In fact, it will be my pleasure."

"Mmmm, mine, too," I said. "Listen, I have to go down to the police station for a while, to finish giving my statements. Somebody is going to go to my office and get Annette out of that bomb, and she'll probably need a ride home. Would you mind?"

"Not a bit, babe. Call me when you're free, okay?"

"You got it," I said. "And by the way, I deserve something nice for dinner tonight."

He was laughing as he hung up.

I limped my way over to where Pennington was still staring at the Cuda. "Dex can fix it," I said. "It'll be just like new."

"I hope so," he said. "That's heartbreaking, to see it like that."

"I'll tell you what," I said. "You get me out of the station within an hour, and I'll let you borrow it for a weekend sometime."

The smile almost broke his face. He grabbed me by the arm and rushed me to his car and back to the station, and I gave my keys to a lieutenant from the bomb squad who was waiting. He and his men took off toward my office, and they called back twenty minutes later to say that they had successfully removed the bomb from Annette.

Twenty minutes after that, I walked out the door. Pennington had taken my statement, I had signed it, and I had a receipt in my pocket that certified that the Tulsa Police Department had received custody of my prisoners. I had made my first actual arrests, and I intended to be proud of both of them for a long time to come.

I called Dex as I got into Pennington's car for the ride home, and he was just getting to the house. He had already taken our truck and picked up the Cuda and taken it back to the shop, and said he would start rebuilding it the next day, after putting the new glass in my GT.

He was waiting on the front porch when I got home, and came down to the driveway and walked me into the house. I went straight toward the bedroom and stripped, then ran the bathtub full of hot water and climbed in. Normally I just get a shower, but that evening I needed to soak.

Dex stayed in the bathroom with me, and even washed my hair for me. It felt so good, but I couldn't help thinking that it wasn't all that long ago when I couldn't bear the thought of anyone touching my head. While the hair on most of my head was still soft and healthy, anyone trying to wash my hair was going to end up touching the burned scar tissues on the left. I had even refused to let my mother wash my hair for me, because I couldn't stand the thought of her feeling that rough texture, or the stumpy spot where my left ear used to be.

With Dex, though, it was more like he was caressing me, and even when his hand brushed the stub of my ear, it actually felt somehow nice.

When I got out of the tub, he wrapped me in a big towel and then waited until I got my eyepatch on before he turned another one into a turban on my head. I followed him out to the kitchen, where I found he had made a stop at Boston Market and picked up roasted chicken and all the trimmings.

We sat down to eat, and I waited until I had answered all of his questions about the events of the afternoon, and then I looked directly into his face.

"So," I said. "Sometimes, when you find yourself in an extremely unpleasant situation, it makes you think about things that you might not have really thought about before. Or, maybe you thought about them, but just didn't want to really think that deeply about them. Am I making any sense?"

Now, I'm sure I've told you before, Dex can read me like a book. If I ever really need to keep a secret from him, I'm probably going to have to go into hiding. He seems to have a natural talent with body language, and he can spot when somebody is lying like nobody I've ever seen. Half the time,

I find myself wondering if he has a secret ability like ESP, because it often feels like he's reading my mind.

The point is, I'm pretty certain he knew exactly where I was going, but he looked at me, all innocent like, and said, "I think so."

I cracked up laughing. "Dex," I said. "Remember when we were at the Center of the Universe? When I was checking out the weird sound thing it does?"

"Yeah." He nodded.

"You really couldn't hear what I said?"

"No, I really couldn't. Like I told you, I tried to read your lips, but—well, your lips are very hard to read."

"That's probably because they're only halfway there. The other half got burned away, but I'll remember that in case I ever need to use it to my advantage. Anyway, the thing is, what I said—what I actually said was, 'I love you.' I figured, since you were telling me you wouldn't be able to hear it, I'd know by your reaction if you really could or not."

His eyebrows rose a half-inch. "Damn, now I wish I could have heard it."

"The point of this is," I went on, "that I said it when I was pretty sure you wouldn't be able to hear me say it, even though I was looking right at you at the time. And now, I feel like a big coward. While I was up there dealing with Danny today, there were a couple of moments when I was pretty sure I wasn't going to come out of there alive. And when I felt that way, I suddenly realized that I've been cheating both of us by not being willing to tell you how I feel, or listen to what you want to say to me. Can you understand?"

"I think I do," he said cautiously, "but I'm going to keep my mouth shut. Right now, I want to hear what you want to say."

I licked my lips. "Dex, what I want to say is that I love you. Abby's been trying to tell me for a while that I was in love with you, and I kept shutting her up, but today I realized that she's right. I'm in love with you."

Dex just stared at me for a moment, then he leaned forward and crossed his arms on the table.

"And does this have any bearing on the future?"

I looked at him and chewed on the inside of my cheek for a couple of seconds, but then I smiled. "I think it does," I said, "if you honestly do want us to have a future together. Like, a real future, a permanent one."

He sat there without saying a word for thirty seconds, then got up and walked out of the room. I didn't know whether I should follow him, or just give him space. For all I knew, I might have waited too long to open up to him. He might be thinking about how to tell me that he didn't want that future, after all.

He came back a couple of minutes later and stopped right in front of me. I slowly raised my eye up to look at him, and that was when he suddenly knelt down. I think my eyeball tried to pop out and run away, because he reached out and took hold of my left hand and pulled it toward himself.

"Cassie," he said softly, "I think I've been in love with you since the day we first met. There was something so different about you, so powerful and strong and—and original, that I knew before you walked away from me that first time that I was going to need to see you again. I knew it. Since then, I have only come to love you more every single day, and while I know that you are strong and capable, I am absolutely terrified that something is going to happen to you, and you'll be gone from my life. I want to have you in my life for as long as I possibly can, and for that reason, I have to ask you a question." He reached into his pocket and came out with his hand clenched in a fist. He held it up in front of me and opened it, and I saw a diamond. "Cassie, will you marry me?"

I stared into his face for a moment, and then I looked at that diamond again. That's when I noticed that it wasn't exactly a diamond ring. I mean, it was, but the ring and pinky fingers on my left hand were fused together after the fire. The doctors said it was either that or take them off, and I'm glad they chose the way they did.

Of course, that meant I could never wear a normal engagement ring again; in fact, they had been forced to cut off the one I'd been wearing that horrible night. Once I got used to the two fingers being one, I had never really thought about it again. Besides, who would ever propose to Freda Krueger? It wasn't likely to ever be an issue again, or so I thought at the time.

The thing laying in Dex's hand had obviously been custom-made. It looked like two rings had been put together, and one side had a beautiful diamond and several smaller ones.

"Where in the world did you find that?" I asked him.

"I had it made about a month ago," he said. "It was right after the night you tried to do shots with Nicole, and you passed out. I used some smooth copper wire and wrapped it around your fingers to get the shape and the size, then took it to a jeweler so he could make this."

I leaned forward and kissed him quickly, then sat back again. "Yes," I said.

The custom rings fit perfectly, and they're the most beautiful thing I've ever seen.

It was only a little after seven, so I got up and went for my phone. I took a picture of the custom ring on my hand, then sent it to Mom's phone.

"I give her two minutes before she calls," I said to Dex, but it was less than sixty seconds later when my phone rang.

"Hey, Mom," I said nonchalantly. "How's it going?"

"Cassie?" Mom asked. "Don't tease me, young lady! What is this picture you sent me?"

"Well, that would be a photo of the custom engagement ring that a certain wonderful man just put on my fingers," I said. "Remember when I told you not to start planning any weddings yet?"

"Yes," she said cautiously.

"I'll let you know as soon as we set the date."

SPECIAL OFFER

BUILDING A RELATIONSHIP with my readers is the ultimate goal with writing. At least, it should be. Without you guys, us writers would just be making up stories for ourselves...which would be weird. That's why I like to connect with my readers in a way many big name authors don't.

I occasionally send newsletters with details on new releases, special offers and other bits of news relating to Sam Prichard, Noah Wolf, and the other varies series and stand alone novels that I write.

And if you sign up to the mailing list today, I'll send you this free content:

- A free copy of the first Sam Prichard novella, FALLBACK (plus the audiobook version)

- A free copy of the first Noah Wolf novella, THE WAY OF THE WOLF (plus the audiobook version)

- Exclusive content and pricing to my mailing list – you can't get this anywhere else. Every book launch I set a discounted price for my mailing list for a couple days. This is exclusive to my list *only,* and something that isn't publicized anywhere else.

You can get the novella's, the audiobook's, and the exclusive discounted pricing **for free,** by at: www.davidarcherbooks.com/vip

NOTE FROM THE AUTHOR

IF YOU ENJOYED THIS adventure, would you please consider taking a moment and leaving your thoughts for others who might also enjoy this book?

It takes only a handful of seconds to leave a review, but can literally make or break a self published career. Please don't feel any obligation to do so, but if you had fun, or perhaps enjoyed yourself at all, then I'd sincerely appreciate it!

Thanks so much,

David Archer

Made in the USA
Middletown, DE
07 April 2018